WAITING FOR
TEDDY WILLIAMS

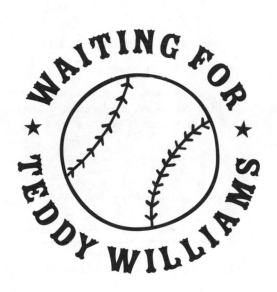

WAITING FOR TEDDY WILLIAMS

HOWARD FRANK MOSHER

Houghton Mifflin Company

BOSTON   NEW YORK

2004

Visit our Web site: www.houghtonmifflinbooks.com.

ISBN-13: 978-0-618-19722-4
ISBN-10: 0-618-19722-2

LIBRARY OF CONGRESS CATALOGING-IN-PUBLICATION DATA

Mosher, Howard Frank.
Waiting for Teddy Williams / Howard Frank Mosher.
p. cm.
ISBN 0-618-19722-2
1. Boys — Fiction.   2. Vermont — Fiction.   3. Drifters — Fiction.
4. Single mothers — Fiction.   5. Baseball players — Fiction.
6. Boston Red Sox (Baseball team) — Fiction.   I. Title.

PS3563.08844W35 2004
813'.54 — dc22   2004042721

Book design by Anne Chalmers
Typefaces: Janson Text, Caledonia, Frutiger Condensed Black, Zebrawood Fill

PRINTED IN THE UNITED STATES OF AMERICA

MP 10 9 8 7 6 5 4 3 2

"Sticks and Stones" and "Nobody's Child" copyright © Annie Mosher.
Reprinted by permission of Annie Mosher Williamson and
of Sam Weedman, producer of the album *Annie Mosher.*

To Phillis

★ THE COLONEL ★

1

TIME WAS, on a summer afternoon in the northern Vermont hamlet of Kingdom Common, when Ethan Allen could walk completely around the rectangular village green and never be out of earshot of the Red Sox game on somebody's radio. That's what E.A. was doing on the early afternoon of his eighth birthday. He'd started at the short south end of the green, where the Voice of the Sox was blaring out over Earl No Pearl's portable, perched on the top row of the third-base bleachers beside the town ball diamond so that Earl could listen while he chalked the batters' boxes and base lines for the Outlaws' game that afternoon. The same resonant and, as it seemed to E.A. in those years, omniscient Voice was broadcasting the game from the dusty pickups angled diagonally against the long west side of the green across the street from the brick shopping block. Backcountry farmers in from the outlying hollows sat in their cabs with the windows down, listening to the play-by-play from Fenway while their wives did their Saturday marketing. As E.A. crossed over to the heaved blue-slate sidewalk in front of the stores, he could hear the Voice drifting out through the screen doors of the IGA, the hardware, the five-and-dime, and the office of the *Kingdom County Monitor*, where Editor James Kinneson sat by the front window, typing and listening to the game. Since there was no local television station in the mountains of northern Vermont in those days, and no cable TV, every Sox fan in the village was listening to the game on the radio.

E.A. stuck his head inside the newspaper office. "Hey, Editor."

Editor Kinneson looked up and smiled. "Hey, Ethan."

"I reckon we're holding our own today," E.A. said, nodding toward the radio on the corner of the desk.

"So far," the editor said. "But you know us, Ethan. If there's a way to lose —"

"We'll find it," E.A. said, and ducked back outside.

Editor James Kinneson always spoke to E.A. as if he were a man instead of a seven-year-old — as of today, an eight-year-old — kid. E.A. would give nearly anything to have it turn out that Editor K was the one. He knew better, though. He knew he might as well wish for the Sox to win the Series. It wasn't Editor Kinneson.

He continued north along the brick block, with the buzz of the big Fenway crowd now coming through the screen door of Quinn's Pharmacy. On the outside of the screen was what appeared to be a baseball. Actually, it was a baseball-size ball of cotton soaked with bug dope to keep away the flies. As E.A. approached, George Quinn II stepped outside in his white coat with his aerosol can and sprayed the cotton ball with a fresh dose of Old Woodsman. E.A. stared at him with his pale eyes. He'd seen the druggist eyeing Gypsy Lee when he thought no one was watching. He hadn't liked the way Quinn had looked at her.

"What are you staring at, E.A.?"

"You," E.A. said.

"Scat," George Quinn II said. Like a man shooing away a mangy stray cat, he gave the aerosol can a squirt in E.A.'s direction, suffusing the air with the smell of citronella. Then he retreated back into the pharmacy while the all-knowing Voice of the Sox announced that after three complete innings Boston led New York 2–1.

To which E.A. replied, "I reckon I won't hold my breath."

"To whom are you speaking, Ethan Allen?"

It was Old Lady Benton, leaning over the rail of her second-story rent above the pharmacy and glaring down at him the way she used to glare at whispering pupils in her third-grade classroom at the Common Academy across the green. She'd spotted him from her porch rocker while pursuing her two favorite avocations, listening to the Sox game and spying on the village.

"I asked, to whom are you speaking?" Old Lady Benton said again.

"Nobody," E.A. said.

"You're patrolling the streets and mumbling your mouth to one of those imaginary companions of yours, aren't you, E.A.?"

E.A. gave her his iciest WYSOTT Allen stare, but she looked right straight back at him, waiting for an answer. Old Lady B was one tough customer. To this day she was feared by all three generations of Commoners who'd had her as a teacher. Everyone knew how she had faced down E. W. Williams and the entire Outlaws baseball team a decade ago, on the night of the torchlight procession in honor of the Outlaws' fifth consecutive Northern Vermont Town Team League Championship. Earlier that afternoon, E.W.'s game-winning home-run ball had struck one of the twin wooden decorative balls on the back of her porch rocker while she was sitting in it. Unimpressed that it had traveled a distance of 442 feet (not counting arc), according to Bumper Stevens's Stanley metal tape measure, Old Lady Benton had refused to return the baseball in question. That night, cheered on by his teammates, E.W. had stood, drunk and swaying, below her porch and called her Battle-ax Benton and worse besides. She had merely come to the rail and said that while she didn't deny being a battle-ax, the ball had nearly taken her head off and therefore she would keep it as a souvenir, thank you kindly. After which E.W. had staggered off and the torchlight procession had fizzled out.

E.A. nearly always knew whether Boston was ahead or behind by a certain subtle inflection in the Voice of the Sox. Now blasting from the porch of the Common Hotel, the Voice was worriedly describing a Yankee threat. Several bat boys, retired from the Green Mountain Rebel baseball bat factory, sat out on the hotel porch in the sunshine in folding chairs listening to the game on Fletch's hunch-shouldered Stromberg Carlson. Fletch liked to tell how, when he was E.A.'s age, in October of 1918, the bell at the United Church had rung of its own accord when the Sox won their last World Series.

With the score now tied, 2–2, at the end of the fourth, Fletch reached back over his shoulder to the windowsill, where the Stromberg Carlson sat, like an old-fashioned breadbox with dials, and turned down the volume. Loud enough for E.A. to hear as he crossed the street, Fletch said, "Here comes that Allen boy again."

E.A. stopped at the foot of the hotel porch steps to eyeball the pensioners. He regarded them and they regarded him. A slender, redheaded boy in jeans and scuffed Keds and a T-shirt and a Sox baseball cap. Not big for his age but wiry, with hair the color of barn paint and a pale blue stare that was already as cold as the ice cliffs on Allen Mountain in January.

"We saw your hit in that pickup game on the common yesterday, E.A.," Early Kinneson said. "Saw you lace that opposite-field triple over first base."

"You keep at it you might take the playing field for the Outlaws someday," said Early's brother, Late.

"Might even crack that other knob offen Old Lady B's rocking chair," Early added.

E.A.'s eyes moved carefully from one seamed face to the next. Then he headed down the lane beside the hotel toward the commission-sales auction barn. Inside the barn a couple dozen local farmers and downcountry cattle buyers stood on the sawdusty floor while Frenchy LaMott, the auctioneer, sat on a high stool above the cattle ring and presided over the Saturday afternoon auction. The Voice of the Sox droned indistinctly from somewhere beyond the ring while Frenchy chanted into a microphone. "Who'll give a thousand dollars for this fine animal, gentlemen? Rose Blossom Princess, a two-year-old first-calf heifer out of the Hansom herd up to Lord Hollow. One thousand. One thousand. One thousand. Seven fifty? Five hundred? Five hundred, boys, and there's a real steal. Four? Four? Four hundred in gold for a really first-class animal . . ." One of the buyers slightly inclined the brim of his porkpie hat. "Beef her," Frenchy said in disgust to conceal his sympathy for the Princess's owner. Little Shad Shadow, Frenchy's softheaded ring man, lifted his blue cattle cane and whacked the doomed Princess from Jack Hansom's equally doomed hill farm out the exit chute and up the urine-stained, cleated ramp to the buyer's truck.

Occasionally Frenchy or one of his cronies from the auction barn got slicked up at the barbershop and came out to see Gypsy Lee. None of them had red hair, but Gypsy did, and E.A. figured his came from her.

"So the Sox have turned a one-run lead into a four-run deficit, folks, as a result of one bad inning . . ."

"One bad inning," Frenchy barked into his microphone. "One hundred, two hundred, five hundred bad innings. Who'll give me a thousand bad innings, boys? Who'll give me ten thousand bad innings since 1918?" He put his hand over the mike and said, "E.A., what you want here, you?"

"Nothing."

"You come to the right place, then," Frenchy said. "Nothing's what these boys" — nodding at the farmers — "have to give and stand to get."

E.A.'s eyes traveled over the faces of the third- and fourth-generation dairymen witnessing their farms and hopes roll down the line to the meatpacking plants along with their cattle. Most were family men from what had once been family farms. Not that being family men ruled them out. Many of Gypsy's regular RFD Escort Service, Inc., gentlemen were family men. Hands in his jeans pockets, E.A. went outside and back up the lane between the barn and the hotel, past the slat-sided trucks filling up with bellowing cattle.

⚾

The Colonel and the boy looked down the green together. On the ball diamond at the south end, the Outlaws were beginning to warm up for their game with Memphremagog.

"You could give me a hint," E.A. said. "At least you could do that."

The Colonel stared silently at the Outlaws, his broken-off sword jutting straight toward home plate.

"You know who it is," E.A. persisted. "Or was. I know you do."

On the hotel porch Early said, "He's doing it again. Talking to that statue."

"What of it?" Fletch said. "He's got to have somebody to talk to, don't he? Why shouldn't it be the fella he was named for?"

"No reason, I reckon."

"No reason at all," Fletch said. "Leave the boy be to conduct his own business in the manner he sees fit."

"Strange business, if you ask me," Late said. "Carrying on a conversation with a statue that's been dead nigh two hundred years."

E.A. figured the Colonel was mad that the Sox were falling farther behind New York. How could he not be? Hadn't he seen it all? Seen Ruth blithely traded away to those very Yankees. Seen Teddy Ballgame never get his Series ring. Seen hopes throughout New England rise higher than the top of Allen Mountain when Fisk waved his home run fair in '75, in the sixth game against the Reds, *willed* that baseball fair, only to watch the team stumble and lose the seventh the next day. Fisk, a story in himself, had played American Legion ball across the river in New Hampshire and had come north to the Common once and smacked a ball off the Colonel's privates, 390 feet from home plate, according to Bumper's Stanley. Granted, Fisk's blast was nothing like E.W.'s 400-foot-plus shot at the Battle-ax, but it was still a hang of a ways for an eighteen-year-old kid to hit a ball. Years later the traitors in the front office had sold Fisk down the river without so much as a by-your-leave. And despite that run in '75, and several other runs nearly as exciting, hadn't the Colonel seen many decades pass since 1918 without another championship flag flying over Fenway? Closer to home, he'd seen the Common's own E. W. Williams, arguably the best long-ball hitter and smartest catcher to

8

come out of New England since Fisk, never make it to the majors at all or even the minors. Lord knows there was no cynicism in that fixed bronze expression, even after all these years. Baseball, of all sports, and maybe of all human endeavors, has no room for cynicism. But when it came to the Sox, the Colonel's hopes were diminished. When the Yankees waltzed into Fenway for a Sunday twin bill, he hoped for a split. When the Sox were slated to play two at the Stadium, he prayed for rain.

As for the Colonel telling E.A. what he most wanted to know, there was less chance of that than of the Red Sox winning the World Series.

E.A. was all but certain that Prof Benton knew. He could see Prof sitting in his shirtsleeves by the open window of his headmaster's office on the ground floor of the Academy, across the street from the long east side of the green, listening to the now nearly listless Voice of the Sox announce, "New York eight, Boston three, after seven." He'd never seen Prof out at Gran's place, or Judge Charlie Kinneson, either, who was no doubt listening to the game in his chambers in the granite courthouse next to the Academy. The judge was Editor Kinneson's older brother and a great favorite of E.A.'s. But the judge wouldn't tell him, either.

Next to the courthouse was the railway station. Only three passenger trains a week stopped there now, though ten daily freights still rumbled through the Common, and a decade ago there'd been twice that many. E.A. supposed it might possibly have been a conductor on the Montrealer. Or maybe an engineer off the Green Mountain Limited. He didn't really think so, though. Most of Gypsy's RFD clients were local.

At the short south end of the green he stopped behind the double-chicken-wire backstop and stared across the street at the Reverend, out cutting the lawn in front of the United Church with a clickety-click push mower to demonstrate to his parishioners that he wasn't afraid of day labor. Showboat stuff, E.A. figured.

Daniel praying in the lion's den. He gave the Reverend a glacial stare, which the man of God pretended not to notice. The Reverend was the only Commoner E.A. had encountered this afternoon who was not listening to the Sox game, and as far as the boy was concerned that was just one more strike against him. He'd offer up his '74 Topps Bill Lee, and maybe throw in his '62 Fleer Willie Mays, if Our Father Who Art in Heaven would turn the Reverend into a pillar of salt right there on the church lawn. E.A. closed his eyes and said a little prayer to this effect. When he opened his eyes the Reverend was still there.

E.A. linked his fingers through the chicken wire and peered through the backstop at the Outlaws, taking batting practice. Viewed through the wire, the scene had something of the quality of an old black-and-white documentary of the early days of baseball. In most parts of the country, town ball was a thing of the past. In Kingdom Common this afternoon the bleachers were filling up fast. Cars and pickups were parked along all four sides of the green. Some radios were still broadcasting the Sox game — 11–4, Yanks.

E.A. pressed his face close to the chicken wire and watched the Outlaws hit. Earl No Pearl was loosening up on the sideline. Drunk or sober, Earl was unhittable, though in either condition he could not find the strike zone, so he had to pitch in a semistupefied state midway between sobriety and inebriation, maintained by one longneck Budweiser every three innings. It was a sobering enough sight for the visiting team to watch Earl warm up, uncorking his 90-mph fastball between sips. Few batters crowded the plate against him.

The Three Shoeless Farmer Boys, Merle, Elmer, and Porter Kittredge, played the outfield and batted barefoot. The book on the Farmer Boys was that you couldn't get a ball by them, in the field or at the plate. It was confidently said in Kingdom Common that if they'd been willing to wear cleats, all three brothers could have gone all the way to the majors. Moonface Poulin at shortstop could have gone all the way too, said the Common, and so could

Squint Currier at second, except for the unfortunate fact that they'd "never had the coaching." Bobby Labounty, now looking at the centerfold of a *Penthouse* magazine while waiting his turn to take BP, had tragically and unfairly been denied his major-league career by an errant arm. Something of a drawback, E.A. thought, for a third baseman. Pappy Gilmore at first, and Cy McCoy, the Outlaws' longtime catcher, had played some single-A ball in Canada decades ago. Both men were now in their fifties. In the estimation of the Common, Pappy and Cyrus could have gone all the way but for their careers having been interrupted by the war. Which war, E.A. had never been sure.

Several of the ball players regularly called on Gypsy Lee, and E.A. supposed that the one he was looking for might have been an Outlaw. If so, he had mixed feelings about it. True, the townies were good old boys who paid him a nickel for every foul ball he shagged during BP, ten cents if he caught it on the fly, and let him go up to the plate and take ten raps when they were through. But when it came to baseball, E.A. was already something of an elitist. Even at eight years old, the birthday boy was certain that regardless of what the Common said, not one of the Outlaws had ever had the ghost of a chance of setting foot on a major-league baseball diamond, as he fully intended to do someday, and wearing a Red Sox uniform at that.

"E.A.'s giving us the hairy eyeball again, Cy," Elmer Kittredge said to the catcher. Elmer winked at E.A. "You're up next, Bubba B. After me."

Bubba B was one of a dozen nicknames the Outlaws had devised for E.A., none of which met with his approval, but he was too happy to be hitting to care much. He swiped Elmer's thirty-eight-inch Green Mountain Rebel and choked up three-quarters of the way to the trademark. Standing in to take his cuts, he felt right at home. This was where he belonged. He drove Porter Kittredge's floating BP pitches out toward short, toward second, even pulled one down the line over third. The Outlaws nodded and said the ball jumped off his bat right quick for a shaver. That he had a right fast bat and he was one to watch. It felt good when the ball met the fat of Elmer's old Rebel. Like the solid weight of a big brown trout on his line in the trestle pool.

"That's eight, E.A.," Porter called in.

He got just ten chances when he took BP with the Outlaws. If a pitch was wide or tight or high or in the dirt, he swung anyway. The tenth pitch was right in his wheelhouse, and he drove it into left field.

With E.A. on the bench keeping the book, the Outlaws jumped out to a five-run lead in the first inning and never looked back. From his station in deep center, the Colonel watched the game with his usual bemused expression. A few cars honked when Elmer Kittredge hit the Colonel's pedestal on the roll, and there was a flurry of polite horn taps when Earl No Pearl struck out the Memphremagog side on ten pitches in the third. But by then the Outlaws were far ahead. Though everyone knew that the competition wasn't what it once had been, any baseball was better than no baseball. So the Colonel said anyway. The Colonel was also fond of saying that while change, like spring, came slower to the Kingdom than to the rest of Vermont, the day would certainly arrive when there'd be no town ball on the common at all.

Then the game was over and the boy started home across the outfield grass.

"Outlaws thirteen, Memphremagog two. New York fourteen, Boston five," he told the Colonel on his way by, hoping for a hint in return. But the statue didn't say a word, and E.A. was as much in the dark as he'd been when he first woke up that morning, remembering that he was no longer seven but eight.

As the Colonel said, everything changed.

2

E.A. BEGAN TO RUN. First he ran around the darkening common a couple of times, bouncing off the balls of his feet, increasing his pace the second time around, pushing himself down the backstretch across from the baseball bat factory and the courthouse and the Kingdom Common Academy before heading out the county road toward Allen Mountain, looming dark against the twilit sky. East of the village he ran between the Kingdom River on his left and abandoned farms on his right, the fields fast growing up to puckerbrush. Earl No Pearl, who never ran except when he was legging out an extra-base hit, and then lumbering more than running, had told him that to stay in training, baseball players ran. So E.A. ran everywhere he went.

In fact, he liked to run. First because he was good at it. At eight he could already outrun much older boys and often had to. Second because he wanted very much to stay in training so he could play for the Sox someday. And third because when he was running, once he hit his stride and was skimming over the cracked old macadam of the county road between the murmuring river and the brushy, disused farms, he no longer thought about his search, or the scoldings the Colonel gave him, or how much he detested Old Lady Benton and Sissy Quinn. He just thought about running.

E.A. crossed the river on the M&B trestle because it was fun and he wasn't supposed to. The 7:46 southbound hooted, but he had plenty of time before it arrived. He scanned the sand beside the trestle pool far below for the tracks of deer, moose, railroad tramps. All he saw was a neat set of raccoon prints and the long, three-pronged indentations of a great blue heron. Across the river he followed the tracks past the old water tank to where the dirt road off Allen Mountain crossed the M&B line. A number of people had been killed there: a farmer in a stalled hay truck, a hobo who fell asleep on the tracks, some kids in a hot rod racing the train to the crossing. The freight rumbled by. As it passed, E.A. read the names on the cars. Gaspé and North Shore. Pine Tree State. Burlington Northern. Santa Fe. Baltimore and Ohio. Southern. Canadian National. Gypsy had taught him how to sight-read from these names, and as often as he'd seen them they still thrilled him.

Gran's place sat in an overgrown field at the base of the mountain, just past Devil Dan Davis's automobile junkyard. Gran's house and eight-sided barn were weathered as gray as the big granite boulders that had tumbled down into the back field from the mountain over the eons. The dooryard was overrun with weeds, but Gypsy Lee had set out some potted begonias — red, yellow, and orange — compliments of an RFD Escort client who worked at a greenhouse in Memphremagog. Gypsy's rig, the Late Great Patsy Cline, assembled from a '51 Chevy, a '53 Ford, and a '78 Pontiac, was parked on the drive sloping up to the hayloft of the barn. Named after Gypsy's all-time favorite singer, the Late Great Patsy Cline faced downhill so that Gypsy could pop the clutch and jump-start her on the run. That was the only way she would start.

"You're late, boy," Gran said when E.A. banged in to the kitchen. "Where have you been? Over in the village consorting with those good-for-nothing baseballers, no doubt."

"I wasn't consorting. I was looking."

"What for?"

"That's for me to know and you to find out."

"Shameful. To speak so to a crippled old woman. Never mind. I know what you were looking for. And who. And you're not about to find him, for he's Gone and Long Forgotten."

Gran cackled, her little round black eyes full of humor and malice, as she peered up at him from the old-fashioned wicker wheelchair with big wooden wheels, to which she had been confined since her stroke, caused by Bucky Dent's fateful home run in 1978.

"If he's gone, why doesn't he have a regular stone?" E.A. said.

"Because he doesn't merit a stone. You'll go the same way if you continue to seek out bad companions. Not to mention playing baseball day and night. The devil's pastime."

"Why the devil's pastime?"

"Did you ever know any good to come of it? Disappointed hopes, is all."

"Where's Gypsy Lee?"

"Primping."

"Who for?"

"How should I know? Where's my newspaper?"

"I forgot it."

"I expected no less."

"I'll pick it up tomorrow."

"Don't bother. Why should a crippled old woman have her newspaper? Her one small pleasure."

E.A. took a rolled-up tabloid out of the hip pocket of his jeans and dropped it in Gran's lap. The *Weekly World News*. Her black eyes snapped as she read the front-page headline: PRESIDENT GREETS ALIENS ON WHITE HOUSE LAWN. The accompanying photograph showed the chief executive watching a gigantic saucer hovering just over the Rose Garden.

Gran's face was as wizened and sour as a dried crab apple. As Gypsy had explained to E.A., Bucky Dent's pop-fly home run had been the perfect excuse for Gran to take to her wheelchair, even though there wasn't the least thing wrong with her. Moreover, Gran claimed that the unwelcome surprise of getting pregnant after she believed she was safely past childbearing age — Gran detested children almost as much as she detested the Red Sox — had further contributed to her permanent posttraumatic stress. "I was going through the change when I had your mother," she liked to tell E.A. with grim satisfaction. "That's probably what's wrong with Gypsy Lee." E.A. didn't think there was anything wrong with Gypsy Lee. He couldn't imagine a better mother, and the only change he'd ever detected in Gran was a rather steady progression over the years from mean to meaner.

Gypsy Lee came in from the parlor. "Hi, sweetie." She ruffled E.A.'s hair and patted Gran on the shoulder and straightened the frayed throw rug on the old woman's lap. Noticing the tabloid headline, she laughed.

"Stranger things have happened," Gran said.

"Like what?" E.A. said, as Gypsy began to fry bologna slices for supper.

"Do you think the *News* would print it if it wasn't fit to print?" Gran said.

Gypsy winked at E.A. "I can't decide who to be tonight," she said. "Any ideas?"

Gran turned the page. Tami Janis Kage, a twenty-one-year-old model in a bikini from Brisbane, Down Under, smiled up at E.A. Gypsy looked at Tami Janis over Gran's shoulder. "There we go. Bingo."

E.A. grabbed his fried bologna sandwich, got his red rubber ball and the old Rawlings glove with the padding leaking out that he'd found under the melting snow on the green three springs ago, and went out to the dooryard. He began to replay the Sox's most recent victory over New York, a month and a half before, throwing the rubber ball against the side of the house and catching it to represent each play. "Twenty-seven Outs" he called this game. As E.A. worked his way through the innings, Gran wheeled herself to the kitchen door, propped it open with her chair, and watched with bleak interest. On the slanted roof above the sideways window of his loft bedchamber, a row of young sparrow hawks, hatched out earlier that summer under the rotting eaves, waited for their parents to feed them. High overhead in the evening sky the dark, short-winged chimney swifts that lived in the village church steeple soared and dipped.

In the top of the seventh E.A. bobbled a ball on the short hop. "Do that often enough, and you can play for the Sox yourself someday," Gran called out.

As E.A. retired the final Yankee hitter in the last of the ninth, a car pulled into the dooryard. There was just enough light left to read its front plate: JESUS 2. The Reverend got out. "Pastoral house call," he announced. "Is Mother at home?"

"No," E.A. said. "She just left for Brisbane."

Gypsy Lee stepped out into the dooryard in a blond wig and a short gold lamé dress. "G'd evening, mate," she said. "Tami Janis, from Down Under."

"Catch," E.A. said, whizzing the rubber ball past the Reverend's head.

"Here. Here now," said the Reverend, hurrying inside with Tami.

By now it was too dark to catch his ball, so E.A. went inside to play high, low, jack, and the game with Gran while Gypsy entertained the Reverend in the parlor. E.A. won five hands and Gran won six. Then E.A. went up the loft stairs to bed with a jelly glass of milk and two Pop-Tarts he'd bought at the dented-can store where he'd gotten Gran's newspaper. He pulled the string of the single bulb hanging from the ceiling. In the glaring light the poster of Ted on his door was bright and alive-looking. Ted was leaning on a bat in the on-deck circle at Fenway, giving the eyeball to a very young-looking pitcher in a White Sox uniform. No doubt Ted was already planning where he would drive the ball.

E.A. reached under his bed and pulled out the White Owl cigar box containing his baseball cards. Most were ragged and stained and dog-eared. Not one could be graded Mint or even Good. Many he'd won by flipping for them in the dives where Gypsy Lee sang on weekends. His favorite was a recent Topps, in near-Good condition, of the great Sox manager G. P. "Spence" Spencer, known to the Red Sox Nation of Greater Boston and New England as "the Legendary Spence." Spence had won more games than any other manager in the history of the Red Sox franchise, and it was E.A.'s dream to play for him someday. In all he had one hundred and twenty-four cards, most of them Red Sox, many of which he could identify by touch from a turned edge, a crease, a bit of bubble-gum residue, or a missing corner.

He slid the White Owl box back under his bed. He snapped off the light and went to his dormer window and looked out over the dooryard at the WYSOTT family cemetery. The moon was not quite full. In its white light the granite stones gleamed pale. The small cedar-wood slab they called Gone and Long Forgotten was just visible in the moonglow. E.A. turned away from the window, shucked off his Keds and jeans, and got into bed.

"Our Father," he began with the best of intentions, but before he reached "Give us this day" he was murmuring, "It's the last of the ninth in the seventh game of the World Series, folks. The next pitch will tell the story. The young batter from Vermont is set. The pitcher is ready . . ." Who was the pitcher? He could see himself waiting in the batter's box, but the pitcher wasn't clear. "He comes to the set. Checks the runners, kicks, and delivers . . ." Then the unmistakable sound of straight-grained ash meeting horsehide and a roar expanding outward from Fenway through Boston, sweeping north over the towns and mountains of New Hampshire and Vermont to Kingdom Common, filling all New England. But exactly what it signified — long-awaited triumph or a long foul ball — Ethan E.A. Allen had no idea. The birthday boy was asleep.

Sometime in the night he came suddenly awake. The moon had shifted around so that its light was coming directly through the slantwise window, falling onto the bare pine planks of the loft floor. The moonlight on the floorboards reminded him of a story Gran liked to tell from her girlhood. As a small child (she said), she'd waked up one night, in the very loft where E.A. now slept, to behold a man standing, sopping wet with his own blood, in the moonlight at the foot of her bed. She didn't recognize him, and after a while he was gone. But the next morning, when Gran told her ma, ma showed the little girl a photo of her dead pa, Outlaw Allen, killed in a running gun battle with revenuers. He was the gory fellow she'd seen standing at the foot of her bed.

"I swear before God above, E.A., there was a bloodstain on the floor when I woke up," Gran always concluded the story. E.A. had never been able to make out the stain, but it was a scary story, and a strange one for a grandmother to tell her only grandson.

E.A. got up and walked across the floor to the window, his arms and legs pale in the moonlight. Outside, everything looked the same. The Reverend's car, JESUS 2, was still parked in the dooryard near Gran's old-fashioned pump, where the Allens drew their water. Beyond, the graveyard stones gleamed faintly. The abandoned hay-loader down in the meadow looked like a big school slide. Along the river the black willows were shrouded in fog.

Then E.A. saw him. He was leaning against the grill of Gypsy's rig at the top of the barn highdrive, looking up at the house. He wore what looked like an old suit jacket over a tieless shirt that might once have been white and old slacks baggy in the moonlight. The red pinpoint of a lighted cigarette stood out against his face. At first E.A. thought he was one of Gypsy's callers. But except for Patsy Cline and the fool's JESUS 2, there was no other vehicle in the yard. E.A. watched the man watch the house. His hair was cut short, not quite a brush cut, but flattened off straight and stiff on top, like Mickey Mantle's and Whitey Ford's, in E.A.'s *Illustrated History of Major League Baseball.* What he looked like was a drifter, up off the M&B line wanting a back-door handout. E.A. didn't like him smoking that close to the buildings. If a match or a smoldering butt got loose, the whole shooting match, house and barn and all, could go up in flames. He decided to run the drifter off the premises.

He slipped into his jeans and sneakers and went downstairs, through the dark kitchen, outside and across the yard to the highdrive. The drifter was still there, smoking in the moonlight.

"Gran doesn't want people smoking around the buildings," E.A. said.

"You say?" The drifter's voice was as raspy as a chain saw. Like he'd already smoked a hundred million cigarettes and intended to smoke this one right down to the butt. Especially if someone told him not to.

"I said, my gran doesn't allow smoking on the place."

"Don't she now?"

"No, she doesn't. You up off the freights?"

The stranger puffed at his cigarette, narrowing his eyes to size up the boy through the smoke. In his chain-saw voice he said, "I saw you hit today. Overstreet on the common." He shifted the cigarette between his lips a quarter inch without touching it. The tip flared. "Keep your hands back," he said.

E.A. looked at his hands. "What?"

"Keep your hands set back even with your back shoulder until the ball gets there and you take your cut."

"I reckon I know what to do with my hands. I went six for ten today in BP. That's two hundred percentage points better than Ted in 'forty-eight."

"If you keep your hands set back from the start," the stranger said, "you won't have to jerk them back just before you take your cut. That jerk throws off your swing."

The cigarette moved slightly. The man was tall. E.A. put him at six two. Maybe six three. Taller than any of the Outlaws by at least an inch.

"What would you know about anybody's swing?" E.A. said. "A drifter up off the railroad."

The outside light came on and the kitchen door opened. The drifter faded back into the barn entry as Gypsy and Tami Janis came out, Tami's heels clacking on the wooden steps. E.A. didn't see how this could be. Gypsy *was* Tami. No, by Jesum Crow. *Tami was the Reverend* — now removing the blond wig, now stepping out of the gold gown and high-heeled slippers.

"God Jesus, will you look at that," the drifter said in a low voice. "Will you just take a gander at that, now." He spit out his butt, took one short step, and crushed it under his beat-up work shoe, as if he were grinding the life out of the cross-dressing Reverend.

"Ta-ta," Gypsy said.

Just before the fool got into JESUS 2, he lifted his hand palm outward and intoned, "May the Lord bless you and keep you and make His everlasting light to shine upon you."

As the Reverend drove away, Gypsy snickered and said something that sounded to E.A. like "horse's ass." Then she stepped back inside the house and the light went off.

The dooryard was quiet. The drifter continued to stare at the house. He shook his head. Then he looked back at E.A. "So you like baseball."

"You bet I do," E.A. said. "I intend to go all the way to the top."

"When you get there," the drifter said, "you won't have time to jerk back your hands and swing. Assume your stance."

"What?"

"Take a make-believe bat and assume your batting stance." Hesitantly, E.A. did as he was instructed. "That's right," the drifter said. "Now. You want to start out with your hands back here."

He took E.A.'s hands and moved them back six inches. He smelled like tobacco, beer, sweat, and the wool of his old-fashioned suit jacket.

The man stepped back, surveyed E.A., and nodded. "Now you're a hitter."

E.A. experimented, moving his hands up and back, up and back. "It doesn't feel natural," he said. "Starting with them clear back there."

"It will. After two, three days, it'll feel as natural as riding your bike."

"I don't have a bike," E.A. said.

The drifter looked at him curiously. At the crossing the 5:15 A.M. local whistled. The man looked off in the direction of the train whistle as he rummaged in his suit jacket. He brought out something that glistened white in the moonlight and tossed it to

E.A. The boy's hands closed around the seams. He stared, unbelieving. ★ **OFFICIAL** ★ **AMERICAN LEAGUE,** the writing said in the moonlight. He smelled it. Genuine horsehide. Hand-stitched. The real article. A major-league baseball.

When E.A. looked up, the drifter was walking across the meadow toward the tracks, his long, cuffless pant legs swishing through the wet grass.

"Hey. Hey, mister!" E.A. trotted partway down the meadow. He could see the local coming, its headlamp glaring through the fog. Indistinct in the river mist, the drifter was trotting alongside an open boxcar. In a smooth, practiced maneuver, he swung aboard the train and vanished.

The local hooted again. E.A. tossed the baseball up in the air and caught it. On the side opposite ★ **OFFICIAL** ★ **AMERICAN LEAGUE** he read, in large blue printed letters, *HAPPY BIRTHDAY ETHAN.*

3

"'It is a truth universally acknowledged, that a single man in possession of a good fortune, must be in want of a wife.'"

Gypsy sat at the kitchen table in the number 8 Outlaws jersey Earl No Pearl had given her, homeschooling E.A. from the classics. They had just started *Pride and Prejudice*, and E.A. could already tell that it was likely to be heavy sledding. Gran would have rescued him. Gran hated the classics, every last one of them. But she was sleeping in, recuperating from the Red Sox's loss to New York the day before.

Gypsy took a sip of coffee from the sixteen-ounce plastic cup Earl had brought her with the picture of his eighteen-wheeler, which had Gypsy Lee's name embossed on its side in red. Earl hauled the Green Mountain Rebel factory's genuine, real-wood, white ash baseball bats to unlikely-sounding places like Muncie, Indiana, and Tupelo, Mississippi. Besides the personalized thermal coffee cup, he'd brought Gypsy all kinds of other souvenirs from the open road, including several belt buckles as big as saucers, in the shapes of leaping deer, crossed shotguns, and more eighteen-wheelers, which Gypsy wore with her size-two jeans; baseball caps embroidered with the names of truck stops from coast to coast; and tapes of Gypsy's favorite singers. Earl No Pearl had promised to take E.A. on a cross-country road trip with him in the *Gypsy Lee* when he turned twelve. "We'll have us a time, I and you," he'd said, winking at E.A. and looking at Gypsy out of the tail of his eye. "See some good country, listen to the ball games over the radio. Get us some of that Californy poontang." E.A. wasn't sure what Californy poontang was but he looked forward to the trip with Earl, seeing good country and listening to baseball as they rolled west.

"Ma, is Earl in possession of a good fortune?" E.A. said.

Gypsy laughed. "Earl still owes forty-nine thousand, eight hundred, and seventy-four dollars on the *Gypsy Lee*. He isn't in want of a wife, either. He's already paying alimony to two that I know of."

"Speaking of Earl, I thought maybe you'd throw me a little BP this morning."

Gypsy ruffled E.A.'s hair, the same fire-engine red as hers. "What morning when the temperature's over twenty below don't you want me to throw you a little BP, sweetie? Okay. We'll compromise. How about a little field trip? A little nature walk, get some life science in. What do you say?"

"Throw fingers? You win, we take the nature walk. I win, you pitch me BP."

"Okey-dokey," Gypsy said. "Rock beats scissors, scissors beats paper, paper beats rock. Ready?"

E.A. nodded.

"I'll count," Gypsy said. "One. Two. Three."

On three she threw three fingers, and E.A. one. Three — paper — covered one, rock, so she won. Gypsy was a veteran sleight-of-hand artist, like Gran before her. She'd wait a split second to see how many fingers E.A. was throwing, then throw whatever beat him. She was so quick he could never catch her at it. She did the same at cards. Nobody could cheat at high, low, jack, and the game as skillfully as Gypsy Lee.

Still, it was worth trying. "Cut the cards? All or nothing?" E.A. offered.

"Sure," Gypsy said. "High card wins." She shuffled the worn deck of Playmate playing cards Earl had brought back from the P and K Service Center in Reno, Nevada. She handed the deck to E.A., who shuffled, set it on the table, and cut. He drew the jack of diamonds he'd spotted shuffling. Pretty good. He handed the pack to Gypsy, who drew the queen of hearts. E.A.'s face fell.

"Hey," Gypsy said. "Look. Who says we can't have our cake and eat it, too? Let's take our coffee up to our special place, do a little field-tripping, then, when the grass starts to dry out in the meadow, I'll pitch to you. Okey-dokey?"

E.A. grinned. "Okey-dokey."

They started up the path beside the barn where E.A. had seen the drifter the night before. This morning that seemed like a dream. Gypsy, barefoot, still in her Outlaws jersey, went ahead of him a few steps. She'd brought along her old Gibson in case she was inspired to do some composing. E.A. considered telling her about the drifter. But somehow he wanted last night to stay between him and the stranger.

Above Old Bill the hired man's trailer they passed through the piney woods, which smelled green and fresh in the early dew, though the season was too far along for many birds to sing, just a lone ovenbird. They came out of the pines into the maple orchard, overgrown with brush, the tops blown out of many of the larger trees.

Their special place was just above the maple orchard and just below the first steep pitch of the mountain. It was a clearing in the woods about the size of a baseball diamond, which Bill called the high mowing meadow, though no one had mowed there in years. From here, on clear summer nights, Gypsy had taught E.A. the names of the stars and constellations. She'd explained the Big Bang theory and told him the old Greek myths about the constellations. Looking over at the Presidential Range of New Hampshire's White Mountains from the high mowing meadow, he'd learned the names of the early presidents — Washington, Madison, Jefferson. Gypsy had told him about Thomas Jefferson's beautiful slave mistress, Sally, who was also his deceased wife's half sister. And about George Washington's wooden false teeth.

For a time when he was small, E.A. thought the jagged peaks with snow on them eleven or twelve months of the year actually *were* the presidents.

On mornings like today, when the dew was heavy, E.A. and Gypsy sat on a gray boulder in the shape of a crouching lion at the top of the meadow. Gypsy had explained that the lion-shaped boulder had been deposited there ten thousand years ago by the Great Wisconsin Ice Sheet. E.A. was the only eight-year-old in Kingdom County, homeschooled or otherwise, who could tell you the difference between an esker and a drumlin. When Gypsy first read him "The Fall of the House of Usher" and came to the part where crazy old Usher's house collapsed into the tarn, he'd known what a tarn was.

Gypsy Lee Allen was as smart as a whip. She knew all about things like the Great Wisconsin Ice Sheet and Edgar Allan Poe because she had gone away to the state university on scholarship for a year before she got pregnant with E.A. and had to come home to support him and herself with Gypsy Lee's RFD Escort Service, Inc. She'd even written a country song called "Knocked Up in Vermont." Then, guessing that nobody would buy another song with the word Vermont in the title after "Moonlight in Vermont," she'd changed the title to "Knocked Up in Knoxville."

As the sun came up behind the Presidential Range, Gypsy strummed her guitar and sang a few bars.

> "Knocked up in Knoxville;
> Made up in Memphis;
> Hitched up in Nashville,
> Tennessee."

Gypsy had a clear, strong voice, with every bit as much vibrato as Loretta Lynn's, and E.A. thought the title change was a good one. Even so, he couldn't imagine Music Row buying a song that began "Knocked up in Knoxville," or WSM, the Voice of the Grand Old Opry, playing it over the American airwaves. But the crowds at the bars and roadhouses where Gypsy sang loved it no matter how many times she performed it for them. She'd dedicated "Knocked Up in Knoxville" to E.A.

They watched the sun light up Kingdom County. It sparkled off the village church steeple and the slate roof of the courthouse. It brought out the emerald of the grass in Gran's meadow and the sheen of the river and the silvery blue surface of Memphremagog, the big lake to the north that stretched twenty miles into Canada between tall peaks.

The rising sun lit up the yellowing tops of the sugar maples below them, and it glinted off all the glass and chrome and shining metal of the old cars and pickups and cranes and logging skidders and dozers and backhoes and draglines and tractors in Devil Dan Davis's Midnight Auto Junkyard.

Gypsy hummed a new song she was working on called "Nobody's Child." E.A. looked off at the September snow on New Hampshire's Mount Washington. Gypsy had told him that the highest wind in the world had been recorded there, 231 mph, in 1934.

"Look, hon."

Near the edge of the maple orchard a woodchuck had popped out of its hole. E.A. put his fingers in his mouth and whistled. The chuck swiveled its sleek head around and whistled back. E.A. made an imaginary rifle with his hands. Bang. He and Gypsy had shot more than one hundred chucks this past summer with Grandpa Gleason Allen's 30.06. Orton and Norton Horton, the state boys who lived with Devil Dan Davis and his wife, R.P., called E.A. a woodchuck because his family ate them, just as they ate muskrats and crawfish and whatever else they could shoot or catch. Chucks from the mountain meadows of Kingdom County had a diet of clover and wild grasses and were as flavorful and clean to eat as western beef, but that didn't cut any ice with Orton and Norton.

Gypsy stopped picking her guitar. She nudged Ethan and grinned. Gypsy Lee Allen was twenty-six, but when she grinned at Ethan, she looked about fourteen. A low-flying gray hawk, a male harrier, was gliding over the field, tracing the contours of the ground, occasionally dipping down so that its wings nearly touched the grass to see if he could flush out a mouse or a snake for breakfast. The chuck sat in the sun with its back to the approaching hawk. Gypsy nudged E.A. again.

The harrier made two strong wing beats and picked up the woodchuck, struggled to rise, couldn't, dropped the chuck. The chuck froze for a moment, like a runner caught napping off first base, then dived into its hole.

Far below, Devil Dan came out of his house, wearing his fedora, and went into the machine shed near the entrance of Midnight Auto. Norton and Orton appeared a minute later, carrying R.P.'s wash out to the clothesline. A growling cough, followed immediately by a deep rumbling, emerged from the shed. Devil Dan appeared in the glassed-in cab of his D-60 bulldozer, headed across the flats toward Gran's meadow.

4

DEVIL DAN DAVIS was a miser and a bad-tempered man who, like his bad-tempered father before him, had lived all his life next to the Allen place at the foot of Allen Mountain. Dan sold used parts and machinery out of his junkyard and did contract jobs requiring heavy equipment like his Blade. His avocation, however, was feuding with the Allens.

Dan's sixty-ton D-60 Blade was the biggest bulldozer ever made — powerful enough, Dan said, to push over a courthouse. He cut logging roads and maple sugaring roads and farm roads and roads into gravel pits, doing great and irreparable harm to the environment. Dan Davis frequently proclaimed that there was no such thing as the environment. A small man with a sharp face like a meadow vole's, Dan averred that the environment was a lie made up by the socialists who ran the government in Montpelier. Dan said that if anyone doubted him he would prove his point by running them over with the Blade. "Can you eat the environment?" he roared out at the March Town Meeting, where he fancied himself something of an orator. "No, you cannot. Can you sell it? No, sir, mister man. Can you put it in the bank and draw down two and a half percent interest on it? Not that I ever heard of."

Every Monday morning Devil Dan changed the crankcase oil of the Blade whether he'd used the machine that week or not. He dumped the old oil into Allen Mountain Brook, which ran into the Kingdom River just below the meadow where Ethan and Gypsy played ball. When brown trout and rainbow trout and suckers and perch and bullpout and bass floated belly-up on the surface of the river, Dan said there were too many fish in the crick to start with — it was good for the fish to be thinned out now and again. Otherwise, they would become stunted and develop overly large heads. Dan said that if there had been such a thing as the environment, which there was not, it would be good environmental policy to cull out the weak fishes from the strong ones. Gypsy said the crankcase oil from the Blade would cull out Jonah's whale, it was that toxic.

On the side of his machine shed, Devil Dan had painted a huge sign that said TAKE BACK VERMONT. Who from? Ethan wondered. Take Vermont back how? When? And where? He had no idea what the sign meant, and neither, Gypsy assured him, did Devil Dan. But "Take Back Vermont" sounded good to the junkyard owner, and to others of his mind who did not believe in the environment.

The older boys of the Common called Devil Dan's junkyard Midnight Auto because late at night they would slip under his high-voltage Weed Chopper electric fence and strip junk cars of their antennas, radios, tape decks, and hubcaps. These forays were fraught with peril because Dan patrolled the yard with his shotgun at all hours and did not hesitate to pepper any trespassers with number-eight birdshot. Nor did he shoot first and ask questions afterward; Dan Davis prided himself on shooting first and asking no questions at all. Also, he kept a free-ranging billy goat with ferocious yellow eyes and large horns, which, along with Orton and Norton Horton, Dan's state boys, was the bane of E.A.'s existence. The goat's name was Satan. Sicced on E.A. by Orton and Norton, who were three or four years older and had shaved heads and swastika tattoos inked on their skulls, Satan Davis would shag E.A. all the way home from the railway trestle, butting him and sometimes rolling him into the ditch. E.A. didn't dare tell Gypsy about these assaults because he was afraid she would shoot Satan, and perhaps Orton and Norton in the bargain, and have to go to jail. Then he'd be out a mother *and* a father.

The goat attacks had continued for more than a year and got-

30

ten worse rather than better until at last, this past spring, E.A. had confided his misery to the Colonel. After thinking for a minute, the old soldier said, "My advice to you, boy, is to cut you a stout ironwood stick, and the next time those rapscallions set upon you, do what you can with it." He'd followed the statue's suggestion and done considerable damage to both boys and gotten in a solid lick to Satan's head as well, before Orton and Norton overpowered him and frailed the daylights out of him with his own stick. But since then they'd mostly confined their assaults to verbal abuse, calling him a woodchuck and a woodchuck-eater from a distance. The goat, too, stayed out of range of the stick. So the Colonel's advice had worked in part, which the statue said was the most any advice had ever worked for him. Scarcely a night went by that E.A. did not append to his prayers to Our Father a short request to drown Orton and Norton and the goat in the river, or burn them up in a glorious junkyard conflagration, or arrange for them to slip and fall under the massive treads of Devil Dan's Blade.

5

E.A. AND GYPSY watched the bright yellow bulldozer rumble down Gran's meadow, throwing up a barrier of earth and stones along the edge of the river to prevent the spring highwater from flooding Dan's junkyard. Dan was bulldozing dirt from the out-field of E.A.'s ball diamond, Fenway Park. Right field looked like the start of an open-pit mine.

The Blade's air-conditioned cab was equipped with a tape deck and a PA system with two large loudspeakers mounted on the roof, over which Devil Dan blasted John Philip Sousa marches. To the beat of "Stars and Stripes Forever," E.A. watched a killdeer run out of the asters in front of the dozer, dragging one wing, like a partridge luring a fox away from her nest. Dan plowed up the patch of wildflowers where the killdeer's chicks were hiding. Then he swerved the machine to the left and got the mother bird as well.

"Oh, that son of a bitch," Gypsy shouted. "Did you see that, Ethan? Did you see what that twisted little Nazi in a fedora hat did to those birds?"

E.A. felt bad for the killdeer, but he wasn't surprised. He'd seen Devil Dan hitch a hose to the vertical exhaust pipe of the Blade and gas out a whole lodge of beavers, seen him shoot a loon fishing on the river last summer.

"I'm sorry, Ethan, but that little SS pissant should be put in jail for the rest of his life."

"He's a pretty bad fella, mom. Remember how he shot that loon?"

"That was the most gratuitously cruel act I've ever witnessed."

"He said it was eating his fish."

"What fish? He'd already poisoned all the fish with crankcase oil. You want to wait until he's finished before taking BP, hon?"

E.A. shook his head. "I reckon I better get it in. It might turn off to rain later."

"You sound like Old Bill, sweetie. 'Turn off to rain.'"

"At least I don't sound like Devil Dan."

"No, thank Jesus," Gypsy said. "Thank the sweet Jesus you do *not* sound like Devil Dan."

E.A. stood at home plate, a slate shingle that had fallen off the roof of Gran's eight-sided barn. Now he crowded the plate like Jimmy Collins, the great player-manager of the old Boston Americans, now he stepped out of the box and looked over the diamond like Teddy Ballgame, checking to see if they had the Shift on. Now he was Pudge Fisk in the sixth game of the '75 Series, adjusting his batting glove, pulling down his sleeves, seconds away from blasting the shot heard round the world. He stepped back into the box and grinned out at Gypsy on the hill, which in fact was an abandoned anthill. Keeping up a steady chatter, *atta girl, atta girl, come to mama*, she glowered in at E.A., tipped back, and spun around, her long red hair swinging wildly. She kicked high, revealing under her Outlaws jersey one slender white thigh, and pitched. The BP ball, wound in black electrical tape, waterlogged, half again as heavy as a new baseball, sailed four feet over E.A.'s head and whanged into the southeast wall of the barn, patched with license plates Old Bill had purchased from Midnight Auto, putting a dent in New Mexico.

The book on Gypsy Lee Allen was that she was wild in every way. Gypsy was just eighteen when she was knocked up, not in Knoxville but in Kingdom County, right down past Devil Dan's, under the railroad trestle. One of her most popular early songs was called "Buck-Wild in the Back Seat of a '54 Chevy." She was wild off the mound, too. Four of her first five deliveries came nowhere near the strike zone, either hitting the dirt in front of the plate or caroming off the license plates on the barn. What's more, though Gypsy Lee had pretty blue eyes that smiled like a cat's when her hair was pulled back, she was nearsighted. She missed most of Ethan's underhand tosses back to her, holding her arm straight out with the glove pocket up as if the ball were a pet bird she was trying to coax into landing on it.

E.A. used a thirty-six-inch, thirty-eight-ounce Ethan Allen model bat made at the local factory, one that Earl No Pearl had split fighting off an inside pitch. Earl had taped it and given it to E.A.

"Come to mama," Gypsy said, sticking out Ethan's glove and missing the ball by a foot.

Out in the gap in left center, the Blade was throwing up a high wall of Kingdom County blue clay along the edge of the river. A little closer, standing in the asters in his black rubber barn boots, Old Bill had materialized. He looked like half of the painting *American Gothic*. Bill liked to shag balls when E.A. took BP, because it wasn't work and it gave him an excuse to complain about getting farther behind. There he was in his slouch hat and suspenders, his mouth already going. E.A. couldn't hear him over the Blade, but he knew what Bill was saying. "Hurry up and throw the ball, Gypsy. I ain't got all day. The longer I stand here the behinder I get."

Gypsy wound up, lifting her hands high over her head. She threw the ball more like a shot put than a baseball. No amount of coaching on E.A.'s part ever made a difference. The pitch was outside, but E.A. swung anyway, just to swing at something. He missed.

"There," Gran called from the kitchen doorway. "You're on your way, boy. You've got all the makings of a future Sox hitter."

Gran was watching E.A. through the 8× scope one of Gypsy's RFD clients had mounted on Grandpa Gleason Allen's deer rifle for her. Having someone look at him through a rifle scope made the hair stand up on the back of E.A.'s neck, particularly given the long-standing WYSOTT Allen gun safety policy of never keeping an unloaded firearm on the premises. Other boys' grans sat around gossiping and telling tales of the olden days. They put up black-berry jelly and snap beans for the Kingdom Fair, complained to each other over the horn about their ailments and their neglectful grown children. Gran Allen read her *Weekly World News* and con-ducted a one-woman jihad against the Boston Red Sox and sighted in on E.A. with a loaded deer rifle.

Gypsy threw the ball straight at his head. Luckily, she didn't throw very hard. E.A. ducked and the ball bounced off a 1947 SEE VERMONT license plate. The next pitch landed on the barn roof. As it rolled back down, Ethan caught it behind his back, a trick he'd worked on with his rubber ball for hours every day last sum-mer. Gypsy clapped.

"Just what the Sox need," Gran called out. "Another clown."

The next pitch was low but hittable. E.A. grounded it over the first-base bag, feeling the vibrating jolt of the rock-hard taped ball all the way up to his elbows. He dropped the bat and tore around the bases, crossing home just as Bill reached the ball. Bill picked up the baseball and stared at it as if it were a small meteorite newly fallen from the heavens. "What I don't see," he said, "is why a fella would want to smack at a ball with a stick and then race clear round Robin Hood's barn just to get back where he started."

E.A. had an idea. "Wait a minute, ma. I'll be right back."

He ran to the house, past Gran with the rifle scope still clapped to her eye, now watching the Blade down at the far end of the meadow, and climbed up to his sleeping loft. He reached under his pillow and took out the official American League base-ball the drifter had given him. As E.A. came back out onto the stoop, Gran said, "That last hit was pathetic. It reminded me of the dribbler Buckner booted in 'eighty-six, just when I was begin-ning to regain strength in my legs again. That set me back another decade."

Upriver from where Devil Dan was building the dike, the

white-headed fish hawk that nested on top of the water tank hit the river hard and came up with a sucker in its talons.

"Try this one, ma."

E.A. flipped the new ball to Gypsy and she actually caught it. There was something about a brand-new baseball, he thought, that defined newness. Just the way a brook trout in its spawning colors defined prettiness and Devil Dan Davis defined meanness.

"Where'd you get this, hon?"

"A fella gave it to me."

Gypsy was too nearsighted to read the inscription. "What fella, sweetie? One of the Outlaws?"

"A fella up off the railroad tracks. A drifter."

"Oh, hon. Some of those old drifters are very perverted men."

"More than the Reverend?"

"Well. Maybe not more than the Reverend. But I don't want you holding commerce with railroad tramps, Ethan."

"I wasn't holding commerce with him. He was standing by the barn and I went out to run him off the property and he gave me the ball."

Gypsy bit her lip. "What did he look like?"

Ethan thought. "Like a ball player."

"What does a ball player look like?"

"He wears pinstripes and a cap with the letters NY on it," Gran called out.

E.A. got set at the plate. "It's an official American League ball, ma. One of those lively balls. Earl says you can drive a lively ball twenty, thirty feet farther than what the Outlaws use for base-balls."

"You sure you want to practice with it? It'll get all scuffed up."

"I just aim to give it one good lick."

"You better aim better than last time," Gran said.

"I don't know about this, hon. This is a special ball. Like our special place up on the mountain."

Gypsy tossed the official baseball up into the air six inches and stuck out E.A.'s glove. "Oops."

The ball rolled to a stop at the foot of the anthill mound.

Gypsy picked it up and bit her upper lip with her lower teeth. Most people bite their lower lip with their upper teeth. Not Gypsy. Leave it to a WYSOTT Allen, E.A. thought. Gypsy's teeth were as white as the osprey's head. Why she hadn't made it to Music City yet, Ethan couldn't imagine. Unless it was him. Taking care of him.

"One lick," he said, leveling the taped bat over the plate waist-high to show where he wanted the pitch. "Try throwing out of the stretch."

Gypsy nodded. Just behind E.A.'s forehead, where he heard the Colonel's voice, the Voice of the Red Sox said, "It's the last of the ninth at Fenway, folks. The final game of the World Series, with the bases loaded and the Sox down by three. Allen's coming to the plate . . ."

Gypsy looked in at the imaginary catcher. She shook off his first sign, shook off another, nodded, came to the set position. Checked the runners.

"Fling the ball, Gypsy," Bill whined. "As much as I'm backed up on my chores, I ain't got all day to stand out here in the cowpies while you make up your mind."

Gypsy pitched the baseball. Which, glory be, came right down the pipe over the heart of the plate. E.A. kept his hands back exactly the way the drifter had told him and waited on it and swung. He caught the ball on the fattest part of the bat and sent it high over Old Bill's head. Bill looked up with his mouth open as the ball kept going and going until at last it landed far out in the meadow where the Blade had dozed the grass down to raw clay. E.A. was astonished. Already he was thinking of running overstreet for Bumper's tape measure. He'd never hit a ball that far in his life. Maybe not even half that far.

"Wow," Gypsy said. "Wowee! You've got your batting shoes on, hon. Where'd it go?"

Ethan was running now, out past shortstop, past Bill. There in the blue clay was the ball, buried halfway up its seams. And here came the Blade, martial music blasting.

"No," E.A. shouted. He broke toward the ball like a base runner breaking for second. Gypsy arrived just in time to snatch him back.

As the monstrous yellow bulldozer came on, Devil Dan's voice blasted out of the loudspeaker. "Stand clear, boy. This machine will dozer you down to Chiny."

The white baseball disappeared under the treads of the D-60, which continued down the meadow. E.A. ran up to where the ball had landed. All he could find was the muddy horsehide cover, the writing and birthday inscription no longer visible. It hung from his hand, as limp as shoe leather. For the first time in three or four years he started to cry.

The D-60 had turned around at the far end of the meadow and was proceeding back in their direction, a windrow of blue clay curling away from the huge steel blade.

Through his tears E.A. did not see how Gypsy got there. But she was standing in the path of the oncoming machine, hands on her hips, refusing to move. "Come ahead," she shouted. "Run over me, you impotent little rat's prick."

"You go, girl," Gran screeched from the doorway. "You tell him where the bear shit in the buckwheat, Gypsy Lee."

"Get outen my way, hoor," Devil Dan shouted through the loudspeaker.

When Gypsy didn't, Dan shut off his machine and climbed out onto the top step. "You and your little bastard get off my premises or I'll run you off with this Cat."

"This isn't your property, it's ours," Gypsy shouted back. "There's a place in hell for you, Devil Dan. To deliberately run over a little boy's baseball."

"A curse on you and yours, Dan Davis," Gran screamed. "Unto the seventh generation."

Dan stood on the top step of his machine and shook his little fist. He was dancing mad. E.A. could see his feet going up and down in place, like the feet of a wind-up toy.

"You and your bastard get offen my property," Dan shouted again, feet hopping.

"This is Allen land. You're on *our* land," Gypsy shouted back.

"What's going on here?" It was R.P. — Rolling Pin Davis — cruising down the meadow, holding her housedress up to the tops of her high buttoned shoes. In her other hand she wielded the formidable culinary instrument from which her name derived.

Whipping her Outlaws jersey up over her head and flinging it down at her feet, Gypsy stood in the meadow in her birthday suit, except for a tiny yellow G-string. Gypsy's breasts were not much larger than a young girl's and she had freckles on her shoulders. "Here I am, Devil Davis," she shouted. "I guess you didn't get enough of me last night. Or if you did you forgot to leave the twenty dollars on my dresser. Pony up. You owe me twenty bucks."

"What's this all about?" R.P. demanded. "Put your shift back on, Gypsy Lee."

"Not until your wayward husband pays me. He wanted me to dance buck-naked for him last night. Then he stiffed me. That was the only stiff thing about him."

"I never —" Devil Dan said, his shiny little dress shoes going fast on the top step of the Blade.

"Look, he wants to dance," Gypsy said. "I'll dance for him."

She ran up the steps of the Blade, shoved Dan out of the way, clambered onto the roof of the yellow cab, and began to do a furious jig. "Here's the River Dance," she screamed. Gran began to clap rhythmically. "The same one we did bare-naked together last night, Devil Dan. Will you pay me for services rendered, or will I have to take you to small-claims court? Uh-oh. Here comes the judge."

R.P. bore down on the machine. She drew back her throwing arm and let fly with the rolling pin, which whistled through the air end over end like an old-fashioned hand grenade, grazing the top of Devil Dan's fedora and crashing through the side window of the cab.

"What are you doing, woman?" Dan shouted.

R.P. clawed her way up the steps, following the rolling pin into the cab, where she set to work on the instrument panel. As R.P.

hammered at the levers and gauges with the rolling pin and Gypsy danced and Gran screeched, Bill remarked, "Well, E.A., I got to get overstreet to the feed store now. You need anything from town?"

Ethan, holding what was left of his official American League baseball, shook his head.

6

IT WAS RAINING in Kingdom County. The wind blew out of the west, off the Green Mountains, and the rain came riding in on the wind, falling steadily on Gran's piney woods, bringing out the evergreen scent, falling on the scarred and ruined meadow by the river and on the brook that ran down the mountain, washing worms and bugs into the current, so the brook trout would bite like crazy in the morning, falling *tick tick tick* on the license plates Bill had used to patch the octagonal barn. E.A. lay in his loft bed and listened to the driving rain and thought over the events of the day. He decided to count his family's blessings and thank Our Father for them, just the way Gypsy had taught him to. They had a falling-down house that they were cannibalizing for stove wood and a rig named Patsy. They had an eight-sided barn patched with license plates of places he longed to see, a barn where, on rainy days, he liked to read books like *Kidnapped* and *Huckleberry Finn* and to practice throwing his red rubber ball through the tire swing. He, personally, had the largest collection of Red Sox baseball cards in Kingdom County, also the leftover hide of an official American League baseball, also a Green Mountain bat with a cracked handle. He had a pretty young ma who wrote beautiful songs about wildwood flowers and knocked-up girls, who pitched him BP and took him fishing and stripped down to her birthday suit and did the River Dance on Devil Dan's earthmoving machine in the broad light of day and, even now, as E.A. was counting his blessings, was sitting in the front parlor dressed as Little Nell, the Queen of the Gold Dust Saloon, drinking assorted Twining teas with Corporal Colin Urquahart, in his full official regalia, from the RCMP barracks in Sherbrooke, Quebec. Corporal Urquahart was known more familiarly to E.A. as Sergeant Preston of the Yukon. Besides being one of Gypsy's most faithful clients, the jovial Mountie was a great favorite of Ethan's, bringing him air rifles and ice skates and hockey sticks and fishing rods, and E.A. was thankful for him, too. For all these blessings, E.A. thanked Our Father, tacking on a request that He reveal the name of Gone and Long Forgotten, if not now then soon.

E.A. went straight from counting his blessings to reciting Our Father Who Art in Heaven. He had never been exactly sure what "deliver us from evil" meant, but he assumed it had something to do with revenge. Gypsy had enjoyed revenge that morning, setting R.P. on Devil Dan and the Blade. E.A., however, still had a score to settle. He and Dan weren't even — not by a long shot. He would dump a ten-pound sack of Shurfine sugar in the gas tank of the Blade. He would set fire to Dan's machine shed with the Blade inside it. He would shoot Devil Dan with Grandpa Gleason Allen's deer rifle and hang him up by his little feet in Gran's dooryard maple like a deer.

E.A. began again. "Our Father who art in heaven . . . thy kingdom come . . ." Thy kingdom come must be Kingdom County, Our Father being somehow connected with the Colonel. E.A. no longer supposed that the Colonel actually *was* Our Father, or his father, either. But the Colonel had been as much a father to him as anyone had. The Outlaws, Earl and the boys, were more like indulgent uncles, or grown-up brothers, than fathers. Thinking about brothers sidetracked E.A. yet again, because he wished he had one, or even a sister. He seemed destined tonight not to get to the end of his prayers, so finally he just slammed through the whole shebang without thinking what any of the words meant, adding a quick P.S. wish for Gypsy to find a good man, like Randolph Scott or Jimmy Stewart in her song "A Good Man Like Randolph Scott or Jimmy Stewart Is Christly Hard to Find These

Days," and a P.P.S. for Gran to get her Series ring at last and be easier to live with, and finally for Devil Dan to fall off the Blade and get squashed under its treads like the official American League baseball.

"All in the fullness of time, boy," the Colonel's voice said as E.A. started to drift off, feeling happy and thrice blessed and dreaming of revenge and baseball.

7

MOST VISITORS to Kingdom Common quickly realized that more ardent Red Sox fans could not be found anywhere else in New England. Three signs within the village limits proclaimed the relationship between the baseball fans of the Common and their beloved team.

Approaching the village from the south on old Route 5, you could not miss the large sign with tall black letters that said, WELCOME TO KINGDOM COMMON, THE CAPITAL OF THE RED SOX NATION. Strangers skeptical of this claim had only to drive another quarter of a mile to the long rectangular green at the heart of the village, with the baseball diamond laid out at its south end, and lift up their eyes not unto the steep hills surrounding the town but to the huge green bulletin board, twenty feet long by fifteen feet high, atop the bat factory, known locally as the Green Monster of Kingdom Common. During the off-season, the Green Monster announced, in white wooden letters a foot and a half high, such uplifting tidings as "236 Accident Free Days" or "Have a Safe New Year" or "Congratulations to Porter Kittredge, Proud Father of an Eleven Pound Future Power Hitter." But from early April until however deep into the fall the Sox held on before being eliminated by bad luck or injuries or mismanagement in the front office, the giant announcement board looming over the mill was used as a scoreboard.

The Green Monster of Kingdom Common was tended by Moonface Poulin. In a box about the size of a kitchen woodbox, located behind the sign, Moonface kept his wooden letters and numbers. Nearby lay his tall, homemade, spruce-pole ladder. True, Moon's grasp of Sox data was more impressive than his spelling. He had never figured out, despite constant reminders, that Chicago was not spelled with two *g*'s or that the *e* between the first and second syllables of the Oakland Athletics was superfluous. But Moon more than made up for these unorthodoxies with his unhurried, deliberate style, his quiet aplomb, and his impenetrable, stately demeanor when posting the scores. Even Gran, one morning in the summer of E.A.'s tenth year, watching Moon's expression out her kitchen window through Gypsy's rifle scope, could not discern from his features whether the Sox had won the critical rubber game in a three-game series with the Yankees the night before until the numbers went up. NEW YORK 12 SOX 1.

Gran was so delighted by her team's humiliating defeat that she inadvertently pulled the trigger of Grandpa Gleason's rifle. The 30.06 went off inside the kitchen with a thunderous detonation, shattering the window. A hole an inch and a half in diameter instantly appeared in the middle of the letter X in SOX on the Green Monster. Whereupon Moonface won the everlasting admiration of the entire village by simply continuing about his business, which was to add, without missing a beat, YANKS TAKE SOUL POSS. OF 1ST PLACE.

Yet even in those palmy summers when the Sox were on a tear, the tidings that blazed forth from the Green Monster of Kingdom Common, however encouraging, were viewed by villagers in the context of a sobering third message, this one lettered in red on the abandoned water tank near the railroad trestle over the river just upstream from Gran's meadow. It said BOSTON RED SOX WORLD CHAMPIONS — 1918. And no news that Moonface Poulin could ever relay to the Kingdom from the scoreboard atop the bat factory could counteract the stark truth that the Sox had not won a World Series since then.

"I am a vengeful fella when need be," the Colonel was telling E.A. on the day Gran shot the Green Monster. "I'll endure so much and then no more. John Bull found that out over at Fort Ti. So did the York Staters who proposed to annex Vermont. When the time comes to act, I'll be all action. Don't you ever misdoubt it."

"Two years have gone by," E.A. said. "Two years have gone by since I first asked you to do something about Dan Davis. I don't recall seeing any action yet."

Lately Dan had been threatening again to dozer down Gran's barn with his Blade. But the Colonel had not seen fit to do anything about it, and now fall was in the air once more. At the far end of the Common the Outlaws were getting ready for their last game of the season. They were playing Pond in the Sky for the league championship.

Across the street in front of the drugstore, Old Lady Benton said, "There. Do you see that, Reverend? He's talking to that statue again."

"That's bad," the Reverend said. "It's unnatural. Holding conversation with a graven image."

E.A. wanted to holler across to the Reverend, was it right and natural to ask Gypsy Lee to put on a long, dark Delilah wig and nothing else but her G-string and call the Reverend her big manly Samson and chase him around her bedroom with a pair of scissors? Not that the man of the cloth had that much hair to start with.

Now Old Lady Benton was saying, "Allowed to patrol the village at all hours of the day and night. Where's his mother, I'd like to know?"

E.A. imagined that the Reverend would like to know the same thing.

"That pair over across there," E.A. said to the Colonel, "is about as bad as Devil Dan. Maybe worse. Can't you help me with them, at least?" He looked up, past the Colonel's extended sword, broken off at the point, at the bronze face under the three-cornered hat. As usual, his old friend was gazing down the common to where the Outlaws were taking BP.

"What is it?" the statue said in that place just behind E.A.'s forehead where only E.A. could hear him. "What is it you want now?" As though he didn't want to be bothered. Or, worse yet, as though he'd already done something for E.A. and the boy was returning to the well once too often.

Though it brought him into full view of the Reverend and Old Lady Benton, E.A. stepped directly into the statue's line of sight. "I'll tell you what I want. I want you to cause Devil Dan Davis to fall off his machine and get run over by those big treads, cleats on them the size of ax blades. And" — raising his voice and glaring across the street — "I want you to cause the Angel of Death to slay his first-born. And locusts to descend on his vineyard."

The Colonel thought for a minute. "Why would you wish for all that misfortune to befall one man?"

"Devil Dan said Gypsy Lee was a hoor and that made our place a hoorhouse and he wouldn't have a hoorhouse next door where R.P. had to look out at it every day. And that Gran's barn's going to fall over onto his property someday, and he intends to dozer it down first."

"Does he now?" the Colonel said with more of an edge to his voice. Ethan knew the Colonel was not happy to have a direct descendant of his, even a WYSOTT Allen, called a hoor.

"I will reflect about all this," the statue said.

"Why do you need to reflect? Weren't you a soldier? I want vengeance and I want it now. Before he knocks down our place. Not afterward, when it's too late."

"I said, I will study on it. Now skedaddle on down to the ball diamond. Those Outlaws need you to shag foul balls, keep score. They shouldn't even be playing this game. They should have clinched the league ten games ago. There was no call to let the race drag on so. The rumdummies are apt to throw it all away now. Just like the Sox, losing that game to those York Staters last night. Your grandma was right to fire a ball through that tally board."

"The state should step in and take him away," Old Lady Benton said.

"I'll see what I can do," the statue said to E.A. "I might send someone to help you out."

47

"With Devil Dan?"

"No. Dan is a no-'count pismire. With your baseball."

"How'll I know who he is?"

"You'll know."

"Your only begotten son, no doubt."

"Misbegotten is more like it. Now see here. If he shows, don't listen to him on anything but baseball. Other than baseball, he's just another loser. But on baseball, listen like your future in the game depends on it."

"Why is that?"

"Because it does. Now scat. They'll be starting up that contest in another few minutes and I don't want to be distracted. Why I should care is more than I'll ever know."

8

JUDGE CHARLIE KINNESON, who umpired the Outlaws' home games, was meeting with the team captains at home plate. E.A. sat on the Outlaws' bench on the third-base side of the diamond, just in front of the small wooden grandstand, copying the names of the Pond in the Sky players into the Outlaws' scorebook. The scorebook was green and flat and dog-eared and stained with beer and Coke and chewing tobacco and mustard, and it dated back one year, to when the Outlaws had lost the championship game to the team they were playing today. The players were mostly the same this year for both teams. Gypsy and Gran, who had come over to the game in Patsy, sat behind E.A. in the first row of the bleachers.

The Pond captain, who was also their pitcher, came over to the bench to get his team's scorebook, in which E.A. was now penciling the Outlaws' roster. A bespectacled beanpole, he looked like the illustration of Ichabod Crane in the matched set of Washington Irving volumes that the American literature prof from Middlebury College who summered in Lost Nation Hollow had given Gypsy for dressing up in white and reciting from Emily Dickinson's *Collected Poems* while she did a striptease.

"What's this all about?" Ichabod said. He was a substitute schoolteacher in the off-season, E.A. had heard. "Who's this kid? What's he doing with my book?"

"Scorekeeper," Earl No Pearl said.

"He's too young to keep score."

"Ask him a baseball question," Gypsy called out from the bleachers.

"What?"

"Ask him any baseball question you can think of."

E.A. saw the sneer come across Ichabod's face, saw his lip curl. "Winningest pitcher in baseball history?" Ichabod said.

"Denton True 'Cy' Young, five hundred and eleven wins," E.A. said, continuing to write. "Here's one for you. Pitcher who threw the first perfect game in major-league baseball?"

"What?" Ichabod said.

E.A. looked up and gave him the sneer right back. "I thought *you* were supposed to be the schoolteacher," he said. "Cy Young again. May 5, 1904."

Gypsy laughed. "Atta boy, E.A."

Judge Charlie K, strapping on his umpire's chest protector, clapped his hands together twice and called out, "Let's get this show on the road, gentlemen. Play ball."

An inning into the championship game, E.A. knew that it was going to be a pitcher's duel. Earl didn't have much to go with his fastball, but he threw so hard E.A. could hear the ball hum from where he stood behind the backstop to keep score and shag foul balls.

The beanpole substitute-schoolteacher pitcher from Pond in the Sky wasn't as fast as Earl. Nobody in the Northern Border League was. But Ichabod came from the side and was sneaky-quick and crafty, with a big, sweeping, yellowhammer curve ball that kept the Outlaw hitters off stride. Though he'd never gone to school a day in his life, E.A. disliked schoolteachers in general. During the Outlaws' games, if he wanted to see a schoolteacher all he had to do was look up at Old Lady Benton, camped out with her binoculars in her green rocker. He did not need to watch a teacher pitch.

In the bottom of the second, with no score, Porter Kittredge hit a high foul ball over the backstop. E.A. dropped the scorebook, grabbed his glove, and made a diving catch. The crowd cheered.

"Ain't you a man and a half, E.A.," Gran called out sarcastically. "Ain't you the grandstander, though."

"Nice catch, Ethan," Judge Charlie K said as E.A. tossed the ball back over the chicken wire. "If I'd made a few more like that one back in my playing days, the Sox might have come calling on me."

At the end of the fifth the score was 1–1. That's when E.A. spotted him again. Though he hadn't seen the drifter for two years, he recognized him immediately. He was leaning against the last remaining elm tree on the common, twenty feet behind the backstop, under an oriole's nest. He was wearing a Red Sox cap and the same ratty suit jacket, once-white shirt, uncreased khaki pants, and battered work shoes, with a cigarette butt in the corner of his mouth and a bottle twisted up in a brown paper bag sticking out of his jacket pocket. As E.A. watched, the drifter took the bagged bottle, unscrewed the cap, drank, screwed the cap back on, and stuck the bottle back in his pocket. All without taking his eyes off the game.

E.A. waved. The drifter nodded. E.A. wished he'd say something. About how much he'd grown in two years, or about his diving catch of Porter's foul ball. From the diamond came the loud crack of Earl's bat. Another foul ball, very high. It descended into the elm tree, glanced off several limbs, and narrowly missed the oriole's nest. Ethan ran to it and got his glove on it, but it was harder to catch a ball falling out of a tree than people might think. The baseball ricocheted off the heel of his glove onto the ground near a trash barrel. The white ball lying there reminded Ethan of the official baseball the stranger had given him on the night of his eighth birthday. He was afraid the man was going to ask about it. Hurriedly, he reached down with his glove, picked up the foul ball, and returned to the backstop. Earl flied to center for the third out of the inning.

Between innings E.A. went around the backstop to give the ball back to Judge Charlie K. "Keep it for a souvenir, Ethan," the judge said. "I've got more than enough."

51

E.A. ran over to the bleachers. "Hold this for me, ma, will you?" he said, handing the ball to Gypsy. He jerked his head toward the oriole's hammock. "Almost hit the bird's nest."

"Well, I'm glad it —" Gypsy started to say. She stopped, stared at the drifter a moment, looked back at E.A. "I'm glad it didn't," she finished.

"I was hoping it would," Gran said. "I could never stand orioles."

E.A. returned to his station behind the backstop.

"Ethan."

The drifter's voice was as harsh as E.A. remembered it. He'd moved a few feet out from the elm tree. "A dead ball like that? Pick it up with your throwing hand. Not your glove."

E.A. wasn't sure what he meant.

"You always pick up a dead ball with your bare hand," the man explained. "That way you don't have to take it out of your glove before you throw it. Saves time."

E.A. realized that the drifter was referring to the foul ball that had fallen out of the elm tree. He didn't sound critical. He sounded like a man stating a point of information to another man. The drifter nodded at E.A. as if to say, okay, now you know. Then he took another swig from the bottle in the brown bag.

Out of nowhere, here came Deputy Warden Kinneson, big hat jutting forward, marching toward the stranger. E.A. did not often see the deputy on foot. Generally he sat in his cruiser outside of town on the county road, waiting for someone to go thirty-six miles per hour on a wooded, unpopulated straightaway.

The deputy's official blue hat bobbed along. E.A. hoped the orioles would let fly all over it.

"You there. In the baseball cap," the officer said. "There's no drinking on the village common."

The drifter was just lifting the bottle to his mouth again. He took a drink, and his ice-colored eyes did not leave the ball field, where the Outlaws were hustling out, the Pond townies hustling in. He watched the two teams dispassionately, like a man watching ants at work.

"You hear me, mister? You don't put that bottle away, I'll have to write . . ."

The deputy's voice trailed off. He took a step back, then another, then turned and walked quickly away. The drifter sloshed what was left in the bottle and lifted it to his mouth and knocked it back, then flipped the sack with the bottle inside end over end into the green trash barrel. Once again his eyes were back on the common, on Earl taking his warm-up pitches.

The championship game stayed tied through the eighth inning. In the top of the ninth, Pond in the Sky pushed a run across, and it began to look like a repeat of last year. A dispirited silence had fallen over the grandstand, over the green lined with pickups and cars. The drifter had left for an inning, but now he was back with a fresh bottle. This time there was no bag wrapped around it. When Pappy Gilmore started out the bottom of the ninth with a foul onto the church lawn, E.A., retrieving the ball, saw the label on the drifter's bottle. Crackling Rose. Like the cover song Gypsy sometimes sang at the hotel.

E.A. watched the stranger watch the game. He was noticeably taller than Earl. A really big man.

"They can't seem to get to old Ichabod," E.A. said to the drifter as Pappy took a ball outside.

"Would that be the pitcher's name? Ichabod?"

"His name is Horace Guyette. But they call him Teach on account of he's a substitute schoolteacher in the off-season. I call him Ichabod. For old Ichabod Crane in a storybook a fella gave Gypsy."

Pappy swung at Guyette's sweeping curve and missed.

"He keeps them off balance with that big yellowhammer hook," E.A. said. He wanted to impress the drifter with knowing what a yellowhammer was.

"They need to lay for his fastball," the man said. "You can't tell what pitch he'll start you off with. But anytime he misses with the curve, the next one is almost always a fastball. That's the pitch your team has to lay for."

Pappy took another ball, a curve inside. Pappy couldn't drive

53

the ball anymore, but he was more patient than the other Outlaws and got his share of walks and singles, loopers over the infield or seeing-eye grounders.

"You mean you have to guess what the next pitch'll be?" E.A. said.

"A good hitter guesses a lot," the man agreed. "But in the case of old Ichabod, there's not much guesswork to it. The last pitch he thrown? To that old man? It was a curve that missed. Now watch. This one will likely be the heater."

It was. Twenty years ago, fifteen years ago, Pappy would have parked Guyette's fastball over in the street in front of the brick block. Now all he could do was foul it back into the screen.

"The other thing is," the drifter went on, "a player like that pitcher? You have to get an edge on him. Rattle him. Call him Ichabod, maybe. A schoolteacher would likely know who your Ichabod was. Call him Ichabod."

Guyette seemed to be tiring. He walked Pappy on the next two pitches. Then he hit Elmer Kittredge, then he walked Elmer's brother Porter. The Outlaws had the bases loaded with nobody out. But just when it seemed that they had the momentum to win, Merle Kittredge and Moonface Poulin struck out, leaving the team one out away from another disappointing season. Slim Johnson got ready to step into the batter's box. Slim was a terrible curve-ball hitter and had already struck out twice on Guyette's yellowhammer.

"Time, Charlie," Earl No Pearl said. He turned to the backstop, where E.A. had just penciled another *K* in the Outlaws' column. "E.A. Leave me see that book."

E.A. trotted around the screen and handed him the scorebook. Earl glanced at it. "Does their book look exactly like ours?" he said.

E.A. nodded.

"Then you go up to bat for Slim. Take four balls. Allen for Johnson," he called over toward the Pond bench.

His heart thumping, E.A. headed out to the plate with Earl's thirty-eight-inch Green Mountain Rebel. It was approaching twilight now. The swifts that nested in the belfry of the church steeple were working the sky high above the common for gnats.

"Allen pinch-hitting for Johnson," Earl said to Judge Charlie K.

The schoolteacher started down off the mound. "See here," he said. "What is this all about? Show me his name in the book."

Earl took the green scorebook out to the pitcher and showed him E.A.'s name at the bottom of the roster.

"Allen, Ethan," Ichabod read aloud. He looked at E.A. "What sort of charade is this?"

E.A., leaning on his bat and watching the confab like Teddy Ballgame in his poster at home, did not like the word "charade." He was not sure what it meant, but it had a nasty, sarcastic ring when the four-eyes used it.

"What is this, a joke?" the teacher said.

"It's no joke," Earl said. "E.A. Allen for Johnson."

The schoolteacher motioned for his scorekeeper, who happened to be his skinnyminnie wife, who, E.A. had heard, also was a schoolteacher. "Bring our book out here, Wilhelmina. Show me that absurd name in our book."

Wilhelmina came out onto the field. There was E.A.'s name in the Pond scorebook. Right where he'd penciled it in before the game.

"This is a farce," Ichabod said.

No, E.A. thought. A farce is a substitute schoolteacher for a pitcher. *That's* what a farce is.

Judge Charlie came striding out, tapping his face mask against his leg. "What's up, gentlemen?"

"This is a mockery," Ichabod said, pointing at E.A.'s name in the book, then at E.A.

"Then strike him out," Charlie said. "Play ball."

On his way back to the Outlaws' bench, Earl No Pearl said quietly, "No fancy-Dan stuff, E.A. The season's on the line. No drag bunts like when I put you in against Woodsville last month. There's a force at every base."

"Just take four balls, E.A.," Pappy called in from third. "Take four and tie her up. Old Earl'll do the rest."

Ethan glanced over his shoulder. The stranger was still there, leaning against the elm, watching. The bottle was back in his jacket pocket.

"All right," the schoolteacher said as E.A. stepped into the batter's box. "Two can play at this game."

Guyette turned and motioned to his outfielders, waving them in. To a chorus of hoots and jeers and angry horn blasts from the Outlaws' fans, the Pond outfield trotted in and sat down on the edge of the grass just beyond the infield. Now E.A. saw with great clarity why Gypsy had always detested teachers, why she'd insisted on homeschooling him. Making fun of boys. Getting the upper hand. Schoolteaching, E.A. realized, was all about getting the upper hand on kids. Still, useless though they were, schoolteachers knew certain things. As the drifter had pointed out, the four-eyes would probably know his Washington Irving.

E.A. lifted his hand and stepped out of the batter's box.

"Time," Judge Charlie K barked.

E.A. said to Earl, in the on-deck circle, "Ichabod."

"What?"

E.A. jerked his head toward the schoolteacher. "Call him Ichabod. Ichabod Crane."

Earl didn't know Ichabod Crane from Nebuchadnezzar. But he cupped his hands around his mouth and called out toward the mound, "Hey, Icherbod. Hey, hey, Icherbod."

"What's that?" the schoolteacher said. "What's that now?"

Earl signaled to the Outlaws' bench.

"Hey, Icherbod," they yelled. "Hey, hey, Icherbod."

The first pitch was a blazing fastball, inside, at eye level. It just missed the bill of E.A.'s Red Sox cap. Fine. E.A. was afraid of Devil Dan's Blade. If the truth be known, he was afraid of Orton and Norton Horton. But not of a baseball. He'd never been afraid of a baseball in his life. His foot didn't go into the bucket.

"Ball one," Judge Charlie K said.

"That's a strike on anybody but a midget," the catcher said.

"It was above the letters on the batter and it was inside," Charlie said in the courtroom voice that had put fear into the hearts of so many drunk drivers, wife-beaters, bar fighters, and officious authorities, as well. There was no further argument from the catcher.

"Hey, Icherbod." The whole grandstand was taking it up. The Outlaws' girlfriends and wives and exes, high school kids, little kids younger than Ethan. Everybody. "Hey, Icherbod Crane."

The teacher missed outside with the yellowhammer, and Judge Charlie barked, "Ball two." But oh Lordy, E.A. thought, how that curve ball had dipped, swooped down like one of the swifts flying over the village. He wondered how a man ever got a baseball to behave like that. E.A. did not see how he could get his bat on a pitch that darted downward like a swallow.

"Two and oh," Judge Charlie said. "Play ball, boys. Night's coming."

E.A. glanced over his shoulder at the drifter. The big man touched the bill of his cap with his index finger.

"That's two, E.A., take two more," Earl called out as the grandstand behind third base started up with their "Icherbod" refrain again. With Gypsy's assistance, Gran stood up on the peeled wooden bleacher, ringing a cowbell and shouting "Icherbod! Icherbod!" She'd gladly have stoned Guyette if given the chance.

The teacher took his time coming to his set. E.A. leveled his bat waist-high, then set his hands back the way the drifter had taught him two years ago. He knew what pitch was coming, and he knew that the four-eyes would let up on it just enough to be sure to put it across the plate. It occurred to him that maybe he should see a pitch there once in order to time it. Then he decided. If it was there he'd swing.

It was there. Straight, medium-fast, standard BP fare. E.A.'d seen quicker pitches from Porter. He kept his eye on the ball, white in the dusk, and he turned on it hard without overswinging and drove it ten feet above the head of the left-fielder, who was sitting on the grass behind the shortstop. Pappy was so surprised that he forgot to run. Elmer, coming hard from second, had to remind him. They crossed home plate five feet apart.

The grandstand was up and shrieking, horns were blowing all around the common, Gran's cowbell was clanging like a five-alarm fire. As Ethan rounded first, the Outlaws poured onto the field. Between second and third they intercepted him in a body, got him up on their shoulders, while he fought like a wildcat, wanting to retrieve the ball. They paraded him all over the field. The whole village cheered. Players, fans, farmers, loggers, big boys, the Outlaws' women. Only the Pond players were silent, heading slowly toward their vehicles. Judge Charlie K, ambling home across the outfield with his umpire's mask tucked under his arm, stooped and picked up the game-winning ball to give to E.A. later. Already the cars and pickups and farm trucks were lining up for the victory procession around the common, drivers plugging in their deer-jacking spotlights, horns bleating.

When E.A. finally fought his way to the ground, he ran to the elm tree. The stranger was gone, but it didn't matter. Because the boy was already thinking, *This is nothing. All this is nothing to what will happen when I do the same thing in the last game of the World Series for the Boston Red Sox.*

9

"WELL?" ETHAN SAID. "You see my game-winning double?"

"I scored it a single in my book," the Colonel said. "On account of the game was over and won by the time you reached first base. Of course I saw it. I see everything that takes place on this so-called common. Including a great plenty I'd rather not witness."

The victory procession was over. The deputy had made them stop after they'd gone three times around the green, citing a noise ordinance. But the celebration was still going strong at the hotel, where the barroom was lit up like Christmas. On Anderson Hill someone was burning leaves.

"I thought you were instructed to leave four go by," the Colonel harangued him. "On my team, a fella that can't take instruction is going to ride the pine, by the hollering Christ child."

"Number one, you don't have a team. Number two, you don't have to swear at me. I'm expected to watch four go by with the bat on my shoulder? Let a four-eyes substitute schoolteacher make a fool of me?"

The Colonel frowned. "I wasn't aware that the fella was a schoolmaster. That throws a different light on the situation. I never favored schoolmasters that much myself. Stuck a Canada bull thistle up through a knothole in the backhouse wall when the old dominie was inside doing his business and got myself expelled from school for good when I was your age. Before I was your age, I reckon. What are you, eight, nine?"

"I'm ten, as you very well know. Don't pretend you don't. Besides which, you've told me that Canada bull thistle story ten times. You're getting forgetful in your old age."

"It's a good story that doesn't get into the history books. Howsomever. To get back to what's important. In baseballdom, a fella that can't take orders will never make the grade. That was more than half of your — of my own trouble. I'd been able to take orders, I'd have been president of the United States. Governor of Vermont at the very least. Now. You say you hope to go all the way to the top. Is that correct?"

"Not hope to. Intend to."

"Fine. Then you need to be able to take orders. Otherwise, what you've got isn't baseball, it's anarchy. I was your manager, you'd ride the pine till the cows come home."

"Well," E.A. said, "you aren't my manager. And you aren't my father, or Our Father, either."

"Maybe not. But for a while I and Gypsy Lee were the only friends you had and don't you forget it."

E.A. grinned. "Everybody in the village is my friend tonight."

Then they were quiet, the Colonel standing, broken sword extended toward the ball field, E.A. sitting on the pedestal. The bonfire on Anderson Hill smelled good. E.A. noticed that the stars were out. He'd better be getting home.

"CANDLEMAS DAY, Candlemas Day. Half your wood and half your hay."

It was February 2, and a gale was blowing out of Canada. As usual on Candlemas Day, Old Bill had come up to the house from his trailer to recite the ancient adage to the effect that by early February a farmer should have used up no more than half of his supply of firewood and hay, with half left to see him through the balance of the winter.

It was winter, all right. Through the blizzard, E.A. couldn't even see Fenway Park. Bill, who loved sayings of all kinds, particularly if they reassured him that his decision to do no work that day was unquestionably right, peered out the window.

"How do you like this Canadian thaw, E.A.?"

"What's a Canadian thaw, Bill?" E.A. said, feeding a couple of split floorboards from the back bedroom and a piece of a cow stanchion into Gran's Glenwood.

With considerable satisfaction, Bill said, "Two foot of snow and a hang of a blow. We won't be able to get out and do much today." Then, "Candlemas Day, Candlemas Day. Half your wood and half your hay. What a winter!"

As far as E.A. was concerned, this winter had been like any other. Cold and long and no baseball, except throwing to his swinging tire inside the empty hayloft. He stayed busy with his homeschooling, Gran read the *Weekly World News*, Gypsy sang on weekends and put on shows at home for her regulars, Earl and

Moonface and the Reverend and Sergeant Preston and a few others. The escort business always fell off in the winter. Sometimes, for fun, Gypsy and E.A. slid down the hill behind the house on flattened-out cardboard boxes.

A few days before Christmas they had taken the bucksaw up through the snowy woods to their special place to select a balsam fir for their Christmas tree. Gypsy could never find one that suited her. The balsams were all full on the side facing the clearing, sparse and ragged on the woods side. If she'd let E.A. climb up and take the top off a taller tree, the way he wanted to, they could have had their pick. But Gypsy couldn't bear the idea of topping a tree. She said that was the sort of thing Devil Dan would do, except that Dan did not believe in Christmas any more than he believed in the environment.

So as usual they'd bucked down a scraggly little fir, and as they were dragging it back toward the sugar orchard and Gypsy was composing a song called "The One-Sided Christmas Tree," which wasn't going anyplace, she said, "Oh, Ethan. Look at this, hon."

In the snowy meadow, on the protected east side of their sitting rock dropped by the Great Wisconsin Ice Sheet, was the perfect imprint of an owl's wings. It was probably a big white Canadian owl. The bird had dived into the snow after a mouse, most likely the night before, and the print of every wing feather stood out as if in a photographic negative. The owl's wingspan was wider than E.A.'s arms when he stretched them straight out from his shoulders. And right there was Gypsy's next great song, "The Snow Owl," which she didn't even know she'd been looking for. She finished it two weeks later, and everybody at the hotel barroom loved it. That also happened to be her twenty-ninth birthday. For a present, E.A. had gotten her new guitar strings out of a mail-order catalog.

In January the State Environmental Board had found Devil Dan in violation of one hundred and forty-six separate regulations. But the state had no funds to take him to court. The day the indictment was handed down, during a midwinter thaw, Dan dozered five more junk cars over the bank along the river.

By the Candlemas Day blizzard, the Allens were not only out of firewood, they were close to out of food. The deer Gypsy had jacked last December was nearly gone, and they were low on maple sugar for table sweetening. Gypsy's escort service was suffering more than usual this winter; Earl was away on a haul, Moonface was in jail for three months for "tumultuous conduct," meaning bar fighting, and she'd had to shut off a couple of the other regulars — the Reverend and the spindly little social services man from Memphremagog — because their requests were getting too outlandish. That was what a hard Vermont winter could do to people, Gypsy Lee said.

One sunny day in March Gypsy and E.A. took a geology field trip to their special place through hip-high snow. Bill had announced the day before that water had begun to run down the ditches. "When the spring water runs down the ditches, the sap runs up the trees," he intoned. "Sugaring time's coming."

The snow had melted on top of their boulder, and as E.A. and Gypsy perched on it, looking out over the Kingdom, she told him again how the ice sheet had come inching down from the north, gouging out the trenches where Lake Memphremagog and Lake Willoughby now lay, clipping off the tops of the Green and White Mountains, depositing sand and gravel on the meadow, dropping huge boulders like theirs in its retreating path. She told about the Arctic char that swam down the rivers from the north when the glacier melted and by degrees over the eons transformed into brook trout. "Our own little Galápagos," she said. "Charles Darwin should have come to Kingdom County, Ethan. He'd have had a field day."

E.A. wasn't sure who Charles Darwin was. Maybe a country singer, though Darwin sounded more like a country singer's first name.

"Look, hon." Gypsy pointed at a red squirrel in the top of a sugar maple, biting off twigs and sucking on the fresh sap. "Bill's right. It's sugaring time."

They tapped the trees the old-fashioned way, with wooden buckets and wooden spouts, no plastic pipeline running straight from tree to sugarhouse for the WYSOTT Allens, thank you anyway. No sugarhouse, for that matter. The Allens boiled sap on the kitchen stove. On the kitchen wall hung the new *Vermont Life* calendar depicting children coasting downhill on gleaming new sleds, ice fishermen gathered around a miniature city of colorfully painted fishing shanties, steam rising at twilight from hillside maple-sugar houses, sleigh rides and hay rides and multicolored fall hillsides.

How about a calendar showing the Allens burning their house and barn for stove wood to boil sap? E.A. wondered. Gypsy entertaining her gentlemen callers? Gran reading Nostradamus's latest prophecy in the *Weekly World News,* with an out-of-season buck hanging in the otherwise empty woodshed to get them through until May, when they could shoot woodchucks, catch trout, forage for cowslips and watercress and leeks?

Now they were burning boards from the big bays in the hayloft. "If Davis is going to dozer down our place, he better do it soon," Gran said. "Otherwise, we'll have it all burned up."

11

"TYPICAL APRIL DAY in the Kingdom," Judge Charlie K remarked, looking past his portable radio on the windowsill at the monstrous snowflakes drifting down onto the village green. The radio was broadcasting an early-season Yankees-Sox game. The reception was terrible, but E.A. had been able to make out just enough of the play-by-play to know that the Sox were ahead 5–2 in the sixth.

The big courtroom, where Gypsy was being arraigned for poaching, was one of Ethan's favorite places in the village. Over the crackling broadcast, the old-fashioned propeller-blade ceiling fans made a steady, comforting hum. The courtroom was cool in summer and warm on cold days like today, the fans keeping the heated air from collecting up under the stamped-tin ceiling, the tall steam radiators clanking and hissing and grumbling. E.A. couldn't count the times he'd been here with Gypsy Lee. She was forever in court answering one minor charge or another, and for years she'd brought him along. Their court appearances had become an integral part of his homeschooling. They even had a special textbook, *How to Represent Yourself at the Bar Without Having a Fool for a Client*, which Judge Charlie K had given Gypsy a few years back. It was autographed by the author, none other than the judge himself. *How to Represent Yourself* had sold over two million copies and made Charlie rich. Now in his seventies and retired from the Vermont State Supreme Court, he presided over the local docket with a grandfatherly benignity, though he could still be tough on occasion — mainly with overreaching prosecutors and the local constabulary. Charlie made no bones about being a defendant's judge. If a good old Kingdom boy or girl was guilty, the state had better be prepared to prove it.

Ethan looked away from the snow outside the window to Exhibit One, leaning against the front panel of the judge's bench. Exhibit One was a full-size stuffed whitetail buck with a handsome set of twelve-point antlers. Its hindquarters caved in, it was propped against the bench in a semi-sitting position.

E.A. and Gypsy sat at the defense table in the front of the courtroom, to the right of the judge's bench. On the left, at the prosecution's table, sat Warden Kinneson. The warden was also sheriff's deputy, village night constable, zoning administrator, dogcatcher, truant officer, and Judge Charlie Kinneson's third cousin. Today he was wearing his green wool game warden's jacket with its official insignia, even though the courtroom was very warm. Gypsy wore her Loretta Lynn coal-miner's-daughter flour-sack dress. E.A. wore jeans, sneakers, and a Red Sox sweatshirt and cap. Judge Charlie wore a red L.L.Bean hunting shirt, neatly pressed slacks, and loafers. Warden Kinneson was bringing this case himself, as was customary with nonfelonies in Kingdom County. The court stenographer, a humorless woman named Yvette DeBainville, was poised to record the proceedings.

"Your Honor," the warden began. "I'm going to start here by requesting that this boy at the defense table with the female defendant remove his cap in the presence of the officers of the court."

"Leave it on," Gypsy whispered to E.A.

"What officers of the court are you referring to, warden?" Judge Charlie K inquired.

"Why, I and you, Judge."

"Warden," Charlie said, "this is an alleged violation of a fish and game law, not a murder trial. Furthermore, this is a country courtroom in northern Vermont, not Saint Peter's Basilica. Finally, you are a part-time sheriff's deputy and game warden, not an officer of this or any other court. State your case so I can get back to my ball game."

Warden Kinneson sighed. He stood up, shuffled some documents, and turned to Gypsy. "Miss Allen. Walking across the common this afternoon, I noted that the left front fender of your vehicle was dented in. Did you hit a deer?"

"You bet I did," Gypsy said.

"When you hit that deer, Miss Allen. Did you go off the road?"

"Did I ever," Gypsy said. "Off the road and across the meadow almost all the way to the river before I nailed that sucker." She gestured at the twelve-pointer with the collapsed rear end.

"So you admit that in direct violation of" — the warden pulled out his book of fish and game regulations — "Statute Two-oh-one b — 'It is unlawful to take, shoot, net, snare, spear, jacklight or otherwise disturb protected species, except during the stated legal hunting season and hours, with an approved and registered weapon' — you ran down and injured this deer with your automobile."

"I admit no such thing. I hit a stuffed deer, on my own property, that you use to decoy and entrap law-abiding citizens. I knew the deer was stuffed and I did it to teach you a lesson. How can somebody possibly injure a dead deer?"

"Moreover," said the warden, "the deer, which was thrown through the air approximately thirty-five feet, landed in a stand of cut-down marijuana stalks left over from last year, one of which I confiscated and now produce as Exhibit Two."

Warden Kinneson put a plastic garbage bag containing the offending plant on the judge's bench.

"My invalid mother has permission to grow a modest amount of *Cannabis* in her medicinal herb garden to alleviate the pain and suffering caused by Bucky Dent and the Boston Red Sox," Gypsy said. "Check it out."

In fact, Gran's permission to grow marijuana had come not from the state or county but from the Student League for Legalizing the Propagation and Use of Cannabis, with headquarters in Missoula, Montana.

"Now let me get this straight, cousin," Charlie said. "You set up this stuffed quadruped down in Gran's weed patch to bait Gypsy into going after it so you could arrest her. Is that right?"

"I had very good reason to suspect her of jacking deer, Your Honor. What she did when she saw the buck was up to her. I didn't make her run it down."

"Gypsy, why don't you tell me what happened in your own words. You can sit down, deputy."

Gypsy didn't tell everything that had led up to the fateful encounter with the deer in the meadow, but E.A. remembered it all very clearly. The trouble had started one evening several weeks before when he and Gypsy were out in Patsy Cline on an NFT — a nocturnal field trip — as part of his homeschooling. Gypsy was driving the back roads of Kingdom County, telling him the habits of various night-feeding animals, while he sat in the passenger seat holding the Battery Beam.

Ahead of them, eyes appeared on the side of the road. Gypsy slowed down and handed E.A. some cotton to put in his ears. "Our hearing's very precious, sweetie, almost as valuable as our eyesight."

As she pulled even with the animal, E.A. switched on the Beam. The floodlit deer trembled, peed in fright, but didn't run. Gypsy got out of Patsy, leaving the motor running. It was always better to leave the motor running. E.A. handed out Grandpa Gleason's 30.06. She rested it on the roof of the rig, found the transfixed deer in the scope, and blasted it to Kingdom Come. The explosion reverberated through the corridor of trees along the woods road. With the cotton in his ears E.A. felt it more than he heard it, felt the reverberation down through Patsy's frame deep into his chest, as the deer collapsed in its tracks, shot through the heart and dead before it hit the ground.

In less than sixty seconds they had bundled it up in Bill's old overcoat and slouch hat and sat it upright in the front seat between them with just the tip of its snout sticking out between the turned-up coat collar and turned-down hat brim. That's when the flashing blue lights of Deputy Warden Kinneson's truck came up behind them.

"I know that deer's here somewhere," the warden said after

searching the rig for the third time. "You're going to court, Gypsy Lee Allen."

"You can't take us to court for jacking a deer without producing the deer," Gypsy said. "Isn't that right, Bill?"

She gave the animal wedged between herself and E.A. a nudge. "Old Bill's been drinking a little of his private shine," she explained. "That's why he fired the gun out the window. Celebrating."

"Celebrating," the warden said, shining his powerful flashlight on the figure in Bill's hat and coat. "It looks to me like he's passed out altogether. Well, get him home. This time you were lucky."

By the following afternoon, word was all over town that Gypsy Allen had fooled Warden Kinneson into mistaking a dead jacked deer for Old Bill. Every place the warden went — the hotel dining room for his morning coffee, the barbershop, the post office, the courthouse lobby — men asked him if he'd stopped any body in an overcoat lately. Or remarked that even Bill Applejack didn't look that much like a deer. Or inquired if he'd seen anybody in a slouch hat, a fella with a long black nose. Or tipped an imaginary hat to him. So it was probably in a state akin to desperation that the warden borrowed the mounted deer from the hotel barroom, citing official county business, and set it up in the meadow one night while Gypsy and E.A. were off on a fishing expedition to the county hatchery, also presided over by the warden, who lived next door.

They'd sneaked into the hatchery from the back side, and Ethan had boosted his mother over the wire fence, Gypsy trying not to giggle, and had gone directly to the long cement holding tank containing the warden's prize brown-trout brood stock. Gypsy tossed a handful of dry dog food onto the surface, which instantly boiled with big trout.

"Okay, hon," she whispered. "Fling in."

Courtesy of Sergeant Preston of the Yukon, aka Corporal Colin Urquahart, E.A. had a short steel casting rod, thirty-pound line, and a red-and-white spoon with three gang hooks, which

Gypsy Lee's RCMP client had confiscated from a poacher in Megantic, Quebec. E.A. flipped the spoon into the hatchery holding tank and cranked the reel once. Then something attacked the lure, something nearly large enough to yank the rod right out of E.A.'s hands. "Atta boy, Ethan, don't give him any slack," Gypsy said. "Good, good, you've got him coming your way, sweetie." The trout jumped and fell back into the holding tank like a springer spaniel diving into the water for a duck, splashing them both all over.

"Jesum Crow!" Ethan said. "That thing must weigh eight pounds."

"It's probably a state record," Gypsy said. "Oh, honey, get him just a little closer, I've got just the medicine."

E.A. reeled. With its dorsal fin out of the water, the fish swam toward the edge of the brood pen. E.A. backed up and dragged it onto the walkway above the tank. It came off the hook and started to flop back toward the water.

Crack. The shot from Gypsy's derringer rang into the night. The fish quivered, then lay still. "Quick, hon, grab it and run. Give me your pole."

Ethan held the dead fish — he figured it was closer to ten pounds — in both arms. As they made for the fence, a light came on at the warden's house, a couple of hundred yards away. A floodlight illuminated the holding pens. E.A. heaved the fish up and over the fence, then he and Gypsy followed and raced down the hill into the woods. They jumped across the brook that ran out of the hatchery and cut through another patch of woods to the Late Great Patsy Cline, parked on a logging trace, headed downhill. E.A. threw the fish in back. It was nearly as long as the seat. Gypsy slid in behind the wheel while E.A. pushed Patsy to get her rolling. As she picked up momentum, he leaped in. Gypsy popped the clutch once, popped it twice. On the third try the engine engaged and they were off down the mountain.

"That's what I call fishing, hon," Gypsy said. "We could have gotten our limit if Mr. State Record Brown Trout hadn't come off the hook and I hadn't had to plug him."

E.A. wondered what the limit for hatchery fish might be. Ten? Twelve? Twenty pounds?

"The county shouldn't confine fish like that, Ethan. It's a very bad thing to do. Like keeping animals in a zoo. In the daylight their little fish eyes are so sad. This fish is much better off dead and about to be eaten. It won't have to live in confinement anymore."

Speeding down the mountain, they began to laugh. When they were sure they weren't being pursued, Gypsy pulled over and let E.A. drive, while she rode shotgun with the 30.06 and the Battery Beam in case they spotted another deer. Two deer in the larder were always better than one.

E.A. loved to drive Patsy Cline. It made him feel very grown-up and protective of Gypsy, the way a son should be. Nocturnal driving sessions were part of his homeschooling. Driver's ed, Gypsy called it. E.A. was fairly sure he was the only eleven-year-old taking driver's ed in the state of Vermont.

As they approached Fenway and saw the reflection of the deer's eyes, Gypsy working on the first line of "Caught in the Headlights," a new song about a double-dealing two-timer, she knew immediately that something was wrong.

"Hold on, sweetie pie, hold on here. Switch back." They worked the switcheroo without stopping, E.A. sliding over her lap as she slid under the wheel, a neat maneuver they'd practiced before in case a cop stopped them during driver's ed. Gypsy, now back in the driver's seat, swung Patsy into the lane toward the meadow. The deer stood immobile.

"Its eyes don't shine right, hon," Gypsy said. "It's a setup. Take the clip out of the rifle. Gun safety always comes first, you know."

Gypsy was big on gun safety. She'd stressed to E.A. that any number of things could go wrong when you were handling high-powered weapons after dark in a speeding automobile. She'd actually made him take Warden Kinneson's gun safety course for new hunters twice.

Gypsy mashed down on the accelerator as they bounced across the Fenway infield. The Late Great Patsy Cline tipped up precariously when her right wheels ran over second base. They sped into the outfield, where the deer stood stock-still near Gran's herb garden. *Why doesn't he run?* E.A. wondered, holding the Battery Beam in one hand and the 30.06 in the other.

Gypsy blasted the horn. "Am I head-on, Ethan?"

"A tad to the right," he said.

⚾

"So, Gypsy," Judge Charlie was saying, coughing hard, "you ran over a dead, stuffed deer on your own property?"

"She just admitted that she did," the warden said. "And was found with an illegally acquired ten-pound brown trout to boot. And the deer landed in an illegal substance. She broke about five, six laws. Maybe more."

"That depends on which laws the warden has in mind, Charlie," Gypsy said. "Our Father's laws or the trivial little technicalities in the warden's fish and game book? Which Our Father didn't think were important, or He'd have mentioned them to Moses or had Jesus tack them onto the Sermon on the Mount. Did the dear blessed Christ, after he divided the loaves and the fishes, say, 'Now, folks, you can only take these particular fishes by rod and reel during the hours from half an hour before official sunrise to half an hour after official sunset'? Did Our Father announce, out of the burning bush, 'Moses, old boy, thou shalt not take, shoot, net, snare, spear, jacklight, or otherwise disturb protected species except during the stated legal season and hours, with an approved and registered firearm'? I don't think so. Moreover — you got a cold, Charlie? Gran has an herb that's great for that nagging cough — moreover, Gran has permission from that outfit in Montana to grow her medicinal herb. Finally, the warden's going to have to show me the regulation in his book that says it's against the law, even *man's* law, to kill a deer that's already dead."

"Well, warden?"

"I'd just like to ask the defendant —"

"Cousin, for the last time, this is not a criminal trial and Gypsy Lee isn't a defendant."

72

"I'd just like to ask Miz Allen here if she thinks it's good parenting to take a young boy out jacklighting and have him hold the light?"

"Yes, I do," Gypsy said immediately. "First of all, we weren't primarily out jacklighting. The main purpose of our little adventure was an educational field trip for E.A. to study the native fishes of Kingdom County. As for holding the light, it's an Allen family tradition. I held the light for Gran back before Bucky Dent took her out of commission. She held the light for her pa, Outlaw Allen, and Outlaw held it for his pappy, Grandpa Gleason Allen before Grandpa Gleason went insane and tried to blow up the rest of the family in their beds. My great-great-great-great-grandfather down there" — she motioned out the window at the Colonel, standing cold in the snow — "held the light for his father. Only back then the light was a pine-link torch and it was moose and wolves they were after, not deer. They were WYSOTT Allens, too," she added. "They just didn't know it."

"Gypsy," Judge Charlie said. "I've always wondered. What does WYSOTT stand for?"

"Why, you ought to know that, Charlie. It stands for Wrong Side of the Tracks Allens."

The judge smiled. "I guess I'd forgotten. What's the Y for, though? Wrong side of the tracks doesn't have a Y in it."

"Well, I'm not completely sure, but I think the Y got shoehorned in there to make WYSOTT easier to say."

"Your Honor," Warden Kinneson said, but Charlie held up his finger. The ceiling fans went around and around, the flat wooden blades moving just fast enough so that E.A. couldn't follow them individually, though he bet Ted Williams could have. Ted could see the rotating seams on the ball coming up to the plate.

On the windowsill the Sox game was still crackling. New York had gone ahead in the top of the ninth on a grand-slam home run.

"Ethan?"

E.A. jumped.

"Yes, sir?"

"When are you going down to Beantown to straighten those guys out?" The judge jerked his thumb toward the radio. "They need your help."

"Please, Your Honor —"

"Hold your water, warden. What could possibly be so important that you have to interrupt a baseball conversation?"

"I just wondered. What your ruling was?"

"Well, I have been thinking about exactly that. Gypsy, I'm finding you guilty of killing a dead deer. The fine will be five dollars, waived, because" — looking at the game warden in a way that reminded E.A. of Ted on his poster, staring out at the rookie pitcher — "because I do not ever, ever, as long as I am the sitting judge in this courtroom, wish to preside over another case in which a citizen of Kingdom County has been entrapped into breaking the law. Furthermore, Gypsy, you have this court's permission to shoot and consume any deer, live or dead, that you catch in Gran's herbal garden, depriving her of medicinal solace for the pain and suffering caused by those sorry losers" — he nodded at the radio — "in 'seventy-eight, 'eighty-six, and 'ninety-four. What's that, cousin? Stop mumbling and speak up."

"Well, since you ask, Judge, I was saying that this is an outrage. It's a mockery of how a courtroom should be run. I'm going to complain to the judicial review panel."

"What is an outrage, Mr. Deputy Warden Dogcatcher Truant Officer Kinneson, is for you to persecute this hard-working single mother and songwriter slash singer. What is an outrage is for you to haul her and her redheaded boy into court when there are jackers skulking along I-91 every night of the week spotlighting deer and selling the venison to five-star restaurants in Montreal and Boston. What is outrageous is that because you aren't smart enough to catch those professional poachers, you go after Gypsy Lee and E.A. I'm fining you fifty dollars for bringing a frivolous charge in front of this court, and that I'm not waiving. From now on, you leave these good people the hell alone on their own property."

12

ANOTHER SUMMER arrived, and the Fourth of July came and went with no sign of the drifter or of anyone else to help E.A. with his game. A week after the Fourth he woke up at dawn and decided to go fishing. As he looked out the slanted window of his bedchamber, he saw the drifter leaning against the rail fence of the Allen family cemetery in his worn old suit jacket and grimy shirt, baggy slacks, and scuffed work shoes. Red Sox cap. Dragging on a cigarette stub. Just standing there, looking at the grave markers.

E.A. got dressed fast and went out to the cemetery.

"Hey," he said, touching his finger to the bill of his cap.

"Hey," the drifter said back, touching his cap.

"You may as well hear it right now," E.A. said. "Devil Dan Davis ran over that new ball you gave me with his Blade."

The drifter shifted his Lucky Strike. He smelled like the cheap booze at the dives where Gypsy sang. "His Blade," he said, not quite a question.

"His D-60 bulldozer." E.A. glanced over toward Midnight Auto and the open-sided machinery shed. "Biggest bulldozer made — weighs sixty tons. Another five minutes, it'll be light enough to see it."

"What does he need a sixty-ton dozer for?"

"Ma says he uses it to wage war on the environment, except Devil Dan doesn't believe in the environment. He shoves junk cars over the riverbank. Built up that big levee out in center field so the highwater won't flood his junkyard. Drives logging roads up mountainsides, knocks down buildings on the Historical Register."

"The what?"

"The Historical Register. A list of all the old rundown buildings in the county dating back to I don't know when. Gran's eight-sided barn's on it, only we've had to burn quite a bit of the barn lately for firewood. Devil Dan said at Town Meeting he didn't believe in the Historical Register. Said he'd knock down the Washington White House if they'd pay him enough."

The drifter stared over at Midnight Auto, at the hundreds upon hundreds of junk cars and trucks acquiring color in the strengthening light. "How did this fella come to run over your baseball?"

"Gypsy — that's my ma — was pitching to me down at Fenway. The ball diamond over yonder. She was throwing BP?"

The man nodded.

"I wanted to hit that new ball one good lick. See how far it'd go. I caught it right on the sweet spot of the bat and drove it over Old Bill's head, he's our hired man."

The drifter nodded again. One thing Ethan liked about him was that he didn't ask too many questions. He didn't crowd a boy with questions the way the Colonel did, or a schoolteacher. Not that E.A. knew for sure what a schoolteacher would do, never having attended regular school. But he was pretty sure that pressing a fella with questions he didn't want to answer was a schoolteacher's style, and he didn't want any part of it. Questioning E.A. Allen tightly was a sure way to get him to clam up.

It wasn't just not asking questions that made the drifter different from most grownups. Earl and the Outlaws didn't ask him many questions, either, except to tease him. But the drifter actually seemed to listen. He waited for E.A. to finish what he was saying, and he thought over his replies. Listening was unusual. Gypsy listened to him, and the Colonel listened, but just to find out whether he was going to say what the Colonel wanted to hear, and then got mad if he didn't. But the stranger seemed genuinely interested.

"Dan was building that bank, and he swerved out of his way to run over the ball. Gypsy shucked off her top and did the River Dance on the Blade's roof. Old R.P. Davis, that's Devil Dan's wife, smashed the dozer's instrument panel all to pieces with her rolling pin."

The drifter was grinning a little. "That must have been quite a show."

"Dan called me a little bastard."

"Did he?" The man narrowed his eyes through his cigarette smoke. "That's harsh language. How come your pa didn't deal with him?"

E.A. shrugged. The stranger was studying him, using the cigarette smoke as a screen so that E.A. couldn't read his expression. But then he looked back at the slate stones in the cemetery. "Gleason Allen, 1860 to 1922, blown sky high while trying to blow up his loving family," he read aloud.

"Gypsy's got a song about him," E.A. said. "She wrote it when she was a little girl. It starts out, 'Grandpa Gleason, crazy and mean, got blown up to smithereens.'"

They looked at the stones. BABY. MOTHER. SISTER. OUTLAW ALLEN — Outlaw his given Christian name — MURDERED BY REVENUERS. And old Patrick Allen, who, with a few of his drinking cronies, decided one night to annex the province of Quebec to Kingdom County. They got as far as the first farmstead across the border before they were gunned down in their tracks by local farmers.

The drifter was looking at the wooden marker with GONE AND LONG FORGOTTEN scratched on it. "That's my pa," E.A. said.

"Your pa?"

"Yes. Well, I think so. Sometimes Gypsy calls him Mr. Nobody."

The man looked at him. "You want to hit a few balls?"

"You mean like BP?"

The drifter nodded. "I got a few baseballs in my coat pocket. Not official balls like the one Davis run over. But they'll do. You want to hit a few?"

"You bet I do," E.A. said.

⚾

The boy and the drifter walked toward the baseball diamond laid out in the meadow. Over at Devil Dan's, Norton and Orton Horton were hanging out R.P.'s wash. The skinheads stared at E.A. and the drifter.

"This isn't a bad ball field," the tall man said.

"Gypsy and I laid it out. Bill was supposed to help but didn't on account of his bad back."

E.A. looked up at the man with pale eyes. "I got to ask you something, mister. Before we get started. The Colonel — the statue overstreet — said he might send somebody. A fella to help me along with my game."

"Hold on here. You're overrunning me on the base path. You say the statue told you this?"

"You bet. Ethan Allen, over on the common. He's my — let's see — great-great-great-great-great-grandfather. I used to think he was my real father on account of we had the same name. And when I said my Our Father Who Art in Heaven I'd think of him. I asked him to do things for me, but he never did jack. Not that I could see. Him or Our Father Who Art in Heaven, either."

"What'd you ask him to do?"

"Well, to help the Sox win the Series so Gran could walk again."

"That would be a tall order."

"I know. I didn't really expect he'd pull that off. So I asked him to help Gypsy make a record and get to Nashville. When he didn't step up to the plate on that one, I all but begged him to smite down Devil Dan and his first-born and his oxes and asses for running over my official American League baseball with the Blade. But he hasn't seen fit to smite Dan yet, either."

The drifter looked over at the Davis place. He stared at Norton and Orton, and they stared back at him. After a minute they looked away.

E.A. wondered if he'd told the man too much. That he'd think E.A. was crazy for talking to a statue. Maybe not toss him any BP after all. He wished he hadn't blurted those things out, didn't know what had come over him. But all the man said was, "Usually, you want something done like what you asked that statue for, your best bet is to tend to it yourself. Like in baseball. You have to find a way to get on base, make something happen. Same with learning the game. Maybe I can show you a thing or two you'd be a while coming to figure out yourself. Mainly, you have to do it on your own."

E.A. wondered if the drifter was suggesting that he should smite down Devil Dan himself, pop him some morning with Grandpa Gleason Allen's deer rifle when he was emptying crankcase oil from the Blade into the river. Maybe rub out the two skinheads, Orton and Norton, at the same time. It was an appealing idea.

The man walked out to the mound. E.A. stood at home plate and took several hard practice cuts. He said, "You'll be surprised to see how far I can drive the ball this year. Since I hit that game-winning line drive on the common? I've grown a lot. You can see that."

The man was looking at the anthill pitching mound. "You've grown some," he said.

Bill emerged from his trailer behind the barn. The drifter looked up and touched his cap with his index finger. Bill nodded.

"Put your glove on, Ethan. Warm me up a little."

The man stood on the mound, took a scuffed baseball out of his jacket pocket, and tossed a few practice pitches to E.A. He caught Ethan's returns barehanded.

"Sixty feet eight inches, maybe nine," he said.

"What?"

"Your mound is sixty feet nine inches away from home plate. It's long by three inches."

"How do you know?"

From the other pocket of his jacket the drifter produced a steel tape measure. "Come here and hold this on the rubber," he said.

E.A. held the reel on the pitcher's rubber while the drifter walked backward, unwinding the bright yellow tape. He put the end down on the front of the plate. Ethan looked at the tape emerging from the spool: 728¾ inches. Sixty feet, eight and three-quarters inches. The man's estimate was off by a quarter of an inch.

"Stand in," the man said. E.A. assumed his batting stance. He was careful to set his hands back behind his ear.

Without winding up, the drifter brought the ball in his hand back like a catcher gunning out a base runner attempting to steal second and threw. It was a perfect BP pitch, waist-high and out over the plate. Ethan waited, stepped, and smacked the ball over second base. A solid single.

The man reached into his jacket for another ball. This one Ethan hit sharply on the ground between short and third.

He swung around and bunted the next pitch ten feet down the first-base line to show that he knew how to advance the men he'd already put on first and second. On the next pitch he hit a fly ball to center field.

"Where are your base runners?" the drifter said.

"The guy on third tagged up and scored. The guy on second advanced to third. Man on third, two out, one in."

The man nodded.

"Put something on them," E.A. said. "Put some mustard on them."

The drifter threw the next pitch a little faster. Ethan was ready. He lined the ball straight back at the mound as hard as he could hit it. As fast as a boxer slipping a punch, the drifter jerked his head aside. At the same time he reached up and snagged the ball barehanded.

Ethan stared. He did not believe there was a ball player in Kingdom County who could have caught that hit in his bare hand. Not Earl. Not Moonface. Not Pappy Gilmore in his prime. He had never seen a man's hand move so fast.

"Jesum H. Crow," E.A. said. "Where'd you learn that?"

"Nowhere."

"Nowhere?"

"Nowhere. Smart base running, which base to throw to, some parts of hitting, you can learn. Quick hands, you've either got or you don't got. The side's retired, Ethan. One run in. You want to go again?"

They played three more innings. Ethan's team scored once or twice each inning. Old Bill shagged the balls in the outfield, muttering and grumbling, in no way surprised by the drifter's presence. E.A. had never seen Bill surprised. He suspected that if the Red Sox manager, the Legendary Spence, showed up one morning to pitch BP, Bill would be entirely unastonished. Bill lived in a perpetual state of mild disgruntlement in which surprise had no place.

By now the sun had been up for half an hour. The osprey that nested on top of the water tank by the trestle had caught a trout and taken it back to its nest. Orton and Norton were cleaning out an old pickup. Later they'd count bottles at Dan's redemption center at the back of the junkyard, polishing off any leftover beer in the cans. Devil Dan was getting ready to go out with his flatbed and pick up more wrecks. Gypsy and Gran were sleeping in.

"That's good for this morning," the drifter said, dropping the half-dozen balls one at a time back into his pocket.

"Well?" E.A. said.

"Well what?"

"How'd I do? Hitting?"

The man shrugged. "Fair."

"Fair? I never missed once. You want to know the book on me? I never strike out. One way or the other, I get my bat on the ball."

The man lit a Lucky with a wooden match, which he flipped still smoldering into the grass. He squinted at E.A. through the smoke. His eyes were smoke-colored.

"The book on you," he said, "is you swing at a lot of pitches."

"So what, as long as I connect? Yogi'd drive 'em someplace if they bounced in front of the plate."

The drifter dragged on his cigarette. He took a bottle of Crackling Rose out of a pocket and unscrewed the cap and had a drink. Wiped the mouth of the bottle on his jacket sleeve and passed it to Bill.

"Ethan," the man said, "a hitter has to be very patient." He said this in a patient voice, as though to illustrate what he meant. He sounded, again, like one man talking factually to another. He could have been commenting on the weather.

"Hitter has to wait for his pitch," he continued. "That's why your team couldn't do nothing against that schoolteacher fella. They was swinging at too many curve balls, too many pitches just out of the strike zone. Look." He pointed up at the wooden tank where the osprey sat watching the river. He whistled, and the bird turned its white head their way. "See that customer up there eyeballing us?"

E.A. nodded.

"Watch him."

As they watched, the bird rose into the air and began to circle above the river. Suddenly it went into a plunging dive, hit the surface so hard it vanished momentarily in the spray of water, and took off with another trout wriggling in its talons.

"That's a hard way to get your breakfast," Bill observed.

"Ethan," the drifter said, "how many times you ever see her dive and miss?"

Ethan thought. "Never."

"Why come?" said the man. "I'll tell you. Because she's patient. She'll work a pool for ten, fifteen minutes, like a good fisherman, then go along to the next, come back later, work it again for as long as it takes. She watches. If a hatch of flies comes over the water, she'll work harder. She knows the fish'll be coming up to feed. I don't know how she knows, but she does. She's careful to keep her shadow off the surface, and she can see right down into the water several feet on account of her eyes are naturally tinted, like a fancy pair of sunglasses. She can see eight times as good as I and you can see. But none of that would matter if she wasn't patient." It was the most he'd ever said to E.A. at one time.

"How is it," E.A. said, "you come to know so much about ospreys?"

"I read up on them in a bird mag."

E.A. looked at the stranger in his tramp clothes. He did not look like the sort who read *Audubon* or *Nature*, bird magazines like the ones the Memphremagog optometrist who visited Gypsy brought her from his waiting room, six or eight months out of date but still interesting.

"Where?"

"Where what?"

"Where'd you read that bird magazine?"

The man paused, then said, "In college."

E.A. was surprised. He would not have guessed that this man had been to college any more than he would have supposed he read *Audubon*. He didn't talk like Judge Charlie K, say, or Editor Jim Kinneson, or even Gypsy, who had spent that year at the state university before getting knocked up with him.

E.A. said, "Gypsy says I can go to college. Get an all-expense scholarship for my baseball. Paid for by the state."

"I had something like that," the drifter said. "But I never got beyond college ball. To take your baseball as far as you can, you have to learn to be very patient at the plate."

"I guess I'm patient enough," E.A. said. "I never missed one pitch you threw."

The man shrugged. "Them was BP pitches."

"Fine," the boy said, reaching for his bat. "Throw me your best pitch. Game situation. I guarantee I can get my bat on the ball. Drive it somewhere."

The man looked at E.A. Then he nodded.

"Oh Lordy," Bill said.

The drifter went back out to the mound in the morning sunshine. Ethan stood in.

"You all set?"

E.A. nodded.

Again the big man threw with no wind-up. Before E.A. could swing, the ball cracked into the side of the barn, between a blue-and-white Montana Big Sky Country and a Rhode Island the Ocean State plate, bending them back and leaving a hole as big as a fist in the multicolored southeast wall.

E.A. had never seen a thrown baseball travel that fast in his life. All he could do was stare at the hole.

"Look, Ethan. The time'll come when you'll drive a pitch like that into the river. But that telephone pole you use for a bat? It's way too much timber for you."

E.A. rapped the taped handle of the bat on home plate. "It's got good wood."

The drifter shrugged. "Like Ted said. What good's wood —"

"If you can't handle it," Ethan finished. "Hey. This was a good morning."

"A man should have a lot of good mornings like this in his life," the drifter said. Then, "Well, I'll see you when I see you."

He started down across the meadow toward the tracks.

"Wait. Mister. What else should I work on? Besides being patient?"

"That's enough for now."

The 9:30 local was coming, whistling as it slowed for the crossing before the trestle.

"What's your name?" Ethan called out.

Just before the drifter swung through the open door of a Pine Tree State boxcar, E.A. thought he heard him call back, "Teddy." Teddy seemed an odd name for so big a man.

"Did he say his name was Teddy?" E.A. asked Bill, who was still staring at the hole punched in his license-plate tableau.

"I couldn't swear he didn't," Bill said.

The train was on the trestle now. Bill muttered something else, something about his damaged license plates. But E.A. was thinking about what the drifter had said just before he left. A man should have a lot of good mornings in his life. Not a boy. A man. He felt strangely alone as he headed up to the house from a good morning of baseball.

GYPSY WAS WAITING for E.A. in the dooryard, watching the freight train wind out of sight over the trestle. E.A. had no idea how long she'd been there.

"Ethan, who was that guy you were playing baseball with?"

E.A. shrugged. "He's the fella who gave me that new baseball a couple years ago. I think he said his name was Teddy."

Gypsy bit her lip and frowned. "Well. I've told you before. I don't want you hanging out with tramps and strangers. I don't care if he says his name is Joe DiMaggio. Understand?"

"Why not, ma? He's just a —"

"Because I said not," Gypsy said abruptly. "That's reason enough." And with that she turned and hurried into the kitchen.

E.A. sulked for the rest of that day and the next, avoiding Gypsy or shooting baleful looks at her and at Gran, too, for good measure.

Finally she sat him down at the table and said, "Look, sweetie. I know you're mad at me. I'll tell you what. I'll let you practice with that guy, assuming he ever shows up again. But you have to promise you'll only do it when I'm home, and you won't go any-where with him. Is that fair?"

"I reckon so," E.A. said, still mad.

"Well, I reckon it better be, sweetie," Gypsy said good-naturedly. "It's called a compromise. Like the Missouri Compro-mise we studied. Remember?"

"I don't like compromises."

"Nobody does. But it's that or nothing. Okey-dokey?"

"Okey-dokey," E.A. said after a pause. Then he grinned at her, and she gave him a hug. Gypsy was the one person E.A. couldn't stay mad at for long, as much as he would have liked to. The important thing was that he could continue playing ball with the drifter.

E.A. spent most of the rest of that summer waiting for the man called Teddy. He showed up half a dozen times, always early in the morning, always to play baseball. He brought the balls and, the second time he came, a new Green Mountain Rebel Little League bat, which he gave E.A. to keep.

Until Ethan started playing with Teddy, he thought he knew something about baseball. What he learned that summer was how imperfectly he understood the game.

Teddy would appear just after dawn, always on a fair day. Bill was usually ready to shag balls, though the two men rarely spoke to each other, and Bill rarely spoke of the drifter to E.A., and then only as "that fella" or "that Teddy fella."

There he'd be, leaning against the barn or the cedar rail fence around the family graveyard or walking up from the tracks by the river. E.A. would run down and they'd work out at Fenway for an hour or so.

Their routine was always the same. First they'd play catch. Then Teddy would throw him a few dozen pitches while Bill shagged balls in the outfield. After that they'd sit on the back seat of a '38 Packard Bill had once owned, along the third-base line, and the drifter would drink from the pint in his jacket pocket while E.A. drank from the bottle of Hires root beer Teddy always brought him. Root beer for breakfast.

As the daisies and orange hawkweed and black-eyed Susans in the meadow gave way to purple vetch, chicory, steeplebush, and, finally, New England asters, E.A. became more comfortable taking instruction. For one thing, Teddy didn't give much advice.

Often he offered none at all unless E.A. asked. But once, in mid-summer, haying time, Teddy told him there were two kinds of ball players. Major-leaguers and players who couldn't take advice. "There are very few major-leaguers, Ethan, who can't take advice."

"Okay," E.A. said. "How come I can't drive your slower pitches? I'm listening."

"Take a shorter stride when you swing. Don't get out on your front foot so soon."

E.A. nodded. "What's happening when I pop the ball up?"

"Move your right hand counterclockwise around on the bat handle a little. That keeps your right hand on top when you swing."

E.A. tried it. "It doesn't feel right."

Teddy shrugged. By the end of the summer E.A. had stopped popping up.

"How come I couldn't pull that pitch?" he said one morning.

"It was on the outside corner. Go with the pitches. Hit 'em where they're pitched. That pitch, you want to poke it over the second baseman's head."

That was the gist of Teddy's hitting advice. Fundamentals. The same for fielding. E.A. would go out to shortstop. Teddy would hold the Green Mountain Rebel in one hand, his glove on the other, ball in the webbing of the glove. He'd flip the ball up in the air and swat it out to E.A. one-handed. Nothing very hard. E.A. would field the ball and zip it back to him at home plate. Over the course of the summer Teddy showed E.A. how to keep his feet closer together when he fielded the ball and plant his back foot to throw, how to do a slick little slide-step over second base when executing a double play. Sometimes they worked on base running. Teddy showed him how to get a good jump on the pitcher, how to come up standing out of a slide.

"Why don't you ever teach me anything about throwing?" E.A. said one day in late August when the first splashes of red had appeared in the soft maples along the river.

"You throw pretty good already," Teddy said.

That was as close to a compliment as E.A. ever got, but Teddy never criticized him, either. If a grounder squirted under his glove, all Teddy said was "That's baseball."

By degrees E.A. came to trust the big man, though he had no more idea who he was than he'd had when he first saw him. The Colonel refused to say whether this was the fella he'd promised to send, and if Old Bill knew anything more about the drifter than E.A. did, he wasn't telling.

Teddy rarely spoke about anything but baseball, and when he did he immediately connected it to baseball. He never asked Ethan about school and didn't seem interested when Ethan told him one morning that he was being homeschooled. He never talked about fishing or hunting. He never asked about Gypsy or Gran.

Otherwise, little changed at Gran's place that summer. E.A. continued to watch Kingdom Common carefully, patiently, with unflagging persistence. In a more detached but no less curious way, the Common watched E.A.

The Common was watching the man E.A. knew as Teddy as well. No one approached him. There was something forbidding about the big, laconic, watchful stranger who seemed to appear out of nowhere. An air of something almost dangerous hung about him. As if you couldn't quite tell what he might or might not do. But to E.A. he never seemed forbidding, much less dangerous, though all they ever spoke of was baseball. And that was fine with both of them.

E.A. continued to keep score for the Outlaws and to take BP with them. They noticed that he was choosier at the plate and that he hit the ball sharper. Once against St. Johnsbury, when Moonface didn't show, E.A. played an entire game at shortstop. He got two singles and a walk and didn't make an error in six chances in the field.

When E.A. reported on the game to Teddy, he shrugged. "Town-team ball," he said. "There's a big difference between town-team baseball and even, say, single A. That's a different world, Ethan."

"I reckon an eleven-year-old boy who can go two for four and field his position without a miscue in a men's league game has got a shot at A ball and more when he grows up," E.A. said.

"Time will tell," Teddy said.

All in all, it was a fine time in the life of Ethan E.A. Allen. He had just two problems. Their names were Orton and Norton Horton.

Orton and Norton had lived with Devil Dan and R.P. Davis for as long as E.A. could remember. They were foster children who had been removed from their own home in southern Vermont and shipped north to "live in bondage," as Gypsy put it, with the Davises. Other than doing R.P.'s laundry every morning and counting empties at Devil Dan's redemption center, their main job was to help Dan around Midnight Auto, cleaning out junk vehicles and salvaging anything of value. If the brothers Horton found a dime under a floor mat, they were not allowed to keep it. At random intervals, Dan ran a metal detector over them and their room, and they had to turn out their pockets for R.P.'s inspection whenever they entered the house. Under different circumstances E.A. might have sympathized with Orton and Norton. But they routinely tormented him, lying in wait under the railroad trestle or iron bridge and shagging him home with rocks in the summer and ice balls in the winter, rabbit-punching him in the back of the neck, drenching him with water bombs made from condoms they found in the glove boxes of cars wrecked by teenagers, and, worst of all, siccing Devil Dan's watch-goat, Satan Davis, on him.

Orton and Norton never hunted or fished or played baseball. The one time E.A. had invited them over to join him at Fenway, Norton had thrown his ball into the river, then heaved E.A. in after it. At fifteen, Orton was still in the fifth grade at the Common Academy. His fourteen-year-old brother was mired in grade four. The headmaster, Prof Benton, who was as kindhearted and jovial as his mother, Old Lady Benton, was hateful, had early on in their tenure at the Academy taken the Horton boys under his wing, assuring them that he wished to be their best friend in the world. When Norton set fire to the contents of their best friend's office wastebasket while he was reasoning with Orton over the propriety of sliding a hand mirror hidden between Miss Lottie Presault's feet while she was helping him with desk work, then looking up her dress and shouting "Miss Lottie wears red undies!" Prof calmly put out the blaze.

He told Judge Charlie K and Editor James K, over their regular six A.M. coffee in the hotel dining room, that, evidence to the contrary notwithstanding, he believed Orton and Norton were not bad boys at all but just needed a break. He added that in his opinion there was no such thing as a genuinely bad boy. Charlie took issue with this pronouncement, citing himself as exhibit A, an assertion his brother the editor did not contradict. Moreover, Charlie said, during his several decades as a defense attorney he had represented many bad boys and later, as a judge, had sent not a few such incorrigibles down the line to the state reform school without a moment's hesitation. At this the headmaster pounded his fist on the table and said by God, Orton and Norton were good, skylarking country boys, and he would stand by them until Doomsday.

Doomsday arrived the following Wednesday afternoon when the skylarking country boys tiptoed into Prof's office while he was taking his customary after-lunch snooze, tied him to his chair, stood on his desk, and peed first into the wastebasket, then on him. For this, Prof summarily expelled them and declared them officially uneducable and unofficially (to the judge and the editor) depraved. After that they worked full-time for Devil Dan.

And if, now that E.A. was old enough to outrun them, Orton and Norton were not quite the bane of his existence, they were a constant source of anxiety and often appeared in his prayers to Our Father, whom he fervently beseeched to annihilate the brothers from the face of the earth. He was more or less resigned, however, to having to put up with them until he turned fourteen or fifteen, at which point he believed he would be able to kill them himself and bury their skinny, underfed, tattooed remains up on the mountain where they'd never be found. Not that anyone would look real hard.

One morning in September when Teddy was giving him BP, E.A. smacked a long foul ball into Devil Dan's junkyard. As usual at this hour, Orton and Norton were out hanging up sheets and blankets under R.P.'s all-seeing eye. The ball came to rest beside Dan's 1943 Bucyrus Erie crane, which he called the Hook, and which he occasionally used to haul a wrecked tractor-trailer or a derailed boxcar up an embankment or out of a deep ditch.

"You want to fetch that one back, Ethan?" Teddy said.

Orton and Norton had already started for the ball.

"Not really," E.A. said. "There's two of them. Plus that goat."

Teddy nodded and started toward the crane himself. Norton and Orton watched him.

"Hey, mister," Norton shouted. "What you looking at?"

Teddy took his time answering. "Right now I'm looking at you boys."

He continued to look at them as he walked over and picked up the ball.

"Who give you permission to trespass on us?" Orton said.

Then, for the first time, E.A. heard Teddy laugh out loud. He looked right at the Horton boys and laughed.

Finally Orton yelled out, "E.A. — you, E.A. Allen. This old drunk ain't always going to be here to protect you. You're on our list, boy."

Teddy and E.A. finished BP while the Horton brothers finished hanging up the wash. E.A. figured that sooner or later he'd have to pay for this morning. But he was delighted that someone had faced down the brothers.

After practice he and Teddy sat on the Packard seat in the mild fall sunshine, E.A. sipping his Hires, Teddy and Bill drinking from Teddy's Crackling Rose bottle. The sun felt good on the back of E.A.'s neck.

Over at Midnight Auto, Orton and Norton had started hoeing out the inside of a car totaled in a head-on wreck at Memphremagog over the weekend. Three elderly people, the driver and two passengers, had been killed on their way to services at the local Pentecostal church.

"Them boys are bullies, Ethan," Teddy said, pointing the neck of his bottle at the brothers. "Time's coming when you're going to have to go up against them."

"I know," E.A. said.

"What are you waiting for?"

"To grow a little more. One more year, two at most, I figure I can take them both."

Teddy nodded. "Well, I'll tell you how to put an end to that bullyragging right now."

E.A. thought about the two shallow graves high on the mountain. Maybe three, the third somewhat wider to accommodate Satan Davis.

Teddy said, "The thing with bullies — or for that matter with anybody you go up against — you have to get an edge. The way you did with that schoolteacher pitcher. Ichabod. Once you get an edge, they'll be afraid of you."

"I've tried to fight them. Pitched into them three, four times. Right now they're too much for me."

"Sock my hand."

"What?"

Teddy held up his right hand like a traffic policeman. "Go ahead. Sock it. Hard as you can. You won't hurt me."

Ethan wound up and reared back. Teddy reached out and grabbed his wrist before he could throw the punch.

Still holding his wrist, Teddy said, "You don't want to telegraph your punch like that, Ethan. The other fella, he'll see it coming a mile away.

"Do like this." Teddy's left hand, closed into a fist, moved so fast Ethan couldn't follow it. The fist stopped an inch shy of E.A.'s jaw. "That's the one they don't see coming."

He dropped E.A.'s wrist and stepped around behind him. Reached over E.A.'s shoulder and took his left hand. "Make a fist."

E.A. did. "Like this," Teddy said, and showed the boy how to throw a short punch straight out from the shoulder, then another with the same hand. Two short jabs.

"Put your shoulder into it but don't wind up. There. Go for the nose. Straight on, hit the nose both times. One, two. Other fella'll put his hands up to protect his schnoz, it'll be spouting like Old Faithful. When his hands come up, you take a short sideways step toward him, like this." Teddy nudged Ethan's left sneaker with his steel-toed work shoe. "That's right, like stepping into a fastball and driving it. Only instead of driving a baseball you throw a right to the breadbasket. That will double him up. Then you come up with your left hand. Don't wind up. Use all short punches. That's it. Two left jabs to the schnoz, step, one right to the breadbasket, one more left to the jaw. He's done."

"What about the other one? He'll pile on."

"No doubt. When he does, you have to be ready to take a punch or two. That's all right. In a go-round, Ethan, you have to be prepared to take a punch. But as soon as the bigger one goes down, turn tail and run."

"I'd take any pounding rather than run."

Teddy nodded. "I understand. But turn tail and run — until the boy chasing you starts to get winded. Then let him catch you and serve him the same. Two jabs to the nose, hook to the gut, uppercut."

E.A. thought. "Only thing is, like I said, those boys don't mind getting beat up all that much. They'll just lay for me again, with Satan Davis."

"That's where the edge comes in. Get something on them and get it quick, the way you did that pitcher from Pond a year ago. Once you get that edge, it makes them afraid of you. That's what stops the bullying. Stops it in its tracks. Ethan, listen. Everybody has a weak point. You find their weakness. Let 'em know you know what it is. Then they'll back off. What do them boys do first thing every morning?"

"I don't know."

"Yes, you do. Think."

E.A. thought. "Well, first thing, they hang up R.P.'s wash."

"All right. You watch when they do that. Then we'll talk again."

"What about Satan Davis?"

"What about him?"

"Even if I whip the bullies and get an edge on them, he'll still get me down and roll me around."

Teddy looked over at Midnight Auto. The goat was standing on the roof of a 1956 Ford Power Wagon, staring back at Teddy with his yellow eyes. "You just watch what them skinheads do every morning and report back to me," Teddy said. "I'll tend to the goat."

14

E.A. WATCHED, and the next time Teddy showed up, they made their plan. After BP they started down the river road toward the iron bridge to the village. As they passed Midnight Auto, Orton and Norton stared at them from a '72 Firebird they were cannibalizing for seat covers. They each had a used beer going from Dan's redemption center.

When E.A. and Teddy reached the T where the Canada Post Road off Allen Mountain crossed the M&B line, Teddy headed down the tracks. He passed the old water tower, stopped on the trestle, looked back, and waved. Then he continued across the trestle toward the village, and E.A. turned back toward home.

As Ethan came abreast of Midnight Auto again, Orton and Norton sidled out into the road. One on each side of him, cutting off escape in both directions.

"Where you going, boy?" said Orton, who'd positioned himself on the village side. "You got to pay the toll. Ten cents. Otherwise, you're goat bait."

Ethan started walking toward Orton. When he reached the state boy he jabbed him twice in the nose, two short punches, no wind-up. Orton's nose was already spurting blood as he lifted his hands to his face, just the way Teddy said he would. E.A. took a short step and delivered a right to Orton's midriff, then a left hook to the jaw, and Orton was down in the road. Meanwhile, Norton was rabbit-punching his neck.

E.A. twisted away and sprinted toward home. Then he slowed

down, and when he heard Norton panting behind him, he turned and let the younger skinhead run straight into his first jab. He thought his left hand might be broken. Fighting now with his right, he went for the breadbasket. But Norton, though his nose was bleeding, kept coming. He was all over E.A., whose left hand hurt so much he couldn't lift it. It was time for Teddy's contingency plan. E.A. stepped back, and when Norton charged, E.A. kicked him as hard as he could kick, right "where the sun don't shine," as Teddy had put it. Norton howled, went down, rolled on the ground. Now Orton was up and headed his way, leading Satan Davis on a chain. E.A. still had time to get away, beat him home. But he wasn't finished.

"Orton and Norton Horton," he said in a sharp, carrying voice. "I know what you boys do every morning. I know why you have to hang up those sheets."

Orton stopped short and jerked back on the chain. Satan kept trotting and dragged him several steps down the road. Ethan stood his ground.

"What about our sheets?" Orton said.

"You hang out your sheets every morning because you pee the bed every night. You ever punch me again, or shag me home with rocks, or put Satan Davis on me, I'll have it all over town that you boys pee the bed every night. Anybody doesn't believe me, I'll invite them out here to see you hanging up your sheets."

Orton and Norton were trying to pull Satan back toward Midnight Auto when they spotted Teddy, standing in the river road between them and the entrance to the junkyard. He'd come up out of the meadow, his pant legs wet from wading back across the river.

"What you staring at?" Orton yelled. "You old drunk."

"Sic!" Orton shouted and loosed the goat. Old Satan charged straight toward Teddy, who punched the goat once, hard, right between its horns, driving it to its knees. The dazed goat staggered back toward the junkyard, bleated, and took refuge inside a doorless bread truck. Orton and Norton had taken off across the meadow.

Teddy lit a cigarette. "How's your hand, Ethan?"

"I think I broke it."

"Bend your fingers back. Now the other way. Over your palm, toward the wrist. No, it's not broke. It was broke, you couldn't do that. Besides, it ain't your throwing hand. Long as it isn't your throwing hand, we can live with it."

That afternoon Devil Dan drove his four-wheeler into the WYSOTT Allen dooryard. He spun around and around the yard at a furious pace until Gypsy and Ethan came outside. He stopped, facing them, still aboard the running ATV.

"That little bastard of yours took his ball bat and frailed hell out of my state help this morning," he screamed. "Then he half-kilt my prize goat."

"That's too bad," Gran called out through the open doorway. "Now Satan Davis won't be able to service R.P. tonight."

Dan shouted, "I'll dozer down these buildings by snowfall. We'll settle up, you can bet."

"We'll settle up right now, you impotent dwarf," Gran shrieked, and tossed Grandpa Gleason Allen's rifle to Gypsy. And to E.A.'s delight, as Devil Dan spun out of the dooryard, his ever-loving ma put one right through Dan's hat.

All around, it had been a grand day for the Wrong Side of the Tracks Allens.

15

"You don't ask me to throw you BP much these days, hon. You aren't losing interest in baseball, I hope. Baseball's your ticket to college."

"He probably doesn't want to end up beaned and wearing a metal plate in his head for the rest of his natural life like that imbecile Don Zimmer," Gran said. "Zimmer handed the Yankees the 'seventy-eight playoff game on a silver platter."

"We know, ma," Gypsy said. "Bucky Dent's pop-fly home run." Gypsy yawned. She'd had a busy night. First the Reverend had pulled in and wanted her to dress up like Potiphar's wife in the Bible and "give Joseph the works." He'd left about ten. At eleven Father LaFontaine had shown up and requested "Christ's Temptation in the Wilderness," with a very different outcome from the original story, since Father L never got past the second temptation, the Appearance of Salome in Gypsy's West Texas cowgal outfit.

"It wasn't just Dent's home run," Gran complained. "Instead of lifting that rag-arm Torrez, Zimmer left him in to get hammered some more. The game got out of reach, and I knew right then I'd never walk again. All because of Don Zimmer and that metal plate."

"Ma, Don Zimmer does not have a plate in his head. That's one of those convenient Red Sox myths to explain the unexplainable. Like Harry Frazee trading Ruth to New York to finance *No, No, Nanette* — the Curse of the Bambino. The fact is, the Sox's slump is a mystery. Sort of like the Virgin Birth."

"Hogwash," Gran said. "In both instances. I can explain the Virgin Birth and I can explain why the Sox ain't won a Series. As far as Mary goes, she got knocked up, same as you did with E.A., Gypsy Lee. Then she went and made up a story to tell that gullible young nail-driver. As for the Sox, it's all a plot to keep me wheel-chair-bound."

It was early in the morning. E.A. had grown two more inches over the past winter. He was thinking more about girls, especially before going to sleep at night. At times he almost wished he could go to school so he could get to know some girls.

"I always want you to pitch to me, ma. I haven't lost interest in baseball."

They went down to Fenway in the morning dew, Gypsy still in her cowgal boots and fringed buckskin dress.

"Tiant's spinning a beauty this afternoon, folks," Gypsy announced. "He's ready. Checks the runners. Twists, looks right up at the center-field scoreboard — *wow*, how's he do *that?* — delivers. How come you don't swing at so many pitches anymore, hon?"

"I'm learning to be patient, ma."

Gypsy grinned out from under her cowgirl hat. "I'll try to do better. Get more pitches over the plate."

"You do fine. It's good practice for me to lay off the ones out of the strike zone. Not get down on the count."

Gypsy pitched. The ball was outside two inches. E.A. took his short stride, thought about it, held off.

"Good eye, hon. Walk's as good as a single, right? You want one from Eckersley? The Eck winds, hair flying, throws. Uh-oh. Good ducking, honey boy. We wouldn't want you to go through life with a metal plate in your head."

"Don't worry about me, ma. I'll get out of the way."

"That's what the Zim said," Gran said.

Gypsy pitched. "Oh, my goodness," she said. "I had no idea you could hit a ball that far, baby. Well, twelve was the biblical age of manhood. The age of Our Lord when He went up to the temple and held discourse with the Pharisees."

"It's the age you started going down to the trestle to hold another kind of course with Gone and Long Forgotten," Gran said. Then she cackled. "I got you both beat. I started going to the trestle when I was nine."

Gypsy and E.A. sat on the catwalk of the old water tower by the trestle, just below the osprey's nest, dangling their feet and legs in thin air, the hot tarry scent of the railroad ties in the air around them.

In the olden days, coal-driven steam locomotives had stopped here to fill their boilers. Forty steam trains a day had come through Kingdom Common on the Montreal-to-Boston line. Now only six daily freights, pulled by diesel engines, used the line.

Along with the high mowing meadow, Fenway Park, and Allen Mountain Brook, the water tower was one of E.A.'s favorite places. Ever since he was five, he and Gypsy had often climbed the rickety wooden ladder and sat on the catwalk next to the rusty metal spout. It was a fine place to view the surrounding countryside. Below was the siding where the steam trains had pulled off to take on water. To their left, the Canada Post Road crossed the tracks and joined the river road. The high trestle spanned the river to their right. Across the river, beyond the line of soft maples and willows, lay the big pasture behind the commission-sales barn. Then the village.

The water tower was covered with faded messages. The largest, in red letters touched up every two or three summers by Moonface Poulin, was the ever-present reminder of the last ultimate triumph of the Sox. Just below, LYD PI K M was all that was left of the old Lydia Pinkham patent medicine ad. At abandoned homesteads on the mountain E.A. had dug up a few large shards of Lydia Pinkham bottles, but none intact, though he had unearthed a Dr. Atwood's Bitters that was worth twenty-four dollars in his bottle book. Under the LYD PI K M were some initials in faded hearts. One was especially intriguing: G A + F V. Ethan figured G A might be Gypsy Allen. But who was F V? Fred? Frank? He didn't have a clue. Maybe G A was Gloria Alexander, Bobby Alexander's mother over in the village. Except that she wasn't an Alexander until after she married Bill.

Gypsy strummed a chord of "Nobody's Child," the song she'd been working on for a long time. Then she stopped playing and looked off toward Jay Peak. "When we go to Music City, sweetie, we'll mosey down through the Smokies. See some wild country. Go over to Merlefest, too, in North Carolina. 'Nobody's Child' is the one I'm going to win Merlefest with. It's more geared for the festivals than the Top Forty."

"It's a great song, ma. The songs in the Top Forty all suck."

"Well, in general they do. Except when they play an oldie but goodie."

The 9:30 A.M. southbound whistled. A minute later the lead diesel pulled into sight. The water tank vibrated as the train passed below, mainly Burlington Northern and Canadian Pacific boxcars now, though a few Atlantic and St. Lawrence lumber flatbeds, the yellow boards stacked tall and partly covered with tarps. Three open automobile carriers went by, loaded with brand-new pickups straight from Detroit, being shipped east to Boston through Canada.

Gypsy's red cowgirl hat was tipped back now, and she looked like one of the Lovett Sisters on the cover of the *Big D Jamboree* CD of songs from the '40s and '50s that E.A. had gotten her last Christmas out of a music mail-order catalog.

"Detroit," Gypsy said, shaking her head. "Reminds me of that old song 'Detroit City.' That was one of his favorites."

"Whose favorites, ma?"

"Gone and Long Forgotten's. He loved to have me sing it 'cause it's about a natural-born loser. Hometown guitar-picker lights out to make it in the big city. Detroit. Pardon me. *De*-troit. Let's get it right here, folks. Anyway, he goes up to *De*-troit from wherever, East Jesus or West Overshoe or Kingdom Common.

And what happens? God love him, he falls flat on his face. What he forgot, see, was he was taking his own sorry self right along with him. Not that Mr. Nobody even got that far, come to think of it. He didn't have the guts to try. I'm sorry, hon. I shouldn't bad-mouth your relation. There's only one problem."

"What's that, ma?"

"He was a no-good, gutless, self-destructive son-of-a-bitching loser, pardon my French."

"Ma?"

"What, hon? I'm sorry I went to rant there for a minute. When I get my Allen up, I can't seem to help myself."

"I know, ma. What I wanted to ask, when are you going to Nashville?"

"Not until you're grown-up, hon. Don't worry, I wouldn't ever leave you."

"I'm not worried. But I'd like for you to go soon so you don't wait till it's too late. Gran and Bill and I'd be all right for a while. I want you to go, ma. Like the guy, the natural-born loser, in 'Detroit City.' Only you'd make it. I know you would."

"How do you know that, lovey?"

"Well, for one thing, Our Father told me. I mean the Colonel."

"Oh, E.A. Maybe you just thought he said that."

"He really did, ma."

The train whistled at the crossing in the Common. Gypsy sang a line of "The Wreck of the Old Ninety-seven."

"Ma, tell the story about you and Gone and Long Forgotten."

"Oh, that's a sad, sad tale, darling."

"I like to hear it."

"Well, as young kids together, he and I would jump off the trestle into the big pool below. Sometimes we'd wait until a train was coming and the lead locomotive was on the trestle, whistle screaming, air brakes shrieking, then jump hand in hand. Just don't ever let me catch you doing such a foolhardy thing, sweetie."

"That's where you and my pa went skinny-dipping, isn't it?"

"Yes, hon. We were as wild as two young birds of the air."

"Weren't you afraid of tramps?"

"Not with Mr. GALF there. Plus that's where Our Father blessed me eternally by giving me you, hon. The best thing that ever happened to me."

"I thought it was Mr. Gone and Long Forgotten who gave you me."

"He was just the instrument of the Lord, hon. Only Our Father can give precious life, and all life is precious. I used to tell that to Mr. Gone and Long Forgotten when he killed snakes and frogs and pigeons. Anyway, you were conceived under that very trestle. Romantic, huh?"

"Well, it is, sort of."

"Bobbi Gentry could've gotten a good song out of it."

"You got two good songs out of it, ma. 'Knocked Up in Knoxville' and 'Nobody's Child.' I know you'll get the handle to 'Nobody's Child.'"

"Yes. Companion songs, lovey. To showcase your ma's versatility. You see, Our Father gave me the gift to write them. It would have been wrong not to use it and multiply that gift, like the good steward. We're all stewards of our own gifts. You're the steward of your gift for baseball."

"Did Mr. Gone and Long Forgotten have a gift?"

"I guess you'd have to say he was pretty good at what we did under the trestle, 'cause he helped me make a fine redheaded boy. Apart from that, anything else he was good at, he wantonly threw away."

"Tell about racing the train, ma. Sing 'The Kingdom County Accident.'"

"That's a sad and tragic song, hon."

"They love it when you sing it out."

"People have gruesome taste. Okay, here we go:

> It was the summer of 'eighty-four.
> We wasn't really kids no more.

When we took it in our dumb brains
To race the seven-thirty-five train."

Gypsy stopped. "I don't know, hon. I can't go on. He had a souped-up jitney, and he'd start up on the mountain, on the Post Road, and race the train to the crossing. I did it with him just once. It was a big rush, an even bigger thrill than jumping off the trestle. We bounced over the rails a heartbeat ahead of the locomotive. To tell you the truth it scared me half to death. You know what scared me most? That if we lost I'd never write all the songs in me. Finally I got Gone and Long Forgotten to promise he'd never do it again, but one evening when it was raining he did it one time more."

"And he's buried under the marker?"

"Mr. Nobody's buried beneath the marker, all right."

"Ma? How come sometimes you call him Mr. Nobody?"

"Because he was afraid of being somebody, hon. Afraid to be a father, a husband, and a success. Afraid to use the talent Our Father in His infinite wisdom had given him. Afraid to pay the price of his talent. Oh, hon. He was a low-down coward like the dirty little coward that shot Mr. Howard and laid poor Jesse in his grave. Pardon me for badmouthing him, baby. But he was no man."

"Do you think Mr. Nobody ever would have changed?"

"I don't have much faith in change, baby. He was a son of a bitch through and through. Start to finish. I'm sorry. I guess that's the WYSOTT Allen in me."

"Old Lady Benton says I'm a bad seed. I guess I get that from Mr. Nobody."

"Old Lady Benton can go screw herself, sweetie pie. I'm sorry for the language, but she can. I'll tell her so next time I see her. You aren't a bad seed, you're the most precious gift a mother could ever receive. I shouldn't have told you all this, baby doll. It isn't right for a ma to spill the beans to her only begotten boy about getting knocked up by a no-good, low-down, two-timing loser."

Gypsy laughed and sang:

"Knocked up in Knoxville.
Made up in Memphis.
Hitched up . . . in Nashville
. . . Tin-nessee."

E.A. hummed along. But he never did have much of a singing voice, and besides, he had an idea. A good one. Sitting on the water tank in the hazy morning sunlight, listening to Gypsy warble "Knocked Up in Knoxville," he believed he'd hit on a way to find out what he most wanted to know.

16

PICKUPS WITH BIG, dark, heavy-antlered bucks in their beds cruised slowly around the sere common, displaying their trophies. It was late in the afternoon of the opening Saturday of deer season in Kingdom County. Men, and some women, too, in red-and-black-checked or hunter-orange jackets and pants went in and out of the hardware store and the IGA and the hotel. E.A., who had already gotten his deer with Gypsy several nights before, was talking with the Colonel. But not about hunting.

All villages hold many secrets, the Colonel was saying, and Kingdom Common was no exception. In the Common, many years before E.A. was born, there had been a murder. The murdered man, Orie Gilson, was a farmer who was mean to his help. Everyone in the village knew that the murderer was his hired man, assisted by a few of his drinking cronies. For more than half a century the *Kingdom County Monitor* had offered a standing reward of $10,000 for information leading to the killer's conviction. But no one would talk to the police. To the outside world the murderer's identity remained a mystery, though the greater mystery was how an entire town could keep such a secret for so long. Sooner or later, you'd think, somebody would talk. A world-class busybody like Old Lady Benton. The Reverend, only slightly less proficient at gossiping and casting blame. Or Judge Charlie K himself, at the time a young defense lawyer just out of law school. But no Commoner had ever breathed a word to anyone beyond the county line, and no arrest was ever made. The reward went unclaimed.

The Colonel loved to natter on about the village's other mysteries. What had become of the loot when twenty Confederate soldiers had ridden hell-for-leather out of Canada in 1864 and robbed the First Farmers' and Lumberers' Bank of Kingdom Common of nearly $100,000? Most of the raiders got away, and the money never turned up. How had the Colonel's sword been broken off, and why hadn't it been replaced? Some said Noël Lord, as a boy, had cut it off with a hacksaw after the sword severed his hand when he drove his father's moonshine cart into town and the oxen ran into the statue. But the Colonel wouldn't say.

So it wasn't surprising to E.A. that the knowledge he most wanted — which, like the identity of Gilson's killer, was surely known to most of the village — was withheld from him. Though as the Colonel himself had told him, while a village could keep a secret from outsiders forever, it could not keep a secret forever from one its own and, WYSOTT Allen or not, E.A. was one of the village's own. Sooner or later, E.A. told the statue, he would find out.

"I'm old enough to know his name now. It wouldn't kill you to tell me."

"Looky here, boy. It's Gypsy who has to tell you. That's why nobody else will. This matter is between you and your ma. From what you tell me, she's already given you enough to go on so's any enterprising boy could easy figure out the rest."

"I don't know anything much about him."

"You know a lot. You know when you were born. You know there was a wreck less than a year earlier. Say you knew that Yaz had hit three out of Fenway against the Yankees on a certain day in a certain season but you didn't know the exact day. What would you do?"

"Look it up in the record book."

"That's correct. You'd look it up."

"I didn't know there was a record book where you could look up no-good, cowardly sons of bitches," E.A. said.

But if the Colonel heard him, he didn't reply. The wind had picked up and it was beginning to snow.

"And me standing out here without a cloak to my name," the Colonel said, which was the end of their conversation.

ⓘ

"Hello, E.A. You call for this snow, did you?"

"Hey, Editor K. No, I didn't have to call for it."

"That's the truth," the editor said, looking out the window at the thickening flakes. "Snow is about the one commodity there's no shortage of up here in the Kingdom. You need more baseball stats?"

"I need some stats, I reckon."

"The archives are yours to ransack, son. Let me know if you find anything interesting."

"Okey-dokey," E.A. said, and headed down the steps into the basement.

The basement of the newspaper office was a catchall for every kind of old-fashioned machinery and memorabilia, including the huge hand press and Linotype that Editor K's father and grandfather had used. The tall black volumes containing old issues of the paper were ranked on shelves along one wall. They dated well back into the nineteenth century.

Ethan looked at the dates inscribed on labels pasted to the spines of the black books. He was born in September, and Gypsy had said that the Kingdom County Accident had taken place a month before he was born. He found the volume for the year of his birth, found August, and then it was simple. Nothing in the August 8 issue, but the headline for the next one, published on the 15th, read TWO LOCAL TEENS KILLED AT M&B CROSSING ON RIVER ROAD. Below was a grainy photograph of a crushed car upside down in the field by the river. The trestle loomed in the background. Under the photograph the article began:

Recent Academy graduates René DeLabreure and Ferdinand Viens were fatally injured last Tuesday when the car they were riding in was struck by the Montreal–Boston through freight at approximately 4:15 P.M. at the ungated crossing on the River Road just north of Kingdom Common. A third teen, E. W.

109

Williams, the owner of the car, is in critical condition at the North Country Hospital in Memphremagog. One of the engineers said that the wrecked car appeared to be racing the train to the crossing.

The newspaper story went on to say that the River Road crossing had long been considered extremely hazardous, with two other fatal wrecks there over the years, one in 1938, another in 1957. Recently the sheriff's department had received reports that high school boys were racing the trains but had not been able to confirm it. Viens, DeLabreure, and Williams had played on the school's championship baseball team.

All E.A. could think of, however, was the initials on the water tank. G A and F V. Gypsy Allen and Ferdinand Viens. Son of Mr. and Mrs. Ferdinand Viens, Sr., County Road, Kingdom Common.

He was certain of it. Ferdinand Viens, eighteen, of Kingdom Common, had been his father.

"E.A.? You finding what you need?"

"I'm okay," he called up to the editor as he skimmed over issues for October and November of that year and read that the Williams boy had pleaded guilty to manslaughter and been sentenced to ten years in prison.

He said it again as he came up the steps a few minutes later. "I'm okay."

E.A. stood by the door in his Red Sox cap, his pale eyes looking straight at the editor. "Where can I find Mr. and Mrs. Ferdinand Viens Senior, Editor K?"

"Fern Viens Senior? Well, E.A., Fern and his wife left here years ago. They went back to Canada to live, where Fern's folks were from. I don't know where they are now. Or even for certain if they're still alive. They were an older couple, you know . . ."

But E.A. was already out the door of the newspaper office and headed across the street to the common.

"So," the Colonel said, his voice a little muffled by the snow and wind. "You found what you were looking for."

"His name was Ferdinand Viens," E.A. said through his tears, not understanding why he was crying, since all he knew that he hadn't known before was a name that meant nothing to him.

"Who was Fern Viens?" E.A. asked the Colonel.

"You know who he was. He was one of those fellas killed in that wreck out to the crossing."

"Who *was* he?"

"I don't miss my guess, you just read who he was."

"Where can I find out about him?"

"Ask Gypsy — she can tell you. If she will."

"Well, she won't. His initials and hers are up on that tower."

The Colonel said nothing. E.A. figured he hadn't known about the initials, and if there was one thing the Colonel couldn't bear, it was not knowing some piece of village scuttlebutt.

E.A. shivered, pulled his yard-sale mackinaw closer, hopped from foot to foot. "The only other thing I know about him, he played ball for the Academy. He played for that state championship team — the one Earl and E.W. Williams who hit the home run up onto Old Lady Benton's porch played for. That E.W. was sentenced to ten years in prison. He was driving the car."

"I know who was driving the car," the Colonel said.

"What I'm asking you," E.A. said, "is where can I find out more about Fern Viens. Besides Gypsy. I'm not going to bother her with this."

Across the street from the long east side of the green, dim in the snowstorm, the lights in Prof Benton's office in the Common Academy blinked on.

"There is your answer," the statue said.

"Where is my answer?"

"His high school annual, rummy," the Colonel said. "What would you do without me to cipher out your affairs for you?"

"Any chance of enticing you over here to play for us, E.A.?" Prof asked. "We'd love to have you, you know."

E.A. shrugged. He and Prof were standing in front of the trophy case in the foyer of the Academy. This was the first time he'd ever set foot in a school in his life, and he felt as if he were six years old and today was his first day of classes.

Prof grinned. "Well," he said, "you can't blame me for trying."

As Prof led E.A. upstairs to the library, the scents of chalk dust and sweeping compound and generations of unwilling kids packed close together caused Ethan to stop and catch his breath.

Prof told him where the yearbooks were and asked him to turn off the library lights when he was finished and check in at the office before he left. Then E.A. was alone in the long room full of musty-smelling books. He had no trouble finding the yearbooks. Gypsy Lee's was there with the others. E.A. had been afraid that through some terrible quirk it would be missing. He took it down, opened it, and found Gypsy's picture. She didn't look any different then than she did now. Long red hair, straight small nose, cat's eyes. Gypsy Allen, class salutatorian. Nickname, Gypsy Lee. Hobbies, singing and baseball. Baseball? As far as E.A. knew, Gypsy had never had the slightest interest in baseball until he came along. Gran was the baseball fanatic in the Allen family. Gran and the Colonel. He flipped through the pages. René DeLabreure. The other boy who'd been killed.

Ferdinand Viens.

Fern was a slight, serious-looking, dark-haired boy. He appeared to be scarcely older than E.A. himself. Looking at him was more like looking at a picture of a dead brother. How could someone so young, so frail-looking, have been his father? Hobbies, baseball, 1, 2, 3, 4. Nickname, Lefty. So Fern Viens had been a southpaw.

E.A. realized that Gypsy's listed hobby had nothing to do with sports. It was meant as a joke. Fern Viens was a baseball player, and he was her hobby.

Suddenly E.A. dropped the yearbook. His eyes swam. He made himself pick up the book again and open it to Fern's page. Just across from his dead father's picture was a photograph that could not have astonished him more had it appeared on a major-league baseball card.

"Edward 'Teddy' Williams," the caption read. "Baseball, 1, 2, 3, 4."

There was no doubt at all in E.A.'s mind, as he stared at the photograph of the young man with the buzz cut, pale eyes, and arrogant expression, that "Teddy" Williams, the driver of the car his boy-father Fern Viens had been riding in when he'd been killed at the crossing, was the drifter who'd been teaching him baseball.

18

IT WAS MAY DAY in Kingdom County. Ethan was headed up Allen Mountain to collect wildflowers for a May basket for Gypsy. He hiked along the Canada Post Road past brushy, overgrown fields and cut-over woodlots. Near the edges of old clearings in the woods were spring beauties, hepaticas, deep purple violets, tiny yellow woods violets, and white violets with blue centers. Gypsy loved wildflowers of all kinds and had written many songs about them.

As part of E.A.'s homeschooling, Gypsy had taught him all about the history of the Canada Post Road. It was built shortly after the American Revolution by the Colonel and his brother, General Ira Allen, principally to smuggle cattle back and forth over the Canadian border. In the 1840s and '50s the road was traveled by fugitive slaves en route to Canada from the Allen homestead, Vermont's northernmost station on the Underground Railroad, run by Ethan's great-great-grandpa, Emancipator Allen, until he was hanged with John Brown at Harpers Ferry. This setback did not prevent Emancipator's son, Patrick, from leading the Irish Fenians on their ill-fated raid in 1872 to annex Quebec. Later, during Prohibition, Outlaw Allen ran whiskey down the Post Road from Quebec in large Packards, Buicks, and Cadillacs. The night before the Volstead Act was repealed, Outlaw had been killed at a fork in the road high on the mountain by federal revenuers lying in wait for him.

As E.A. approached the scene of Outlaw Allen's demise, he

noted that the right fork, which led due north to the Canadian border, had been flooded by a new beaver dam across a small tributary of Allen Mountain Brook. He took the left fork, toward the mountaintop and Long Tom.

To the degree that it resembled anything at all, Long Tom resembled a culvert pipe the length of a football field and large enough to drive a small car through. In fact, Tom was the world's biggest cannon, capable of firing a rocket-assisted shell halfway around the earth. This invention was the masterwork and crowning life achievement of Dr. Budweiser "Buddy" Allen, Gran's scientist brother. Perched on the mountaintop above a sheer drop of more than a thousand feet to Lake Memphremagog, Long Tom had a spooky, derelict look. The cannon was pointed almost due south toward its last target, the White House, which Dr. Budweiser had been preparing to shell "to wake up the president," just before being assassinated (Gran claimed) by the CIA. The epitaph on his stone in the family graveyard read: DR. BUDWEISER ALLEN. THOUGH IT REALLY DOESN'T MATTER HE WAS MAD AS A HATTER BUT HE HAD A SMART BRAIN. Gypsy had composed it when she was in junior high school.

E.A. set down his May basket and climbed up inside Long Tom, where he lay back in the dim coolness and looked out at the sky. Inside Tom, E.A. could close his eyes and imagine being shot out of the mouth of the cannon — not like one of Great-Uncle Buddy's gigantic shells with a smiley face and the message "Hello Mr. President, from the Green Mountain State" embossed on its fin, but like a clown he'd seen shot out of a pretend cannon at the Cole Bros. Circus. He imagined that it was night and he was zooming high above New England, and that he'd never learned what he found out in the Academy library, that none of it had ever happened. On he flew. Far below was Fenway Park, with the looming Green Monster, over which he would someday hit another shot heard round the world. He sped over Yankee Stadium, the tiny pinstriped players racing perpetually around the bases like mechanical players in an old-fashioned toy baseball game. West to

Comiskey Park and to Kauffman Stadium in Kansas City, on to the Kingdome in Seattle. Someday he'd play in all of them.

"Hey in there."

E.A. started up so fast he bumped his head. He crawdadded out of the cannon and dropped to the ground. There was the drifter, in his usual garb, standing near the edge of the cliff above the lake.

"Who you hiding from?" Teddy said. Then, "Whoa. Whoa, there, Ethan. What the —"

E.A.'s feet had scarcely hit the ground before he started charging. Teddy held him off at arm's length as E.A. windmilled his fists, trying to reach him, pound him, silently socking the big man in the side, the shoulder, with short punches, the way Teddy had taught him, the way he'd fought Orton and Norton, as though he meant to drive the drifter right over the edge of the cliff.

"Ethan, hold on. Hold up here. What's wrong?"

Teddy was too big for him. Too powerful. E.A. didn't know a man could be that strong, even as Teddy was trying to be gentle, move him back from the dropoff.

"It's you, you son of a bitch," the boy said, not loud, still trying to swing. Teddy had him by the wrists.

"What'd I do?" Teddy said. "What you think I've done?"

"You know what you did," E.A. said, struggling. "You killed my father."

They stood facing each other, Teddy ready to grab him again if necessary.

"Going to college," E.A. said through his tears. "Wanting to teach me baseball because we were friends. Lies! You were never in college. You were in prison, that's where you were. For killing my pa."

"Whoa, Ethan. Who put that idea in your head?"

"Tell me you weren't in prison. Let me hear you say it."

"I can't tell you I wasn't in prison. I was. But I never killed your father."

"I read it. Right in the *Monitor.*"

Teddy said nothing.

"You lied to me," E.A. said. "You lied to me about everything. Probably lying when you said I could do something with my baseball. Get somewhere with it."

"Ethan, I didn't ever go to college a day in my life. And you're right, I was in prison. Eight years, and I'm still on parole. But I'll tell you two things straight out. No matter what you heard, I never killed your father. And I'll never lie to you again about anything."

"That's the truth," E.A. said. "Because I'm going home now. And I don't want to see you around the place. Ever."

"Ethan. Did you ever pretend something was so when it wasn't? That's what I did about going to college. I shouldn't have. But I'm not lying about your father."

Teddy started down the Canada Post Road.

"How do I know whether to believe you or not?" Ethan called after him.

Teddy said something E.A. didn't catch.

"What?" E.A. called. "What's that?"

Teddy stopped and turned back. "I said, ask Gypsy Lee." Then he continued down the mountain, leaving E.A. standing beside Long Tom, more confused than ever.

19

TRADITIONALLY, Kingdom County farm families paid their property taxes with maple syrup income or by selling off some young stock or mature timber. Not the WYSOTT Allens. For as long as there had been WYSOTT Allens, they'd paid their taxes by peddling moonshine or running whiskey, a tradition first Gran, and then Gypsy, had faithfully continued to honor by smuggling American booze north into Canada, where it was worth about twice its value in the United States.

They started out just after sunrise in the Late Great Patsy Cline, with Gypsy driving, E.A. navigating, Gran and Old Bill in the back seat. Gran had a rule of the road, which was that they had to stop at every yard sale and garage sale they came to. Gypsy liked yard sales, too. She'd outfitted E.A. at them for years. Some of his favorite Red Sox caps and T-shirts had been bought off three-legged card tables in backcountry hollows and mill-town tenement yards. In St. Johnsbury they stopped at a sale outside a dented-can store. Gypsy bought a mildewed set of Raymond Chandler paperbacks and Gran bought *The Illustrated History of Spiritualism*. E.A. bought a baseball card, a dog-eared 1942 Topps Johnny Pesky.

They kept to the back roads because Patsy wasn't registered, though Bill had stuck a 1958 See Vermont plate on the back just before they left home. At the liquor store in Lancaster, New Hampshire, Gypsy bought ten fifths of Seagram's. A yellow tomcat weighing at least twenty pounds lay on the counter.

"How much you want for that cat?" Bill said to the clerk.

"We don't need any cats," Gran said.

"What I like about a cat is they don't require much choring," Bill said.

"You can have him for ten dollars," the clerk said. Bill paid her, and they took the yellow cat along.

In Franconia they bought ten fifths of Home Comfort. In Woodsville fifteen half-gallons of Jack Daniel's. In Lebanon another six gallons.

By midafternoon Patsy was riding on her springs. The cat, which Gran had named Bucky Dent, was lolling upside down in her lap, all four paws in the air, purring from the Seagram's Gran had been feeding it. At various yard sales en route they'd picked up a set of Boswell's *Life of Johnson* for Gypsy, an ancient three-fingered baseball mitt for E.A., and a 1934 Philco upright radio with tubes as big as shotgun shells for Gran to try to bring in the Red Sox on.

They arrived home at dusk, detouring out around the village to avoid encountering the deputy. After dropping off Gran, Bill, and the intoxicated Bucky Dent, Gypsy and E.A. started up the Canada Post Road toward their rendezvous. Gypsy drove, with E.A. holding the Battery Beam in case they spotted a deer or a moose.

They crept up the mountain. Twice they stopped so E.A could get out and lay some long hemlock planks, which they'd hidden in the woods, over ditches where the culverts had been washed out, just as Outlaw Allen had done many years before. Near the fork in the road, E.A. spotted the lights of a vehicle coming out the River Road far below. It passed Midnight Auto and turned up the Canada Post Road. Gypsy put the rifle scope on it. "It's our dear, beloved deputy," she said.

E.A.'s heart began to beat faster as Gypsy drove up the right fork toward the new beaver bog he'd discovered on May Day. While the warden's four-wheel-drive truck could probably negotiate the gullies where the culverts had been, no vehicle that was not amphibious could get through that bog. Just beyond an old log landing, the road ended and the flat, black water stretched away into the darkness behind the beaver dam. Gypsy backed into the landing and cut the lights.

Ten minutes later they heard the warden's engine whining as he gunned his truck up the mountain. The lights of the peace officer's vehicle flared into view. It bowled along toward them, the siren shrieking as it passed the landing where Gypsy and E.A. waited in the dark. The truck shot off the new beaver dam, landing in five feet of water. The siren continued to scream after the lights went out. Gypsy and E.A. stayed just long enough to ascertain that the warden was uninjured, which to judge from his very inventive language seemed to be the case, before heading back out to the fork and taking the left branch.

When they reached the mountaintop, E.A. was startled to see three large men in RCMP uniforms standing beside Long Tom in the headlights of a truck.

"Don't worry, hon, it's not what you think," Gypsy said.

The biggest officer stepped up to the window of the rig. "Miss Gypsy Allen, I presume," he said, and E.A. recognized the reassuring baritone of Sergeant Preston of the Yukon — Gypsy's Corporal Colin Urquahart.

"Good evening, officer," she said. "I believe that you and my son are already acquainted."

"We've met at your place once or twice, eh?" Sergeant Preston said, winking at E.A. He waved to the other two officers. "Boys, here's the good stuff for the annual barbecue. Get a load out and help me transfer it."

To Gypsy he said, "And yes, Gypsy Lee, I know the drill. I'm going to pay you in American currency."

Driving back along the Post Road, Gypsy was in such a good mood that E.A. came close to asking the all-important question. The property tax money in her pocket, she sang "Sticks and Stones."

"There was old John Crow the whiskey runner,
Sold his soul to the drink one summer.

And my friend Richard, down in the trailer,
Lost both arms to an old hay baler."

Very inspiring. But to E.A. the time still didn't seem quite right. Next week Gypsy had promised to take him wild-orchid poaching to celebrate her thirtieth birthday. That might be the right venue. In the meantime, the warden would have to hire Devil Dan to derrick his truck out of the bog with the Hook. They passed the deputy walking down the mountain, drenched to the skin and waving wildly for them to stop.

But of course they didn't.

20

WILD WOODSFLOWER GULF lay in a crease high on the mountain. Here, in a sequestered hollow, several kinds of lady's slippers grew undisturbed. Undisturbed, that is, by anyone but E.A. and Gypsy, who privately farmed them for an orchidist at the Montreal Botanical Gardens who had a summer home on Lake Memphremagog.

They left Patsy at the fork where the warden had taken the wrong turn and fished their way up the steep brook that rose in the gulf. Gypsy fished one pool, E.A. fished the next, then she hopscotched around him to the pool above. They'd fished this way for years. The pools were tiny stone washbasins, pockets under overhanging yellow birch roots, dark curves in the shadows of looming hemlocks. The trout were small, with backs the color of new maple leaves, red speckles ringed with turquoise, and orange stomachs. Gypsy was as adept at brook fishing as she was awkward at baseball. She could pluck a trout out of a run only a few inches deep, and she had a sixth sense for where they'd be lying.

Besides his fishing pole, E.A. had a sack and shovel. Tiny blue butterflies — azures, Gypsy said — congregated around damp spots on the trail beside the stream. Spotted wood frogs lived in the lush bankside ferns. A moose had preceded them up the mountain, its muddy hoof prints six inches deep. The sun broke through and everything glistened — the leaves, the maroon and yellow and blue stones in the streambed, the dark hemlock trunks. A winter wren whistled, the longest birdcall in the world. Gypsy shook her head, said she wished she had *his* wind and vibrato. A Blackburnian warbler flashed from tree to tree, its fiery throat gleaming.

They startled a partridge and her brood. The mother bird flapped off, dragging a wing. The chicks ran a few steps in the opposite direction, then grabbed dead leaves and turned upside down under them, lying perfectly still. How in the world could she get that wonderful adaptation into a song? Gypsy wondered to E.A. There had to be a way.

They came to more forks in the brook, each time taking the larger branch. Finally the stream was just a seep and they ran out of fishing. Ahead was the gulf, a ravine about one hundred feet deep and three hundred feet long. Beside a deer path winding up the south wall of the chasm, between jumbled boulders covered with moss, grew hundreds of yellow, pink, and showy lady's slippers. These wild orchids were notoriously difficult to transplant, but Gypsy knew exactly how to do it successfully and never took more than six or seven specimens of each color. The Canadian botanist paid her fifty dollars apiece for them. The same amount he paid her per hour to pose as Persephone, bedecked with a floral crown and little else, while he photographed her.

"The trick here, hon, is to get plenty of dirt around their roots and bring back enough extra woods dirt for each plant to think it's still growing back in the Vermont forest, even though it's in a conservatory belonging to some horse's ass in Montreal."

Exhuming a saffron-colored orchid, E.A. wondered if he'd ever be able to stand living in a city, even for part of the year. If he was going to play major-league baseball, he'd have to figure out a way. He slipped the gorgeous exotic into the burlap bag and spaded up a pink lady's slipper. As a small boy, he'd thought the pink ones were elves' shoes.

"Ma? How come it's against the law to dig these flowers up?"

"Well, a lot of orchid poachers aren't very conservation-minded, hon. They'd clean out a patch the way old Huck Lapointe cleaned out the trout in that beaver pond up behind his place a few years ago. It's a good law so far as it goes. But it's still just man's law.

The day I open up Matthew, Mark, Luke, or John and see where Our Father Who Art in Heaven or his Loving Son says 'Thou shalt not pick, destroy, transplant, or sell the showy lady's slipper,' I'll never dig up another one. I promise."

"Ma?"

"What, sweetie?"

"If I asked you something, would you answer it?"

"Always, hon. Are you starting to have dreams about holding commerce with naked girls? That's entirely normal, sweetie. I'm really happy for you."

"No, ma. Well, yeah, but we've been over all that before. It's about Teddy. The drifter."

"Oh." Gypsy brushed her red hair away from her eyes. "What do you want to know about him?"

E.A. took a breath. "Did Teddy kill my father? In that wreck with the train?"

"Teddy kill your father? Oh, hon. No. Jesum Crow, sweetie. Where on earth . . . you thought Teddy killed your father?"

E.A. nodded.

"Honey boy, who do you think your father *was*?"

"I know who he was, ma. His initials are on the water tower with yours. They're pretty faint, but you can make them out. Plus I saw the write-up on the accident in an old *Monitor*. And his picture in your yearbook. Ferdinand Viens."

Gypsy's hands shot to her mouth. "Fern Viens? Hon, those aren't Fern Viens's initials on the tank. And Teddy Williams never killed your pa because —"

"Because what, ma?"

"Because those initials aren't F V, Ethan. They're E W. For Edward Williams. Teddy Williams *is* your father."

★ TEDDY ★

"Now i get it," E.A. told the Colonel. "He came back on my eighth birthday to try to set things right."

"I used to watch him from out here," the Colonel said. "He had the smoothest swing, the quickest hands, the best throw to second I ever saw. Ages past, the House of David came here to play our boys. Ran all over us, needless to say. Fisk played here. Rich Gale, Bill Lee, a passel of them. Teddy was as good as the best. The accident was on the eve of the day he was slated to go down to Worcester, I believe it was, for his big tryout. Instead he went to the hospital and then to prison. Well, there are worse things he could do than come back to show his boy how to play ball."

"I told him I never wanted to see him again," Ethan said, wishing more than anything that he hadn't.

"That doesn't matter. He wants to see you. For better or for worse, he's your pa. Now skedaddle. BP's beginning down yonder on the ball field."

⚾

As the Colonel had predicted, Teddy came back, and E.A.'s thirteenth summer turned out to be a good one. E.A. heard that Teddy was running a lathe at the bat mill and staying at the hotel. They didn't talk about the accident again, or about Teddy's being E.A.'s pa. Two or three evenings a week he'd appear at Gran's and they'd go through BP and fielding practice, and around dusk he'd drift back over to the village. Sometimes Gypsy watched them for a minute from the dooryard, but Gran stayed inside, hunkered over the yard-sale Philco, trying to pick up the Red Sox games through the mountain static. One night in late June Boston blew an eight-run lead and lost to Seattle 12–11. The Sox never bounced back from that loss and neither did Gran.

Ethan made the Outlaws. It was getting harder to recruit new players, interest in town ball was waning, and teams were dropping out of the Northern Border League. Even in the Common attendance had fallen off. In another five or six years, E.A. figured, town ball would be a thing of the past. But when Moonface got drunk and stumbled into the Colonel's pedestal and broke his toe, E.A. began starting regularly at shortstop.

What was the book on him? Well, that he had a quick bat. It was hard to get a fastball past him, though he'd still occasionally swing at a hard pitch up and out of the strike zone. In the field he was nearly flawless. He rarely made an error, and he held his ground on Cy's throws down to second to nail stealing base runners. He had some trouble hitting curve balls. He didn't shy away or stick his foot in the water bucket or get out on his front foot too fast, and he saw the ball all the way to the bat and tried to go with the pitch. But the craftier curve-ball pitchers could get him to pop up or ground out weakly three out of four times with a hook on the outside corner. Still, by mid-July he was hitting .340, second-highest on the team after Earl, and leading the Outlaws with walks, steals, and on-base percentage. The men called him the Kid. Kid Allen, like a prizefighter. But they teased him less than they used to. He had a knack for being in the right place to make a big play in the field and for knocking in the game-winning run or scoring it by taking an extra bag with his daring base running. He had an instinct for the game, they said. And he had the most heart of any player anyone, including the elderly bat boys on the hotel porch, could remember. Nothing daunted him. In any clutch situation he wanted to go up to the plate. In the field he wanted the ball to be hit to him.

True, E.A. had Gypsy's slender build. He was never going to

be as rugged as Earl, much less Teddy, and this troubled him. He wasn't sure he'd ever be able to hit the really long ball. Also, at night, and even during the day, he was confused by thoughts about "holding intimate commerce with girls," as Gypsy had put it. But since he didn't attend school and lived outside the village, he knew few girls, and none well, and in fact had little commerce of any kind with them. Mainly E.A. concentrated on baseball, as he always had, working hard on his game, bribing the Outlaws to give him extra BP in exchange for duplicate baseball cards, working out on his own, and continuing to run everywhere he went.

At first Gypsy wouldn't let him go to away games with the Outlaws because she correctly suspected that they drank and drove. Not only did they drink prodigious quantities of beer coming home from games late at night, they drank en route *to* their games as well. E.A. wheedled and begged to go along, but to no avail until the Outlaws had to play a double-header in Woodsville, New Hampshire, one Sunday with only eight players, and he talked Earl into making him the designated driver. That was fine with Gypsy. At thirteen he drove as well as or better than most of the men on the team anyway. Certainly he drove better sober than they did drunk. Usually he drove Pappy's big Buick, driving forty-five or fifty at most, to New Hampshire and western Maine, up into Canada (Pappy drove through the checkpoints), over into upstate New York. Anyplace they could pick up a game.

Teddy continued to practice with him regularly, but he didn't come to many of E.A.'s games. Teddy had little interest in town-team ball. When E.A. admitted that curve balls tied him in knots, Teddy threw him breaking pitches by the hour, spotting them wherever E.A. requested. He continued to give the boy very little advice. This was part of what made him a good teacher. When E.A. punched a breaking ball on the outside corner over first base and was mad at himself for not driving it into a gap, Teddy said, "That's about all you can do with that pitch, Ethan. That was a good piece of hitting."

He never gave E.A. any advice at all about throwing but

continued to insist that they toss together before every workout. They'd start twenty feet apart. Then thirty. Fifty. Sixty. As if, E.A. thought, playing catch was some kind of father-son ritual. Once Teddy asked E.A. if his arm ever hurt him. Ethan said no.

In September, orange-and-black monarch butterflies began to congregate in the high mowing meadow. As part of E.A.'s home-schooling, Gypsy borrowed Big Earl's Rand McNally Road Atlas and traced out the southward flight of the monarchs, teaching him history and geography along the way. "Now they're going over the old Erie Canal, hon — Clinton's ditch, they called it. It opened the way for westward expansion. Here's Gettysburg . . ." And she told him all about Pickett's charge and gave him a wonderful book to read called *The Killer Angels*, about General Robert E. Lee and General James Longstreet and an incredibly brave young man from Maine named Joshua Chamberlain.

Once again color was appearing on the mountainside, creeping down from the top, past Wild Woodsflower Gulf, past Warden's Bog, the first blush of the maples gradually intensifying to vivid reds and yellows. Bill said it hurt his eyes to look at the fall foliage. He didn't know why the leaves had to bother to change; it seemed like a lot of trouble to go to, just to drop off a few days later. Gypsy said the only other place in the world where the fall foliage was as bright was a province in northern China. Gran said the Red Sox could all go to China in a handbasket. Maybe they could beat the Taiwan Little League All-Stars, though she had her doubts. E.A. was studying algebra and Latin that fall, which Gypsy said he needed for his college boards. He didn't mind. Gypsy had been a whiz at algebra and Latin.

Late in the afternoon of the last day of September, Teddy showed up at Gran's with his bat bag, his metal spikes lashed through the canvas handles by their laces. E.A. figured his father would be heading out for the winter right after their workout. He missed him already. That afternoon, while Bill stood in the outfield and complained about the fall colors, they played a game of Twenty-seven Outs, the '48 Sox against the '48 Yankees. Ethan fielded and hit for the Sox. On one defensive play, with Joe DiMaggio on second, Berra singled to left center. E.A. ran out from short and took the cutoff from Bill, whirled and nailed Joe D at the plate by ten feet.

"He's coming back to third — throw it!" E.A. said, racing to the bag.

Instead, Teddy faked a throw to third, then sprang up the line four or five steps and tagged Joe on the back, just the way he'd shown E.A., ball in the hand, hand in the glove, tag with the glove.

E.A.'d never seen a man move that fast in his life, much less a six-foot-three man weighing nearly two hundred pounds. Teddy moved the way Bucky Dent, Bill's cat, had pounced on a weasel in the woodshed last winter.

"I'd say you got him dead to rights, E.W.," Bill said. It was the closest thing to a compliment E.A. had ever heard from Old Bill.

Afterward Teddy got a bottle of Hires for E.A. out of the springhouse, and they sat on the Packard seat while E.A. sipped the icy root beer, which tasted like nothing else on earth but root beer. Bill and Teddy sipped Crackling Rose. Bill said he hoped they were satisfied, he'd lost an afternoon of work, and now he might better not try to do anything except sweep out the barn, because if he did it would all just be catch-up. Crickets chirped. Up at the house, Gypsy was patiently at work on the second verse of "Nobody's Child," the guitar chords floating softly down over the ball grounds.

"Why don't she go to Nashville?" Teddy said suddenly. "See what she can do with them pretty numbers?"

"She has a boy to raise is why," E.A. said. "She didn't up and walk out on that boy is why."

"E.W. didn't exactly walk out, E.A. They put him away in prison," Bill pointed out.

Teddy was turning his big, mahogany-colored catcher's glove over in his hands. E.A. secretly hoped he'd give it to him to practice with during the off-season.

E.A. sipped his root beer. Gran's octagonal barn glowed in the sunset, the low rays reflecting off Bill's multicolored license plates like sunshine on a crazy quilt. It was a handsome building, with a dormer over the highdrive to the hayloft and a cupola. On rainy days E.A. stood between the soaring bays on either side of the loft and played Twenty-seven Outs off the back wall. Or threw his red rubber ball through the swinging tire. Recently Devil Dan had driven the D-60 right up to the side of the barn and lifted the blade above the row of windows in the milking parlor and menaced with it while Gypsy drew a bead on him with Grandpa Gleason Allen's 30.06 Springfield from the kitchen door. E.A. had no doubt she'd use it if Dan so much as touched the barn with the Blade. Then she'd be in prison and he'd be all but orphaned. He wished Teddy would stay for the winter.

Tracing his finger across the cold mist on the Hires bottle, he said to Teddy, "You headed out tonight? On the eight-oh-six?"

"Maybe, maybe not," Teddy said. "I've been thinking."

"Thinking what?"

Teddy nodded at the red-and-gold mountain. "You recollect what I said to you up there this past spring?"

"How could I forget? A boy doesn't find out every day of the week that his pa was a jailbird."

"Do you recollect what I said about no more fibbing to you?" Teddy said. "About being in college and such?"

"Yes."

"Have I?"

"Have you what?"

"Told you any stretchers this summer."

E.A. considered. "Not so far's I know."

"Tell me again what you want, Ethan."

"You know what I want. To do what they say overstreet that you could have but didn't."

"Which is?"

"I don't want to jinx it."

"There's no such thing as a jinx. Say it."

Bucky Dent rubbed against Teddy's spike, and he pulled his foot away. E.A. could tell he was uncomfortable with the cat and so

132

could Bucky Dent, who now jumped up on Teddy's lap. Teddy picked him up and tossed him aside. The cat purred and arched its back with pleasure.

Teddy looked back at E.A. "I was saying. There's no such a thing as a jinx. All that happy horseshit about not mentioning a no-hitter in progress? That saying it's a no-no? I don't hold with none of that. Pitcher has a no-hit game going and gets away with a mistake, fastball down the center right in the hitter's wheelhouse, I point it out to him. 'Do that again, bub, there goes your no-hitter,' I tell him. I'll ask you again, Ethan. What is it you want?"

"He wants that Lori gal over to the hotel to ask him out, it's all he can think about," Bill said, to E.A.'s surprise. Just when you thought Old Bill was the next thing to brain-dead, he'd surprise you. In fact, he'd had a crush on Lori, the hotel waitress, who was nearly twice his age, for six months, though he hadn't breathed a word about her to anyone, even Gypsy.

Teddy paid no attention to Bill or to E.A.'s red face as the boy quickly said, "Go all the way to the top. Be a big-league hitter. Play shortstop, maybe even catcher."

"It'll never happen."

Teddy said this exactly the way he might say no rain was in sight. Showers before the weekend? Never happen.

E.A. jumped to his feet. "What do you mean? What do you mean, it'll never happen?"

Teddy, still sitting, held up his hands as if to fend off another attack. "Don't you be flying off the handle, boy. I said I wouldn't lie to you again. Not even in kidding. Well, I won't. And you won't ever be a major-league hitter, either. Or a shortstop or catcher."

"You can just bet I will."

"If I said that, I'd be fooling myself and you, too."

"Well, why the hell not?" E.A. was nearly shouting, and despite himself his eyes were reddening. He could feel them smarting.

"I'll tell you why not. One, you ain't quite big enough and likely won't be. Two, you're fast afoot but you ain't quite fast enough. Three, you have a quick pair of hands but not quite quick enough. Your bat ain't quite quick enough, neither. Yes, in the field you're smooth. But you ain't quite smooth enough. Ethan. Listen to me. You could play college and do real good at it. Single A, maybe. Maybe even double A. But not all the way and be a big-league hitter or shortstop, much less a catcher."

Now tears were beginning to come, and as hard as it was for E.A. to hear all this with no warning whatsoever, it was harder yet to think he might cry in front of his father. He clenched his fists.

Teddy grinned. "You going to charge the mound again? Rush me?"

"You think it's funny."

"No, sir. I don't. But I don't think misleading a kid, much less a fella's own kid, is funny, either. Stringing you along to waste five, six, eight years of your youth riding old buses around the South or out West or wherever until you finally find out for yourself in Chattanooga at twenty-seven with your two-twenty-seven batting average that you ain't going one step further. I don't want that for you, Ethan. You don't want that for yourself."

"You don't know what I want," E.A. shouted. Now Gypsy was out in the dooryard, watching. She'd probably thought Devil Dan was on his way to dozer down the barn.

"Yes, I do," Teddy said equably. "Now looky here."

He took E.A.'s wrist in his hand. "To hit the ball really hard, your wrists have to be bigger."

"Gypsy says if Our Father Who Art in Heaven'd wanted me to be bigger, I would have been."

"There you have it."

"I can improve."

"There's no doubt of it. But not enough."

Now E.A. thought he saw what this was about. For some reason Teddy had gotten sick of helping him with his baseball, living in the hotel, running a lathe for minimum wage at the bat factory. Sticking in one spot instead of drifting from place to place the way he was used to. Teddy was tired of being a father, and this was his way of getting out of it. A way to leave and not come back again.

"I can learn to hit the long ball."

Teddy shook his head. "That, you need to be a big old slab-sided, ham-handed, rawboned fella like your pa, Ethan. Six two. Six one, anyway."

"I could get to be six one."

"You could. Five eleven's more likely. Plus you're built like that Yankee fella. Cajun boy out of Louisiana, pitched for them fifteen, twenty years ago. Fella with the good heat."

"Guidry."

"That would be it. Ron Guidry."

"I'd work hard. Harder than any player they've ever seen."

"Yes, and that's in your favor, but it ain't enough."

He reached into his pocket, brought out a baseball, and tossed it to E.A. "Look at it," he said. "Heft it. Now tell me. How do you feel about it?"

"Feel about it?" Gypsy's psychologist client, Dr. Fuller from St. J, was always talking about feelings. His own feelings, mainly. Once a month, regular as clockwork, he'd show up on a Sunday evening and have a cup of tea with Gypsy and Gran in the kitchen and talk about his feelings over the past few weeks, how he needed to "take care of himself" and "nurture the child within" before repairing to the parlor with Gypsy to have her dress up as Sigmund Freud or Carl Jung and "examine his feelings."

"I like it," E.A. admitted. "I like the way it feels in my hand."

"How about the way it looks? You like them neat red stitches? The leathery way it smells?"

E.A. nodded.

"Well, a natural hitter hates the ball. Wants to kill it, drive it out of his sight. He hates the pitcher, too. But you look here. Your wrists ain't too big, or your arms, but you got fairly long fingers, like a pianer player. You can wrap 'em halfway around the ball or more. See? That's good."

"How can it be good if I'm not going to make it all the way to the top? What difference does it make how long my fingers are?"

Teddy lit a cigarette. "I didn't say you weren't going to make it all the way to the top. I said you weren't going to be a big league hitter. Or shortstop. Now, as a pitcher, that might be something else again."

E.A. had never once considered being a pitcher. In all his fantasizing late at night or playing Twenty-seven Outs in the dooryard or in the barn, he was always the hitter or a fielder. Never the pitcher. He'd never pitched to a live batter in his life.

"You said I wasn't big enough. Aren't pitchers big, too? Earl No Pearl? Clemens? Even that Ichabod from Pond is six feet."

"A lot of pitchers are big. Randy Johnson. That old boy from Texas, What's-his-face Ryan. Then again, you got your Guidrys. Got your Martinezes. With a pitcher, Ethan, size helps. But you can be five ten if you've got long fingers, strong legs, whip in your arm. Plus" — he squinted at E.A. through the cigarette smoke — "it's all right for the pitcher to like the baseball."

E.A. thought about this as the sun sank behind the Green Mountains. "I never thought about winning the Series as a pitcher. How do I know you ain't stringing me along?"

Teddy shook his head. "Whoa, boy. Nobody said nothing about winning any Series. Like I've told you, the only guarantee in baseball is there ain't no guarantees. All I said so far is you got fairly big hands, fairly long fingers."

"Do I have a shot as a pitcher or not? I want you to tell me right now."

Teddy stood up and checked the sky to see how much playable daylight was left. He put on his catcher's glove.

"Let's toss," he said, starting for the plate. "Begin in close. Work your way back toward the mound."

I<small>T WAS</small> A<small>PRIL</small> A<small>GAIN</small>, and the ospreys were back, the female bird already sitting on her nest atop the water tank, the male feeding her big spawning rainbow trout that got by Gypsy's homemade fish weirs just downriver. Even with the weirs, there were plenty of trout left for the ospreys and for the fishermen who stood elbow to elbow along the river below the High Falls, if the fishermen knew how to catch them. Most were from Away, outside of the Kingdom, and didn't.

Devil Dan had a trout weir of his own. It directed the current through a narrow sluiceway, where he shot the fish with his automatic rifle, then netted them when they floated up to the surface. He was out doing it today while E.A. threw to Teddy off the mound at Fenway. During the off-season, E.A. had worked on his pitching in the barn, throwing to his swinging tire suspended from the rafters. As the winter progressed, he refined the game, pitching whole simulated innings. Sometimes he pitched like the Sox's great Cy Young, who'd begun his career throwing underhand. Sometimes he was Luis Tiant, spinning around on the imaginary rubber to look out the open barn door and down the highdrive and across the snowy barnyard. He could throw Bill "Spaceman" Lee's sky-high eephus pitch, calculating exactly when it would descend to meet the pendulum arc of the tire, and he liked to do Bill Monbouquette finishing up his no-hitter in '62 against the White Sox's Nellie Fox and Luis Aparicio, and big Dick Radatz in '63, coming in against the Yankees to punch out Mantle, Maris, and

Elston Howard in ten pitches. He was never Calvin Schiraldi, giving up three consecutive singles to the Mets in '86 to let the Series slip right through his fingers, much less poor Mike Torrez pitching to Bucky Dent in the one-game playoff with the Yankees in '78. The barn was as cold as a freezer locker. It seemed colder than the outdoors. But as the Colonel said, any baseball was better than no baseball, and by spring, when Teddy returned, E.A. could throw as hard as most men. He'd grown some over the winter, too. Just fourteen, he was already nearly five foot eight. But if Teddy was surprised by his new height or speed, he didn't say so.

"How come you never give me any throwing advice?" E.A. said as he stood on the old tire strip he used as a rubber. "If you're going to make me a pitcher."

"I'm not going to make you a pitcher," Teddy said. "You have to do that yourself. As for ordinary throwing, you don't need much advice. You throw naturally. When we get to the pitching part, I'll show you what I know."

"They say you were the best catcher ever played in the village."

"I imagine Judge Charlie K was that. No, I take that back. Fisk was the best catcher ever to play in the village. I wasn't close to him."

Ethan, his eyes the color of rainwater on a stormy day — Teddy's eyes — looked right at his father. "How good were you?"

Teddy considered. "I was a good country ball player with a knack for knowing the hitters' weaknesses. Still am. When I was in college" — he looked at E.A. to make sure the boy knew what he was referring to — "when I was inside, the pen down to Woodstock got overcrowded. They bid out a few of us to facilities down South. I wound up in Florida. Warden found out I'd played some ball, and he shipped me over to the big state prison in Texas. They had a top-flight team, the Lone Star Gang, but their catcher got an early release for good behavior and they needed a quality replacement. The Florida warden traded me for two rodeo stars, a bull rider and a bronc buster."

Ethan was impressed. His pa, traded for two convict rodeo stars.

"By and by the Texas warden cut me a deal. If I'd agree to come back and play five more years for the Lone Stars in the winter season, work at the prison in the rec department, he'd put me up for early parole. So I went up in front of the board, and they asked if I was sorry about them two boys in the car with me, and I said I was. But to tell you the truth, I was *more* sorry to have missed those first eight years with you. Four or five years old is when a boy wants to begin to develop his swing. Maybe if I'd of been around then — but never mind that. Now you're a pitcher.

"Listen, Ethan. Racing that train was the dumbest-ass thing a young fella could ever do. But I never meant for them boys to get killed. And I'm sorry I missed them early years with you. Now that's all I'm going to say about it. You have a good winter?"

"Fair," E.A. said. "But Devil Dan" — he jerked his head at the owner of Midnight Auto, stalking along the riverbank with his rifle, looking for fish to shoot — "he says he intends to dozer down our barn and house before another year is out."

Teddy glanced over just as the junkyard owner fired into the river five times in rapid succession. The startled male osprey, soaring overhead, loosed a viscous white fluid right onto Dan's fedora and shiny shoes.

Dan cursed and smote his thigh with his dripping hat. The fish hawk landed near its mate, and before E.A. knew it, Dan had shot the bird off the water tank. Then he killed the female for good measure.

"No!" E.A. shouted. He broke toward Dan. Something jerked him off his feet.

"Ethan," Teddy said, holding his shirt collar. "There's nothing you can do. Nothing'll bring those birds back. There's a better way."

"What?" E.A. shouted. "What way?"

"You'll see," Teddy said. "And you listen. That man isn't going to destroy your barn and house. I give you my word."

Later that day, at Gypsy's insistence, Warden Kinneson came out and investigated the killing of the fish hawks. But by then Dan had burned them, feathers and all, in his illegal open-air dump, and without evidence there was nothing the warden could do, assuming he was disposed to do anything anyway. When he couldn't find the birds he said that the Allens had probably made up the entire story.

ONE SATURDAY Teddy took Ethan up Allen Mountain to the woods above E.A. and Gypsy's special place and showed him a stand of white ash trees, tall and straight and good for making baseball bats. He told the boy that ashes favored sunny, south-facing clearings, out of the wind. Wind stressed their grain. He said that white ash liked a loamy soil, not a clay base. And that a good sawyer could get twenty bats out of one tree.

"How is it," E.A. said to his father as they sat on a log under a yellow birch and looked down the mountainside, "you come to know so much about ash trees?"

"Oh," Teddy said, "when I was staying with my great-uncle, old Peyton Williams, up in Lord Hollow, he cut ash trees for the bat factory down to the Common."

This was the first time Teddy had ever mentioned his family to E.A.

"Teddy? How come you never talk about your people?"

"My people?"

"You know. Your folks."

Teddy shrugged. "I never really knew my people, Ethan. My ma, she passed on when I was little. I don't hardly recollect her at all."

"Then what happened? After your ma died?"

"Well, I got shifted around from one shirttail relation and foster home to the next. Finally I landed up with old man Williams."

"Was he good to you?"

Teddy broke off a yellow birch twig and sucked on the winter-green-flavored inner bark. "He weren't nothing to me one way or the other. He weren't mean when he was sober, and I learned pretty quick to steer clear of him when he was on a binge. I reckon I was a handful myself, Ethan."

"What happened to your great-uncle?"

"He was old when I first went to stay with him, and a year or so after I got sent to jail, he up and died."

Ethan hesitated. Then he said, "What about your pa?"

"What about him?"

"You said your ma passed on when you were little. What became of your pa?"

Teddy stood up. "He dropped out of the picture before I was born. I never knowed who he was." He flipped the yellow birch twig at a nearby ash. "There, Ethan. That's a better than average baseball-bat tree."

"How do you know?"

"I just do. Same's you know how to throw a baseball. Let's go get your pitching in."

Ethan knew from his geology lessons with Gypsy that a great glacial lake had once covered the entire Kingdom Valley from Lake Memphremagog's south end all the way to the future site of Kingdom Common. Where Gran's house and barn now sat there had been one hundred feet of water with melting icebergs drifting in it. As the Great Wisconsin Ice Sheet retreated, the lake gradually withdrew to its present location north of Gran's, leaving the river and, in the adjacent fields, huge deposits of sandy soil.

Trouble was, for a proper pitcher's mound you needed something firmer than sand. Under Bill's supervision Teddy and Ethan brought five wheelbarrow loads of clay from the riverbank to Fenway. They dug down three feet, removing the sandy loam that Gran's *Cannabis* thrived in, and filled the hole with clay, heavy and blue-gray, the color of Allen Mountain on a cloudy November morning. Teddy built the new mound up as carefully as if he were burying a beloved hunting dog beneath it. He got out his tape and made sure that the distance to home plate was correct.

Surveying the finished job, Teddy said, "Pitcher's mound has to be just right, Ethan. An inch high will throw off your stride and cause the ball to rise up in the strike zone, where the hitter likes it. Hold the tape, will you, Bill?"

Bill stood on the new rubber Teddy had lifted from the mound on the common and held the metal tag at the end of the Stanley tape, while Teddy started back toward the plate, unwinding the reel. He squinted and turned his head aside to avoid the smoke from his Lucky.

"You ought to quit smoking," E.A. said.

"I ought to do a lot of things," Teddy said.

It was sixty feet six inches from the rubber to the back of the plate. E.A. wondered, Why the six inches?

"That's baseball is why," Teddy said.

"Baseball," Bill said. "Run your legs off to get back where you commenced from no further ahead than before you started."

"Wrong," Teddy said, straightening the plate. "You're at least one run further ahead, Bill."

Teddy had borrowed the plate from the common, too.

The Kingdom County nights were still cool. Some of the days, too. Teddy hung a round outdoor thermometer on the side of the barn, a green and blue and red affair that looked like a hex sign on a Pennsylvania barn. If the temperature was a degree under sixty he wouldn't let E.A. pitch.

Their routine was always the same. Teddy would stand behind the plate, his catcher's glove belt-high. E.A. would stand twenty feet away and in line with the new mound. They'd start to toss. By degrees E.A. worked his way back. When he reached the mound, it seemed a long way from the plate.

"It'll get closer every year," Teddy told him.

Teddy was careful not to teach the boy too much at a time. E.A. had a naturally smooth, over-the-top delivery. He started with his right foot slightly slanted on the rubber and his left foot a few inches behind it. His wind-up was economical. He threw exactly the same way every time. Teddy didn't let him throw too hard. He didn't let him experiment with breaking balls.

One morning a brand-new pair of size-eight spikes appeared on the mound. Inside each shoe was a new sweat sock. E.A. sat on the Packard seat to put them on.

"Teach me something new today," he wheedled.

"All right," Teddy said. "Wear them socks inside out the first few times."

E.A. looked at him.

"Cuts down on blisters," Teddy explained.

E.A. turned the new socks inside out.

After the boy's arm was loose Teddy said, "Want to pitch an inning?"

E.A. nodded.

"You pick the team."

"'Fifty-two Yankees."

"All right." Teddy squatted down behind the plate and turned his baseball cap backward. "First batter's who?"

"Phil Rizzuto."

"Book on him?"

"Pitch him away. Work the corners."

He got Rizzuto in five pitches. Fanned Billy Martin, fanned Yogi, didn't have to face DiMaggio. From that day on, Teddy let him pitch one or two simulated innings at every workout. Sometimes Gypsy and Gran watched from the dooryard, Gran disputing Teddy's called strikes.

At first Teddy was generous with his strike zone. If E.A. had Mickey Mantle down on the count, one ball, two strikes, and Teddy set up for the next one on the outside corner at the knees and E.A. missed wide by three or four inches, Teddy'd jump up and say, "Mantle swings and misses, strike three."

As the summer progressed Teddy's strike zone shrank.

E.A. began throwing three innings at a stretch. They went through the Yankees of 1960 with Mantle and Maris. The '50 Cardinals with Musial and Mize. Sometimes, on a low pitch, Teddy'd say, "He swings and hits the ball back to the mound." He'd throw a grounder, and E.A. would grab it and fire it back, Teddy stretching out like a first baseman. Or Teddy would flip the ball out of his glove along the third-base line, a surprise drag bunt, and E.A. would sprint off the mound and pounce on it and whirl and make as if to throw to first.

Once, when Gypsy was watching, he began to throw harder.

"Let up," Teddy told him. "Accuracy first. Speed second."

If E.A. threw a pitch in the dirt, Teddy'd nod and say, "Better down there than up in Jackie Jensen's wheelhouse." Or, "Even Joe D won't hurt you down there, Ethan."

The last day they threw that fall, Teddy squeezed him on a couple of pitches.

E.A. stared in at him. "Sir," he called. "Where was that last pitch?"

Earl No Pearl was big on calling the umpire sir, then demanding to know where the pitch was.

Teddy came partway out to the mound. "Don't speak directly to the umpire, Ethan. It won't help you. When your half of the inning's over, have your catcher say to the ump, quiet-like, 'My pitcher's got a late-breaking curve' — or slider, or whatever — 'it catches the corner of the plate.' You just pitch. Don't show nothing in your face over a call. Don't shake your head or slap at the ball with your glove when the catcher throws it back. Don't stare in at the umpire. Just pitch."

"Good sportsmanship, right?"

"Sportsmanship's got nothing to do with it. You don't want to break your concentration is all. Plus, you start getting into pissing contests with the umpire, he'll always win. Even your catcher shouldn't argue too much. I don't much mind locking horns, but I don't never lock horns with the umpire. I'll speak to him quiet,

145

once or twice a game at most. Maybe hold a pitch in my glove an extra half second, give him a good look."

"How come when I miss close you don't jerk your glove quick back into the strike zone, like Cy does for Earl?"

"Because that's the surest way to get a good ump to give the pitch to the batter. The umpire isn't stupid. Or blind, either."

"What if my catcher won't speak to him at all? Or jerks his glove back into the zone? Or won't call the right pitches?"

Teddy shrugged. "Get a new catcher. I'm heading to Texas tomorrow, Ethan. Be back in the spring."

"Well?"

"Well what?"

"Can I do it? Go all the way as a pitcher."

Teddy looked up at the mountain, hazy in the fall mist. Long Tom seemed to hover about halfway between the mountaintop and Gran's farm. "Time will tell."

He touched his cap with his index finger and was on his way.

THAT WINTER E.A. rigged up a plywood mound with a scrap of indoor-outdoor carpet nailed to it in the hayloft. He threw at the tire, into a strike-zone-size square of hay bales, imitating the all-time great pitchers — Walter Johnson, Lefty Grove, Whitey Ford. He began teaching himself how to throw a knuckleball, a screwball, and a split-fingered fastball. Bundled up in his second-hand yard-sale parka, he resembled an Eskimo pitching. He didn't care. Any baseball was better than no baseball.

Pitching made the winter go faster, and so did his advanced algebra and Latin — he and Gypsy were now working their way through Cicero. He even had a couple of dates with Lori the waitress's daughter, April May. One Saturday night at the hotel he won a '58 Topps Ted Williams, in Mint condition, in a contest with Earl to see who could throw a card the farthest. At Christmas he got a postcard with an aerial view of the Lubbock State Penitentiary, with a baseball game in progress on the prison diamond. E.A. thought he could make out Teddy squatting behind the plate in his catcher's gear. The card was signed, "Don't wish you were here hows the throwing coming Yours in baseball Teddy."

"E.A.," Earl said at the Outlaws' first practice that spring, "you want to throw a little BP?"

From then on he threw all their batting practice. At fifteen he could put nine out of ten pitches right down the pipe, hit the corner if that's what the batter wanted, or put some mustard on the pitch. When the season began, Earl surprised him by starting him at short, moving the slower Moonface to second. Moon didn't squawk. E.A. was the best infielder on the team, and curiously, now that he was training himself to pitch, he was hitting the cover off the ball. You couldn't get a pitch by him. He drove fastballs into the gaps in the outfield, went with the curve balls and lined them between first and second, hardly ever swung at the first pitch, let anything outside the strike zone go by. Secretly he still believed he could go all the way as a hitter. At the same time he pestered Earl to let him pitch an inning in a game. Earl said when he was ready. In the meantime they needed his glove and arm at short.

On the day of the Outlaws' home game with a team of all-stars from Ticonderoga, New York, E.A. stopped to visit briefly with the Colonel, who was in an irascible mood from being out in an all-night rain two evenings before. After two centuries, he was taking the weather harder than he once had.

"So what's new with you?" the statue said after grumbling about his aches and pains.

E.A. knew that the Colonel didn't really expect a reply, that he was mainly making conversation. He looked down the common to where the Outlaws were beginning to arrive in their pickups. The team from Ticonderoga was taking infield and outfield in their new uniforms. They were college boys and ex–minor-leaguers and semipro standouts, paid to play for the big paper-mill team across Lake Champlain. They looked sharp, several cuts above any team Ethan had seen in the Border League. The infielders were just finishing, going around the horn taking a last ground ball, firing it in to the catcher, who tossed it back as the fielder sprinted toward home, scooped it up, and flipped it back to the catcher. Smooth.

The Colonel agreed. "Them boys look trig," he said. "Leave me a mitt, will you? So's I'll have something to protect myself with when they tee off on Earl."

The Outlaws were getting ready to take BP as Ethan trotted down to the diamond, his heart beating from the sheer happiness of knowing he'd be playing ball soon, pitching, even if it was only batting practice.

He headed for the mound. But Cyrus the Great waved him in off the field. "Earl's got him a bad right shoulder, E.A. All that skeet-shooting he done yesterday when he was drunk up to the rod and gun club. We was thinking we might have you go for us this afternoon. You up for it?"

The Common watched attentively as E.A. loosened up with Cy along the third-base line. Judge Charlie K walked across the green from the courthouse with his umpire's gear. Editor Jim K appeared with his notepad. Fletch and the old bat boys sat on the hotel porch; farmers and loggers and villagers filed toward the rickety grandstand and ranged around the common in their cars and pick-ups. Old Lady Benton was out in the green Adirondack chair on her second-story porch. And here, back from Texas, was E.W. Teddy Williams, watching from under the old elm behind the backstop. The tree was yellowing on top but still hanging on, much the way town ball itself hung on in the Common.

As E.A. warmed up he heard Teddy's voice in his mind, in that same place just behind his upper forehead where the Colonel talked. "Throw the ball, Ethan. Don't aim it, throw it. Ignore the batter. He don't exist. It's just you and your catcher. Go right at them with your best pitch. Nothing fancy." He wished Teddy were going to catch him. Cyrus was fine, he was as wide as the upright freezer over at the hotel kitchen, and if he couldn't catch a ball he'd fall on it. But he wasn't Teddy.

E.A.'s arm felt good. He looked in at Cy, flipped his glove over to indicate a curve coming, and broke off a neat off-speed bender. "You got her working good today," Cy said. "Put that down around the knees on the outside corner, E.A., it'll do you some good."

Ethan remembered the first time his curve broke for him. It was a cool, sunny morning last August, the sky over Allen Moun-

149

tain a deep Canadian blue, Long Tom on the mountaintop re-
sembling a huge silver rocket. "Hold the ball gentle in your
fingers, E.A.," Teddy'd told him. "Same way you'd hold your galfriend's titty. Snap your fingers and wrist down, like this. A good
hook, see, it drops more than it swerves. The bottom falls out
of it."

E.A., flushing at the thought of touching April May, had tried
a few, holding the seams of the ball loosely with his first two
fingers close together, snapping his wrist, without noticing anything different about the way the ball behaved. On his fifth or sixth
attempt, as the pitch approached the plate, he saw it dip a little,
like a swallow skimming over the river dipping to pick a bug off
the surface.

That had been a great moment, seeing the ball break as if it
had a life of its own. As much as he loved baseball, he hadn't known
that anything about it could make him feel that good. He knew
Teddy wouldn't compliment him, though. Teddy'd seen thousands
of curve balls.

"Ethan," E.A. heard Teddy's voice say in his head, "start your
curve lower so's it drops from the belt to the knees instead of from
the letters to the belt."

"How do I do that?"

"Bend your back a little more and release it from your hand a
tad later. Not much."

"Go get 'em, E.A.," the Outlaws encouraged him. "You let us
help you now, E.A. Don't try to do everything all by yourself. You
don't have to strike 'em all out."

Gran clanged her cowbell, horns honked, and the grandstand
cheered. E.A. Allen took the mound for the top of the first, pitching for his town for the first time. He did not feel intimidated. Not
with Teddy here and Gypsy in the stands and even Gran hunched
in her wheelchair beside the bleachers. At fifteen, Joe Nuxhall had
pitched in the *majors*.

Ticonderoga's leadoff hitter, watching E.A. throw his warm-
up pitches off the mound, smirked out at him. E.A. stared back.

150

The guy was their shortstop, not tall but built rugged. Ethan had noticed that during BP he'd hit two balls into the street in front of the shopping block, and done it from the backstop.

"Play ball, gentlemen," Judge Charlie K called out.

Cy lumbered out to the mound. "Just relax, E.A. You'll do fine. Let your fastball and curve do the talking for you. Start him off with a curve. He'll be looking for a first-pitch fastball."

The leadoff hitter stepped in, crowding the plate. E.A. looked in for the sign. Years ago Cy had lost his index finger to a ripsaw at the bat factory, so he flipped his middle finger and ring finger down for the curve.

E.A. shook off Cy's first sign, and the catcher signaled for a fastball. There was a lot of horn honking. A kid ran up to the Late Great Patsy Cline, nosed against the common in deep left-center field, reached in and gave a blast on the ooga horn, jolting Old Bill out of a sound sleep. *Throw, don't aim,* E.A. heard Teddy say in his head. He threw, and the hitter drove his best fastball deep into the gap between left and center. Barefoot Porter Kittredge caught the line drive over his shoulder going away, but the leadoff man had tagged it hard, and for a moment E.A. wondered if he was cut out to be a pitcher after all.

Cy was already on his way out to the mound. "Don't let that bother you, E.A. That's a long out, that's what that is."

"Well," Early Kinneson said, watching from the hotel porch, "now we're going to see what this boy is made of."

As the old men watched, as half the village of Kingdom Common watched, E.A. struck out the next two batters on six fastballs.

"There," Early said, sitting back in his folding canvas chair. "What does that tell you?"

"Not much," Late said.

Fletch said nothing.

E.A. set Ticonderoga down again in order in the second, but they got three hits and two runs in the third. In the bottom half of that inning, the Outlaws tied the game on E.A.'s single with men on second and third. By the fifth, with the game still tied 2–2, the

Commoners were honking their horns and cheering every time E.A. struck out a batter, now mixing his fastball and curve like a veteran.

It was apparent to everyone that the boy had uncanny control. Cyrus rarely had to move his glove more than two or three inches. It was astonishing to see a fifteen-year-old pitcher moving the ball up and down and in and out, hitting the corners, issuing no walks but rarely giving a batter anything good to hit, either. And E.A. was sneaky-fast, faster than he looked, with that curve ball Teddy had taught him that dropped straight down instead of swerving to the side. At the end of the seventh, the Outlaws were up 3–2.

"The kid's dealing today," Cy told the boys. They nodded, and some of them repeated what Cy had said.

Now the Common was cheering and honking for every out. Gran rang her cowbell, Bill blared the horn on the rig.

"How's the wing, E.A.?" Earl asked as Ethan came in for the bottom of the eighth with the Outlaws still ahead 3–2.

"It's fine. I could go another nine."

"Well, that ain't going to be necessary. If you can last another half inning that's enough."

E.A. had no doubt about that. But he decided to check in with Teddy to see if he had any advice for getting the final three outs. Earlier he'd been surprised to see Teddy talking between innings with Ticonderoga's manager. Now he was back by the elm again.

"Well?" E.A. said.

"Well what?"

"What do you think? Eight strikeouts, no walks, only four hits given up. Do you think I've got a shot?"

"One game at a time. Mr. Leadoff Shortstop got two of them three hits. What I think, Ethan, is you don't want to see him up at the end of the game with runners on base."

"He isn't going to be up. Seven, eight, and nine in their order are up, and they'll be going down."

Teddy shrugged. "If one of them bloops a hit, you've got the shortstop. He's a hitter. A decent journeyman ball player. You've got to find his weakness and get that edge I told you about."

"Curve on the outside corner. He nearly broke his back trying to hit that last one. Other than that, I can't see that he has one. He tagged my fastball good in the first inning."

Through his cigarette smoke, Teddy looked at E.A. "Every hitter has a weakness. Guerin — his name's Guerin — his weakness is he's scairt of the ball. That's what ended his pro career. He was beaned down in Alabama one night playing A ball and never could hit pro pitching again."

E.A. couldn't believe his ears. Guerin stood with his head right out over the strike zone.

Teddy lit another Lucky. "He crowds the plate 'cause every time he goes up to bat he has to prove to himself he ain't afraid, even though he is. Down to Birmingham he was three weeks in the ICU with a concussion. Anymore, it's not about hitting for him. It's about proving something. Move him back off the plate, Ethan, if he comes up again. Then you can throw him your curve on the outside corner, he'll never reach it."

"How do you know all this? About Guerin?"

Teddy shifted his cigarette. "I told the manager I done some scouting," he said. "He has a nephew, the first baseman, he wants signed. So him and I got to visiting."

E.A. frowned. "But that was a lie. About you being a scout. You said you wouldn't ever lie again."

"I said I'd never lie to *you*," Teddy said. "Besides, it wasn't a lie. I was scouting all the time I was jawing with him. Scouting his team."

E.A. laughed.

"You see Guerin in the top of the ninth, Ethan, brush him back with your first pitch."

"What if I hit him?"

"That's okay. Then he can't hit you. He's the only fella you have to worry about."

"I'm not worried about him."

"Good. Tell your catcher you're going to move Guerin off the plate so he don't let the pitch go by to the screen. If he comes up."

E.A. told Cy what he'd do if Guerin came up, and Cy

153

shrugged. Brushing back a hitter was fine with him. Earl did it all the time.

The Outlaws didn't score in the bottom of the eighth, and in the top of the ninth E.A. got the first hitter on a grounder to Moon, the second on a strikeout. Now everyone in the grandstand was on their feet, cheering for another K to end the game. E.A. got two strikes on the number-nine hitter, was one strike away from a victory. Cy signaled for a curve away, off the plate, and E.A., over-eager, hung the pitch on the outside corner. The batter blooped a flare over first base, bringing up Guerin.

"Time," Cy said.

Judge Charlie K held up his hands for time, and Cy went out to the mound. "You still want to knock him down, E.A.?"

"I don't want to knock him down, just move him back."

"All right. I'll set up high and inside, over the letters. Don't slip and throw it down the middle."

"Play ball, gentlemen," Judge Charlie barked.

Guerin stood in, crowding the plate. He did not look like a man who was afraid of a baseball or of anything else.

E.A. came to the set and checked the runner. Cy flipped him the bird for the fastball. Guerin waggled his bat, leaned over the plate further. E.A. kicked and threw.

As Teddy told E.A. later, it wasn't a bad pitch for a brush-back. It just wasn't quite high enough or quite close enough to the fists. It was slightly above the letters, on the inside part of the plate, and Guerin took a short step and hit it over Patsy Cline. It landed on the asphalt pavement in front of the brick shopping block, took one high bounce, and smashed through the plate-glass window of the *Kingdom County Monitor*.

Ticonderoga, 4–3.

E.A.'s first coherent thought, about the time the home-run ball hit the pavement, was that this must be what dying was like. The moment when the wheels of the car hit the black ice on the bridge and you see the railing coming at you. It was the most helpless feeling he'd ever had, even more than when Orton and Norton got him down, or when Gypsy had told him who his father was. Some things in life are final, the Colonel had once told him. A home run was one of those things. A home run in the ninth inning off a pitch that was intended to brush back the batter was not only final, it would be impossible to live down.

The next hitter struck out, but so did Cy, Moon, and Earl in the bottom of the ninth, and E.A.'s pitching debut was over. The players lined up at home plate to shake hands with each other. Most of them, including Guerin, warmly congratulated E.A. when he went through the line. But it was like running the gauntlet, and E.A.'s face was still hot with mortification, though he defiantly looked every ball player in the eye.

"Ethan." Teddy appeared beside him as he headed across the Common. "That was still the right pitch for that situation. Fella just hit it."

"If he hit it, it wasn't the right pitch."

"Yes it was. I'd tell you to throw it again in the same situation. I'd tell you in a heartbeat. Don't be second-guessing yourself."

"If it was the right pitch, how come he hit it?"

Teddy put his arm around E.A.'s shoulder, stiff with rage and shame. "I know how you feel, Ethan. Winning's what matters, and a real ball player hates to lose even more than he loves to win. I never told you this was going to be easy. It's the last thing in the world from easy. But."

"But what?" E.A. said.

"But that's baseball," Teddy said. "Sometimes you win. Sometimes you lose. Today you lost. Suck it up. In the meantime, we're going on a trip."

"Where?" E.A. said, caught off-guard.

"Cooperstown," Teddy said. "Get your traveling shoes on, son. We're going to visit the Baseball Hall of Fame."

"You PITCHED a wonderful game yesterday, honey boy," Gypsy said the next morning at breakfast, removing her blond Hillary Clinton wig. The chairman of the Kingdom County Democratic Party had just left, and he liked to see Hillary do a striptease while giving a spirited talk on universal health care.

"I'm thinking of writing a song about a boy from Vermont who wants to play for the Sox," Gypsy said. "Actually, I'd like to work some baseball into 'The Kingdom County Accident.'"

"Work in the gopher ball he threw to that fella who took him over the wall in the last inning yesterday," Gran said. "It was worth broiling out there in the hot sun for two hours just to see that home run."

"Teddy says a pitcher who throws a lot of strikes gives up more home runs than a wild pitcher," E.A. said. "He says that's baseball."

"That's Bosox ball," Gran said. "You give up a few more round-trippers like that, the Sox'll be beating down our door by the end of the summer. Maybe they can bring Torrez back while they're at it. And Butterfingers Buckner."

"Teddy's taking me to Cooperstown," E.A. announced. "To the Baseball Hall of Fame."

Gypsy frowned. "I don't know, hon. I don't know that I want you riding the roads with E.W."

"I need to see that museum, ma. If I'm going to go all the way."

"Gypsy Lee went all the way down under the trestle, and that's how we got saddled with you," Gran reminded him.

Bill said, "I'll go along with the boys. To Cooperstown."

"All right," Gypsy Lee finally said. "As long as Billy goes, I guess it's okay, Ethan."

"I'm going to get me one of them Big Macs," Bill said. "Them are good eating."

They started out in the pale light before sunrise in Patsy Cline. Teddy drove, with E.A. in the middle and Bill by the door. In the village they drew up in front of the hotel behind Warden Kinneson's green state truck. E.A. went inside. The warden, several of the Outlaws, the judge, the editor, and Prof Benton were having coffee.

"Hey, E.A. That was some game you pitched," Judge Charlie said. "I was proud to call it."

"I didn't win," E.A. said.

"You will," Editor K said. "You'll win your share and then some."

E.A. glanced out the window. He could see Teddy and Bill doing something in between Patsy and the warden's truck. E.A. sat across the table from Warden Kinneson so that the officer couldn't see out the window. From his Outlaws baseball jacket he took a tin can. He said, "Officer Kinneson, you want to make a donation?"

The game warden sat up straighter and squared his shoulders. No man in the state of Vermont set more store in being called "officer" than he did. "Donation to what, E.A.?"

"To the Crippled Little Leaguers' Fund."

The warden reached out and took the can. It was a Campbell's soup can that Gypsy had rewrapped in a sheet of lined paper from her song-writing notebook. On it she'd printed, with a red flow pen, HELP A LITTLE CRIPPLE PLAY OUR AMERICAN PASTIME.

"What is it, like the Jimmy Fund or something?" the warden said.

"It's like that," E.A. said. "Only for kids without any arms or legs."

"Jesum Crow, how do they get around then?"

"Very slowly," E.A. said.

Very slowly, the warden began digging for his wallet. "All I've got's a ten —"

"They won't mind," E.A. said. He reached out and plucked the bill out of the warden's hand and put it in the soup can.

Outside, Teddy was handing something green to Bill, who took it around behind Patsy.

"That ever gets to the cripples, I'll eat my hat," the warden grumbled.

"I thank you, the legless Little Leaguers thank you," E.A. said, and two minutes later he and Teddy and Bill were headed south on I-91 with the warden's official State of Vermont license plate gleaming in the sunrise on Patsy's derriere and ten dollars in spending money in E.A.'s pocket.

E.A. liked sitting next to Teddy, who steered with one hand on the wheel and the other on the ledge of the open window, his cigarette smoke curling outside. E.A. wished Bill hadn't horned in on their trip. He'd have preferred this to be exclusively a father-son outing. Things had gotten off to a good start, though. The license-plate switch and the Crippled Little Leaguer con had gone just the way Gypsy had said they would.

Bill was peering out the window. Newly cut hay fields ran partway up the hillsides between darker green maple orchards, with blue-green spruce and fir higher up. A clear stream rushed beside the highway. The mountains were blue in the distance. "I don't see why they don't have a few nice billboards to look at along the way," Bill said. "Something interesting to break up the scenery."

"Jesus, Bill, people in New York and Boston slave fifty weeks a year to come up here and spend two weeks looking at the scenery," Teddy said. "Relax and enjoy the view."

"I can remember back when they had Burma-Shave signs all along the roadways," Bill said. "It made touring the countryside interesting."

They cut across Vermont from White River to Rutland, where they stopped at a McDonald's. Soon afterward they crossed into New York State, where they stopped to eat again. By noon Bill had consumed six Big Macs, washed down with twelve cups of coffee.

Now they were driving on a secondary road southwest of Albany. The countryside looked like Vermont without mountains and with billboards, which should have made Bill happy but didn't seem to. Teddy drove ten miles under the 55-mph speed limit. When they went around a curve and E.A. leaned against him, Teddy's arms and legs were as hard as ironwood.

Ahead they saw a dark shape in the road. It was a turtle, a snapper, weighing fifty or sixty pounds, and as big around as a bushel basket. The snapper did not appear to be injured; it had simply decided to rest on the solid white line. Teddy stopped in the middle of the road. On one side of the highway lay a swamp with stumps jutting out of the water. On the other side a lane led off into a sandpit. As Teddy and E.A. and Bill got out and walked up to the turtle, a Gray Line bus barreled up behind Patsy Cline and hit its whooshing air brakes. The bus stopped inches from the bumper and continued to blast its horn.

The snapper shifted around to look at them. It was as big as any turtle E.A. had ever seen. He figured the animal liked the heat coming up off the macadam. A tractor-trailer crested a rise ahead. It, too, slowed down and stopped. The words CHRISTIAN LINE INC. VIDALIA, GEORGIA were stenciled on its side.

"Here," Teddy said to the turtle. "Move along."

Bill began telling about various ways to catch and cook turtles. The Christian trucker rolled down his window and hollered at the animal to get out of the road or he'd run it over. E.A. noticed that the turtle had algae between its legs and shell and mossy green pond scum on its ridged back and tail. It gave off a primeval stench of mud and rotting vegetation. Its eyes were dark and undaunted.

The driver got out of the bus. He was a tired-looking older man wearing a gray suit and a blue necktie. "What's the holdup?"

he called. "I've got a busload of church ladies here to get down to Cooperstown."

"We got a situation on our hands is the holdup," Teddy said. "We'll deal with it."

Teddy maneuvered around behind the turtle, which turned with him, like a man and a snapping turtle doing a dance. Teddy reached for its tail, and the turtle whirled around faster than E.A. had ever seen an animal move. It shot out its head and neck and, had Teddy not been quick himself, would have taken off all five fingers of his throwing hand. "Whoa!" Teddy shouted.

"I got a pistol in my glove box," the born-again trucker offered.

Cars were queuing up behind the eighteen-wheeler and the bus.

Teddy squatted down in front of the turtle. He stared at it and the turtle looked back at him.

The Christian driver, a fat man in a Braves T-shirt, was getting down out of his cab, holding a gun.

"You shoot this turtle, Bubba," Teddy said, patting a bulge in his back pocket, "and I'll shoot you. I won't think any more about it than taking a piss."

"I have to take one myself," Bill said. "It's all that coffee."

"Over there in the swamp," Teddy told him. He feinted with his left hand, trying to distract the turtle and then grab its tail. The turtle swiveled its shell around like a tank turret. Then it laid an egg. It was white and about the size of a golf ball.

"I God," said the trucker.

A burly church lady in a purple blouse climbed down from the bus. The nametag on her blouse said DORIS HAKLEY, TOUR GUIDE.

"Sir, sir," she said. "We have a schedule to maintain."

"Maintain your water," Teddy said.

"I can't much longer," Bill whined.

"Ethan," Teddy said. "See that stick jutting up from the water over yonder? Fetch it here, will you?"

E.A. brought the stick, which was about four feet long and as big around as his thumb. Teddy held it out to the turtle. Fast as a Doberman pinscher, the reptile bit it cleanly in two. Then it deposited another egg in the road.

Teddy opened Patsy's back door and got his thirty-eight-inch Louisville Slugger out of his bat bag.

"Oh," cried the woman in the purple blouse. "I'm going to report you to the SPCA if you harm that animal. I'll use my cell phone."

Teddy extended the handle of the bat toward the snapper. The turtle grabbed it. Holding the big end of the bat, Teddy dragged the turtle, its back claws grooving the hot macadam, toward Patsy. Its tracks in the tar surface looked as if a great, prehistoric beast had crossed the road. The church woman dropped her cell phone on the pavement. Teddy told E.A. to get his bat bag and hold it open. He lifted the turtle, still clinging to the Louisville Slugger, and deposited it inside the bag, where it finally let go of the bat. Then he tied off the mouth of the bag and put it in the back seat, while E.A. buried the turtle eggs in the sandpit.

Horns honked and air horns blatted in congratulatory unison. Some of the church ladies on the bus cheered.

Teddy picked up the smashed cell phone. "I believe this belongs to you, madam," he said, handing it to the tour guide and tipping his cap.

"Oh!"

She was looking past Teddy at Bill. Everyone on the bus was looking at Bill, standing on the shoulder of the highway and loosing an arcing yellow stream down into the swamp.

"I told you I was all coffeed up," Bill said, still going. "I don't know what everyone's gawking at."

Cooperstown was situated on a north-south–lying lake that E.A. was fairly sure had been made by the Great Wisconsin Ice Sheet. The museum was larger than he'd thought it would be. First they walked around the circular room where the Hall of Famers each had a plaque listing his statistics. There were all the greats — Ty

Cobb, Honus Wagner, Babe Ruth, Christy Mathewson, and the rest. Carlton Fisk had been inducted in 2000. At the entrance of the Hall was a life-size wooden sculpture of Ted Williams and another of Babe Ruth, made of basswood, by a French Canadian carver from Rhode Island. Bill tapped Ted's statue with his knuckle. "I don't know why anybody would make all this work for themself," he said.

Upstairs they watched videos of famous moments in Series games, toured the Negro League room, examined the home uniforms of each team, enshrined in glass cases, and paused over famous bats, balls, spikes, and photographs of major-league ball parks past and present.

"Is that the way *you'd* throw out a runner?" E.A. asked Teddy as they watched a video clip of Johnny Bench gunning the ball down to second to nail a base runner attempting to steal.

"That's one way to do it," Teddy said.

"Teddy?"

"Yes, sir?"

"Say you hadn't — say you'd gone right into baseball out of high school. Could you have wound up here?"

Teddy stepped out of the way of a contingent of Cub Scouts. He lit a cigarette in front of a PLEASE DO NOT SMOKE sign. "No," he said. "I doubt I ever could have gotten to the majors, you want the truth. The thing is, I'll never know. Look, Ethan. Say you try and don't make the grade. That's nothing to be ashamed of. Only a few ever do. You can live with trying and not making the grade. But you'll *know*. It's the not knowing that eats at you."

"Sir," a museum attendant said. "There's no smoking in the Baseball Hall of Fame."

Teddy dropped his cigarette on the tiled floor and ground it under the heel of his work boot, and a few minutes later they left for home.

⚾

"You were clocked at sixty-five," the New York constable said, but he was lying through his teeth. E.A. had checked the speedometer.

Teddy had been driving exactly forty-three miles an hour.

The cop had sneaked up behind them with his lights off, then switched on his blue flashers. Later Bill admitted that he'd thought a spaceship was taxiing in for a landing behind them.

"You fellas set tight," the constable said. "I'm going back to the cruiser."

"What are we going to do?" E.A. said. He was terrified that Teddy would have to go back to prison.

Teddy shrugged. "We'll be okay," he said. "This asshole's going to ask for a fifty-dollar bill to let us off the hook."

The constable shone his flashlight in their faces. "Where you boys been? What's your business in New York at this hour?"

"We took the boy to Cooperstown for the day," Teddy said.

"Well, you were clocked at sixty-five. You can pay the fine here, seventy-five dollars, or we can take a little ride up the road, pay a visit to the JP."

"I was going forty-five," Teddy said.

"JP don't like to be rousted out in the middle of the night," the constable said. "He might make that fine two hundred and a free overnight stay at the county motel. The one with bars on the windows." He flashed the light full in E.A.'s face. "You ever been in jail, boy?"

From the back came a thumping, scrabbling sound. The constable jumped. "What's that?" He stepped back from the window and put his hand on his holster.

"Something you'd like to see, officer," Bill said. "A specimen of early life here on earth."

"A what? What you got back there?"

"His name's Jolting Joe, we've got him in a sack. He likes to ride that way," Bill said.

"Good Christ!" the constable said, shining his light in the back. "You get out of the vehicle, mister," he said to Teddy, "and keep your hands where I can see them. I want to see who's in that sack."

Teddy got out. E.A. got out, too, though the constable hadn't told him to. When the constable opened the back door, the bat bag appeared to be moving across the floor of its own volition. The policeman played his light on the bag. "You," he said to Teddy. "Open up that sack and let him out of there."

Teddy loosened the drawstrings. The officer leaned forward, tugging at the chin strap of his hat.

"Joe don't seem to want to come out very bad," Teddy said.

As the officer bent over to look inside, the turtle's head and neck shot out of the sack. The constable leaped back, striking his head on Patsy's metal door frame. Immediately Teddy said to the stunned man, "Here, officer. Let me help you back to your car."

Teddy assisted him to the cruiser and eased him in behind the wheel. He reached inside and snapped off the flashers. The turtle, for her part, had lurched out of Patsy and was lumbering toward a depression beside the road filled with cattails.

"Is the cop going to be all right?" E.A. said a minute later as they continued on east at a moderate speed.

"He's going to have a major-league headache," Teddy said.

In the headlights E.A. saw a concrete bridge. "Won't he come after us?"

"Not right away," Teddy said. He held up the keys from the cruiser's ignition and, as they crossed the bridge, pitched them far out into the darkness.

Just beyond the bridge their lights picked up a large green sign with white letters: WELCOME TO VERMONT.

"Thank the Jesus," Bill said.

"Amen," Teddy said, and all three of them began to laugh.

26

JUDGE CHARLIE KINNESON'S private chambers behind the courtroom looked out over the baseball diamond on the west, the Lower Kingdom River and U.S. Route 5 on the south, and the Green Mountain Rebel factory on the southeast. On the walls were reproductions of the famous Orvis trout, leaping out of a boggy green stream with a dark fly in the corner of its jaw; a Frederic Remington painting of two Canadian voyageurs and a wolfish-looking dog in a canoe; and a Montana butte by Charlie Russell. There was a color photograph of Carlton Fisk waving his '75 home run fair and snapshots of Charlie's wife, Athena, and their twin daughters. On the judge's desk, atop a stack of old *Outdoor Life* magazines, sat a small bronze reproduction of Remington's sculpture of a mustachioed cowboy aboard a bucking bronc. In the floor-to-ceiling bookcases between the windows, wedged in with legal tomes and bound reports from each session of the Vermont legislature back to 1848, were scores of books on the American West.

Judge Charlie liked to say that if he'd known, *really known*, what was out in Montana and Wyoming when he was young and right out of law school, he'd never have set foot back in Kingdom County. But the fact was, Charlie Kinneson loved the Kingdom and was as much a part of it as the Kingdom was of him, and today of all days, E.A. was glad that Charlie had not lit out for the frontier years ago. Deputy Warden Kinneson, in his auxiliary capacity as truant officer, had hauled him and Gypsy up in front of the judge for "flagrant habitual truancy over the past eight years." Charlie had put off hearing the case for as long as he could. Now the deputy was petitioning him to order E.A. to attend school and, if Gypsy balked, to remove him from her custody. Because the case involved a minor, Charlie had decided to hear it in his private chambers rather than in the open courtroom. So here they were, a week after E.A.'s trip to Cooperstown with Teddy and Bill.

Ethan and Gypsy sat on an old leather couch also occupied by Charlie's elderly springer spaniel. Charlie sat in a Morris chair by the west window. The deputy, at Charlie's suggestion, sat behind the judge's desk. The judge wore his black steel-capped shoes and blue umpire's shirt because he had an American Legion ball game to officiate later that afternoon in Memphremagog. In his hand he held a manila folder.

"Now, Ethan," Charlie said with a broad smile, "Deputy Warden Kinneson, my estimable cousin and Kingdom County's favorite game warden, truant officer, and dogcatcher — did I get all your titles, cousin? — is alleging that Gypsy doesn't raise you properly at home."

He waved the folder, and some documents fell out on the floor. Charlie ignored them. "Is that what all this boils down to, deputy?"

"We have proof," the warden said, "that Gypsy Lee Allen has been encouraging a minor to break the fish and game laws, stay out of school, and procure clients for her pornographic shows. Plus he don't eat properly and he's running wild all over town, driving without a license and talking to himself on the common and I don't know what all."

"Well," Charlie said, winking at E.A., "those are serious charges. Let's look at them one at a time. Is it true, Ethan, that Gypsy doesn't send you to school?"

"You know she doesn't, Charlie. Never has."

"Moving right along, do you have enough to eat at home?"

"You bet I do," E.A. said. "Venison every meal and all I can eat of it. Except for last winter when we ran out and had to eat moose instead. But that was just as good."

"I don't believe this," the warden said. "*Moose.* This is too —"

"Does Gypsy mistreat you, E.A.? Smack you around?"

"Of course not."

"We aren't claiming outright abuse, Judge. It would be more like neglect. What we're saying here, the boy hasn't attended school a day in his life."

"Warden, before I pursue this further, who is we?"

"We?"

"Yes. You keep saying we. 'We' aren't claiming abuse. What 'we're' saying. Who is this we? The royal we? You and God?"

"Why, no, Charlie, it's I and — I and the state. The state of Vermont."

"Was it the state of Vermont that pronounced you truant officer?"

"No, sir. Elected at Town Meeting. Town officer."

"Warden?"

"Yes?"

"Unless you have multiple personalities — a theory that I, for one, have never entirely subscribed to — I want you to stop refer-ring to yourself as we."

"Well, all right, but what about the psychiatric evaluation in that folder?"

Charlie leaned down and picked up a note, handwritten on yellow tablet paper, that had fallen out of the folder. "Do you mean this scrawled report, signed not by a licensed psychiatrist but by you, that on three occasions this past summer you observed E.A. talking to the statue of the Colonel out on the common?"

"Well, I did."

"Ethan, do you talk to the Colonel's statue?"

"You know good and well I do, Charlie. I visit with everybody in this town, always have. Even the warden."

"Does the statue talk back to you, boy?" the deputy said. "Tell you to set fires, does he? Hurt people?"

"You be quiet," Charlie told his cousin. "I'll ask the questions this afternoon. To tell you the truth, Ethan, I've always been curi-ous. What *do* you and the old Colonel talk about?"

"Baseball, mainly. He loves to talk baseball."

"Well, he lives in the right town, then."

"Charlie, I think at the least you should order the boy evaluated. He ain't right in the head, and you and I both know it."

"No, you and I do not both know it. His mother schools him at home. He's well-fed. He seems well-adjusted. And he knows more about baseball than anybody in the county."

"Look how skinny he is."

Charlie reached over his head and pulled down the 1904 legislative report, a very thick volume. He put it on his desk in front of the warden. "Ethan, put your elbow up here and twist wrists with my cousin. He thinks you're undernourished."

E.A. jumped up, took three quick steps, and set his elbow on the tome, with his forearm and wrist jutting up at a ninety-degree angle.

"What?" Warden Kinneson was saying. "I don't understand —"

Charlie stood up, took the officer's right hand, and placed it in E.A.'s. "One, two, three, go," he said. E.A. slammed the back of the warden's hand down onto the desk so hard that the bronze bronc jumped. Gypsy cheered.

"He had a book to give him leverage, plus he was standing up," the warden whined, rubbing the back of his hand.

"Switch places with him," Charlie suggested. "You use the book."

"Never mind."

"That was a sorry display on your part, cousin," Charlie said. "You let a mere lad beat you twisting wrists."

"All this is about is the boy missing school, cousin. He isn't getting the right academics. I don't know if he's reading up to grade level. I don't even know if he *can* read."

"Don't you?" Charlie picked up an envelope from the corner of his desk. From it he removed a typed letter, which he handed to E.A. "Ethan, would you please read the first paragraph of this letter aloud? To show this versatile peace officer that you're reading at grade level. It's a letter the local sheriff — your boss, deputy —

168

showed me this morning. Addressed to him. From the sheriff of Washington County, over in New York State."

E.A. cleared his throat and read aloud.

"Dear Sheriff Cunningham,
I am writing to inform you that on the early morning of June 9, one of my constables, Fred Hawkins, stopped and searched a speeding vehicle with plates registered to Deputy Warden Kinneson, of Kingdom Common, Vermont, a game warden and a deputy in your employ. The officer, Constable Hawkins, was attacked by an unknown assailant, assisted by your deputy, in the back of Deputy Kinneson's vehicle, after which the Vermont officer fled the scene with two accomplices."

"God Jesus!" the warden shouted. "I swear I haven't been in New York for twenty years. On June ninth I was — I was watching for walleye poachers up where the river comes into Memphremagog."

"I don't care where you were or what you were doing," Charlie said. "I'm going to let you and Sheriff Cunningham and the sheriff of Washington County, New York, thrash this matter out yourselves. It's none of my affair — yet. Now get up from my chair, warden, and get out of this room and don't ever come to me with charges like these again."

"Charlie, I swear —"

"Skedaddle."

Warden Kinneson gave his cousin the judge one last pleading look, then scurried out of the room. E.A. almost felt sorry for him.

"Well," Gypsy said. "I guess he won't try that stunt again."

"Do me a favor, Gypsy Lee. Lay off the poor guy for a few weeks. Give the deer and moose population and the lady's slippers a breather and lay off the whiskey smuggling and let the warden catch his breath.

"Stick around a minute, Gypsy. You, too, E.A. I want to ask you something. Don't take this wrong, Gypsy Lee. Ethan, would you like to go to school?"

"No. It suits me just fine not to."

"Charlie —" Gypsy started, but he held up his hand.

"Let E.A. answer. He's old enough for this to be his decision."

"I can't abide schoolteachers, Judge K," E.A. said. "I don't have the slightest use for the whole pack."

The judge thought for a minute.

"Charlie," Gypsy said, "the reason I don't send Ethan to school is that kids are cruel. I know. I know exactly what it's like for a kid without a father to go to school. I was the frigging salutatorian and it still didn't matter. Can you imagine what Ethan would have been subjected to with a father who's in prison?"

"Teddy isn't in prison any longer, Gypsy."

"No, but that wouldn't matter. They'd still call Ethan the B word. Our depraved neighbor, Devil Dan Davis, calls him the B word. One of these fine days when my Allen's up I'm going to shoot that wicked old son of a bitch. I swear to Our Father Who Art in Heaven I am."

"Ethan, before your wonderful mom gets her Allen up with *me*, would you step outside for a minute. She and I need to talk some turkey."

E.A. went into the small hallway between the judge's chamber and the courtroom. He shut the door hard, with the handle turned all the way to the right, then silently reopened it a crack. He heard Charlie say, "Gypsy, how much longer do you intend to protect Ethan from this town? Don't you think he's old enough now —"

"I don't protect him, damn it. He comes with me when I sing out. He grew up in honky-tonks and roadhouse dives. He plays with the Outlaws. He hunts and fishes all over Allen Mountain. He's well educated and you know it. But I will not subject him to the cruelties of that school or any school."

"You going to let him go to college?"

"I'm going to *make* him go to college. If we can afford it, that is."

"I'll make you a promise, Gypsy. Athena and I will see to it that you can afford it."

There was a pause. Then E.A. heard the judge say, "So Teddy's been teaching E.A. baseball?"

"He has. When E.W. first showed up I wanted to shoot him. But Charlie, I just didn't see how I could deny Ethan the right to know his father. Even a father like Teddy."

"People change, Gypsy. If Teddy's decided to do one decent thing in his life by showing E.A. how to play baseball, more power to him. Nobody knows more about the game than E.W. Williams. If Ethan pays attention — and knowing E.A., he will — nobody could show him more."

"Charlie? How far could Ethan go with his baseball? I'm afraid his heart'll be broken."

"Nobody knows the answer to that question, Gypsy. Only time will tell. But what about you? How do you feel about Teddy?"

"Well," Gypsy said, "let's look at it this way. I got a couple of real good songs out of the son of a bitch."

And right there in the judge's chambers, with E.A. listening at the door, she belted out the chorus of "Knocked Up in Knoxville."

THE RAIN DRUMMED on the barn roof. It beat down hard, puddling up at home plate and around the feed-sack bases at Fenway. On the mountaintop it began to freeze into sleet, glazing over Long Tom. Then it changed into snow. A snowstorm in July.

Teddy stood in the entranceway of the barn, the huge sliding door open to let in light, and watched as E.A. gave the treadless tire off Earl's eighteen-wheeler a push to start it swinging from the thick rope attached to the overhead hayfork rail. E.A. went back to the entrance. As the truck tire continued to swing back and forth, he went into his wind-up, calculating where the tire would be when the ball arrived, like a hunter leading a flushing grouse. He pitched. The baseball sped through the center of the swinging tire, into the backstop of hay bales. Three times E.A. threw. Three times he split the center of the tire.

He glanced at Teddy, standing behind him, the cold rain sweeping in and spattering his old suit jacket and shoes.

"How long did it take you to learn that?" Teddy asked.

E.A. shrugged. "A long time."

Teddy nodded. That was all. But the next time he appeared he had with him a folded square of heavy brown canvas tarpaulin and a paper grocery bag. It was a hot day, a good day for throwing off the mound at Fenway, the heat fine for keeping a pitcher's arm loose. Instead, Teddy jerked his head toward the barn.

Inside the hayloft a million dust motes danced in the sunlight streaming through the entryway. The air smelled hot, like haying time. Teddy unfolded the tarp on the barn floor. It was about the size and shape of one of the kitchen windows in Gran's farmhouse. From the paper bag he removed, one by one, ten paintbrushes and ten pint cans of bright-colored paint: apple red, orange, light green and dark green, lemon yellow, pale blue, ocean blue, grape purple, cotton-candy pink, and black. He shook the little cans of paint. With his jackknife blade he pried off the lids, then took a photograph out of his shirt pocket. E.A. recognized it immediately. It was a photo of Ted Williams's strike-zone chart, which they'd seen in Cooperstown: a frame the size of the strike zone, filled with colored baseballs, each inscribed with a batting average in sharp black numerals. The number on each ball represented the average the great Teddy Ballgame estimated he hit when he swung at a pitch in that part of the zone, from the blue ball on the low, outside corner, inscribed with .250, to the red ball that read .450 in the heart of the frame.

With great concentration, Teddy began painting colored baseballs on the canvas tarp. As he worked he talked to E.A. "See, Ethan, what a pitcher wants to do, he wants to throw strikes. But he don't want to be wild in the strike zone."

"What's wild in the strike zone?"

"Throwing too many pitches belt-high out over the heart of the plate. Even if you're quick and mix up your pitches, the better hitters'll get to you if you let 'em see too many good pitches. This'll teach you how to nick the corners, move the ball in and out, up and down. But" — he rounded out the orange ball, in on the fists of a righty — "mainly you want to keep the ball low. You'll see why when the colors dry here, and we take and paint in the averages in black. The lower down in the zone you throw, the harder the pitch is to hit."

The dust motes danced in the sunlight. The air smelled like old hay and paint and a faint hint of manure. Overhead in the cupola, pigeons muttered and cooed. Teddy frowned, made a few finicky brush strokes to round out a light blue ball, grinned at his son. Later, after they'd inscribed the averages and hung the canvas from the top bale of the makeshift backstop, Teddy presented E.A. with two dozen brand-new baseballs to throw at the simulated strike zone.

Well before the end of the summer E.A. could hit any individual spot on the canvas more often than not. But he never felt any better than he had when Teddy looked up from the canvas with the baseballs painted on it and grinned at him. That was a moment he'd remember forever.

"Ethan."

Teddy stood up and headed out toward the mound at Fenway. It was midsummer, and he was working out with Ethan every evening that the boy didn't have a town-team game.

"Remember what I told you about getting an edge on that pitcher? Old Ichabod? Finding his weakness?"

E.A. nodded.

"Well," Teddy said, "it's the same with a hitter. You can usually figure out his weakness. If you can't figure it out, you can create one. Keep him off balance. Get him guessing and make him guess wrong. Say the first two, three times you throw him your hook you drop down to three-quarters arm. Then in a critical situation, come at him from three-quarters with pure heat. Or come straight over the top, so he thinks it's heat, and throw your bender.

"Another way," Teddy continued, "when you come to your set, watch for the split second when the hitter ain't quite ready for you to pitch. That's when to throw the ball. Don't take the same amount of time to get your sign, get set, and go into your motion with every pitch. Watch your batter a little. Let him get uneasy. Catch him off-guard."

"How can I tell when he's off-guard?"

"Oh," Teddy said, "he might move his hands different. Wave the bat a different way, shift his front foot, jerk his head. Watch his face. You'll sense it more than you'll know it. Every hitter has a weakness, Ethan. It's a hard proposition, hitting a baseball. A good pitcher makes it just a little harder. Once in a while, try to make eye contact with the hitter. The split second you catch his eye, pitch."

"That sounds pretty hard," E.A. said.

"Why, Ethan, don't you know how hard *all* this is? Baseball's the hardest game there is, man. Hard for the pitchers, hard for the fielders, hard for the hitters. Especially hard for the hitters. Hitting a baseball coming at you ninety miles an hour or more? That's the hardest thing there is to do."

By the end of the summer, E.A. had a pitching record with the Outlaws of 9–1 and was throwing well over 80 mph. "Phenomenal" was the word Editor James Kinneson had used in the *Kingdom County Monitor* to describe his pitching.

One afternoon in early September E.A. pitched a no-hitter against Memphremagog, striking out twenty of the twenty-seven batters he faced and having some fun, too, by pitching the last inning like the New York Mets' twenty-game-winning submarine pitcher from Japan, Suzika Koyoto, scaring the opposing batters out of their socks with his sidewinding motion. Immediately after the game a heavyset man in a rumpled suit, with a florid face and a meaty handshake, introduced himself as a scout on retainer with the Red Sox. E.A. had seen him earlier, standing behind the screen with a hand-held radar gun.

"I clocked you at ninety-four on two, three pitches," the big man said. "For a thousand dollars, I can get you a tryout."

"My father's over there," E.A. said, pointing at Teddy standing under the elm, watching.

"I'm not offering the tryout to your father, kid. I'm offering it to you. A thousand dollars gets you a real good look. I'll set it all up."

How Teddy got there so fast was a mystery. One moment he was leaning against the elm tree, watching the man in the suit talk to E.A. The next he was between E.A. and that man.

"Hey," the man who'd identified himself as a scout said. "Who the hell are you?"

"I'm his father," Teddy said. "And he's sixteen years old. It's illegal for you to talk to him. What's more, you don't represent the Red Sox or anybody else. I ever see you around here again, or hear you've bothered my boy, I'll kick your ass back to whatever hole you crawled out of."

"You and whose army?" the man sneered.

Teddy continued to stand between E.A. and the big man.

"So," the man said to E.A., around Teddy. "We'll talk."

E.A. shook his head. "No," he said. And he headed up the common with Teddy.

"It's your career going south," the man called after him.

"Don't you ever, never think of paying nobody a cent of money to play baseball, Ethan," Teddy said to E.A. "Time's coming when people are going to be paying you to play. You just keep working like you have been. It'll all fall into place for you."

★ STAN THE BASEBALL MAN ★

IN THE MEANTIME everything seemed to be falling into place for the Boston Red Sox. They had the pitching, including a four-time American League Cy Young Award winner. They had the American League batting champ, who was also a strong MVP candidate. They had a world-class veteran shortstop, and in Eduardo "Sally" Salvadore they had the best catcher in baseball. As usual, they did not have much speed on the base paths. But the entire Red Sox Nation agreed that the Legendary Spence was the finest manager "money couldn't buy," as the *Globe* had once put it, since Spence had eternally endeared himself to the Nation by many times declining the opportunity to double or even triple his salary by jumping ship to New York or another less parsimonious club.

Not only did Spence's team win the American League Eastern Division by eight games that season, posting the best record in baseball, they walked through the playoffs, and, on a sunny day in October, with the World Series tied at three games apiece, found themselves taking a one-run lead over the Chicago Cubs into the ninth inning at Fenway Park.

Earlier that afternoon, before the game, Spence had sat alone in his clubhouse office, staring at the photograph on the wall of the longtime Sox owner, Maynard E. Flynn Senior. Spence was wearing his uniform pants, spikes, red socks, and an old-fashioned strap undershirt. The man in the photograph, old Flynn, wore a three-piece suit and a Red Sox cap, and he was standing on a marina dock beside a gigantic blue marlin hanging from a block and tackle. The old man had sent the photo to Spence just before the All-Star break, and he'd scrawled across the bottom, "Wish you could be here, Maynard."

There were no baseball memorabilia in the clubhouse office. No signed balls, no pictures of Spence's three previous American League pennant-winning teams, no photos of the manager with his numerous All-Star players. Just the faded picture of the old man and his enormous fish and, on the corner of Spence's battered, secondhand metal desk, the red, blue, yellow, and green macaw that Sally Salvadore had purchased for Spence some years ago from a Venezuelan fruit-boat captain. Sally had named the bird Curse of the Bambino and trained it to say, among other things, "New York Yankees, number one."

"Chalk it up to bad luck," Spence was telling the macaw on this afternoon of all afternoons in the city of Boston. "Set it down to pure misfortune, nothing more, nothing less, that this old baseball whore never got his Serious ring. But all that's about to change, my feathered friend. As of late this afternoon, Boston will be the new World Champions, and then I intend to cash it in, and I and you will strike straight for the Sunshine State. Spend our well-earned retirement persecuting them big blue fish like the one Maynard there claims he caught. This is the year, Curse."

"Maybe, maybe not," the macaw said.

Spence shot the bird a look. But even though the Boston manager was a born optimist who had endured twenty years and more of managing the Red Sox to reach this day, and the team was healthy, with arguably the best pitching, hitting, and defense in major-league baseball, in his heart he shared the bird's skepticism.

The old man in the photograph, who even now was probably ensconced in his skybox high above the stadium, waiting for the game to start, glared at Spence, who glared back. The Big Manager Upstairs (as Spence thought of God) knew that Maynard Flynn Senior had dug deep into his pockets to put together a contending team. Despite more than two decades of barging into the clubhouse to hector Spence after a loss, despite the recriminating telephone calls late at night when the team was on the road, Flynn already shouting into the phone when Spence groggily picked up, railing at him at the top of his lungs for laying down a failed squeeze or using or not using the hit-and-run or lifting or not lifting a pitcher at the first sign of trouble, despite the two times the old man had actually fired Spence — once in October after losing the Series to Cincinnati, rehiring him in time for spring training, the second time at the end of a bad losing season, actually making him sit out the entire year before bringing him back — despite these abuses of his power and many, many others that Spence could not bear to think of at this moment, he and Flynn had always had a special understanding and, Spence had long believed, a shared goal: winning the Series.

To give the old man his due, it was Maynard who had broken the detestable color barrier that had lingered on for so many years in Boston. Not, of course, from any commitment to equality, other than Flynn's equal and unmitigated contempt for all baseball players everywhere regardless of race or creed. But Maynard had worked hard to make Boston a perennial contender, and a perennial contender the Sox under Spence had been. Complaining, criticizing, sometimes literally howling, the old man had nonetheless consistently brought good and even great players to Boston. Just never quite enough of them, in Spence's opinion, to make the Sox World Champions.

For the Legendary Spence, who had won more major-league baseball games than any other active manager, and won every last one of them in a Red Sox uniform, believed something else, too. He believed that despite what he had just told the talking macaw about bad luck, luck had little to do with the fact that a championship banner had not flown over Fenway Park since 1918. On the bottom line, the misfortune and curses and seeming hexes — Dent's pop-fly home run in '78, Buckner's fateful miscue in '86, Harry Frazee's trading Babe Ruth to New York back in 1920 — would not wash as explanations. The bottom line, the reason Boston had not won a major-league championship in three-quarters of a century, was that they had never, at least until now, been the best team in the majors.

Third-best or fourth-best, frequently. Second-best, once or twice. But not *the* best. They had not been as good as St. Louis in '67 or Cincinnati in '75 or the Yankees in '78 or the Mets in '86. No. On Spence's watch and before, they had always lacked one or two key players. And deep in his heart Spence feared that this year might be no different. It was almost as if, in his own shriveled heart, Maynard Flynn Senior did not really *want* the Sox to walk away in October with those elusive rings. As though, along with much of the rest of the downtrodden yet ever hopeful Red Sox Nation, from Rhode Island to northernmost Maine, Maynard would rather lose and hope to win another year than give Spence everything he needed to take his team all the way.

"And this afternoon may not be no different, Curse," Spence said to the macaw, heaving himself out of the spring-shot office chair into which the former journeyman minor-league catcher was just able to wedge his five-foot-eleven, two-hundred-and-sixty-five-pound person, and struggling into his uniform shirt. "I hope the boys prove me wrong. But I wouldn't bet the ranch on it."

The Curse of the Bambino fixed him with its yellow eye. "New York Yankees, number one," it croaked.

"Not this year they ain't," Spence said as the bird hopped onto his shoulder. "I just ain't all that sure we are, either."

Then the two old friends headed up the tunnel toward the rumbling thunder of the most loyal, long-suffering fans in base-balldom, to see if, at last, they could bring that banner back to Boston.

Now, in the top of the ninth, with the Red Sox ahead by one run and Chicago runners on second and third and two outs, Boston's Cy Young shoo-in had just enticed the Cubs' number-nine hitter to pop up to center. That is when Maynard Flynn Senior found himself becoming emotional. He actually leaned forward in his skybox to see the catch that would bring Boston its first baseball championship since 1918.

"Look at this, will you?" he said to his grown son, Maynard Junior. But the big lummox, as his father and nearly everyone else in Boston referred to the boy, who at thirty-eight had been a full-time graduate student for sixteen years, did not so much as glance up from the book he was reading.

The game-ending pop-up floated high over the playing field. Like a big scoop of vanilla ice cream in the drugstore sodas Maynard Senior had loved to order as a lad growing up in Revere. The Sox Gold Glove–winning center-fielder jogged in several steps. And at exactly that moment, Maynard E. Flynn Senior felt fulfilled. Over the years he had known everybody who was anybody in Boston baseball circles, from the great Teddy Ballgame to such illustrious fans as Honey Fitz and old Joe Kennedy. He'd seen Ted hit a home run in his last major-league at-bat, seen Fisk's shot heard round the world in '75. True, his only child, the lummox, had turned out to be a major-league disappointment, a mama's boy with no interest in baseball whatsoever. But the old man understood that in this world you couldn't have everything. And he suddenly realized that however he might have felt in the past, he infinitely preferred to bring Boston its first world championship since 1918 than to have a son he was proud of.

Maynard Flynn leaned forward a little more. He watched the fielder camp under the ball, now at the apex of its high parabola, white as snow against the bright blue New England fall sky. As a boy, the son of a loom operator at Revere Textiles and Woolens, Inc., the old man had played some twilight-league ball. Once, in an exhibition game against the Sox B team, he'd smacked an opposite-field ground-rule double off Lefty Grove. Until now that had been the highlight of his life, even better than the pennants his team had won or his purchase of the cable television station that carried, besides the Sox, the Bruins and the Patriots and that was now worth nearly as much as the franchise itself.

The old man thought fleetingly of that hit he'd gotten off

the great Sox southpaw as his fielder waited for the ball. The runner on third had already crossed the plate. The man from second was rounding third. None of that mattered, though. Neither run would count. The fielder whacked his glove twice with his fist, and then he lost the descending baseball in the sun. He threw up his hands wildly, and the ball bounced off his forehead onto the outfield grass at exactly the same moment that the second runner plated what turned out to be the winning run for Chicago, the Sox going down one, two, three in the last of the ninth. But that didn't matter to the old man. By then nothing mattered to Maynard Flynn Senior. Because before the ball lost in the sun had rolled to a stop, he'd dropped dead in his skybox of what was later diagnosed as a massive coronary but which the entire Red Sox Nation, from the Legendary Spence to old Fletch in Kingdom Common, knew to have been sheer, ultimate disappointment.

"HENCEFORWARD," the lummox intoned, "we shall be conducting business quite differently."

Standing in front of the new owner's desk, with the Curse of the Bambino perched on the shoulder of his Red Sox warm-up jacket, Spence tried to recall whether he had ever heard anyone say "henceforward" before. He didn't think so.

Maynard Flynn Junior looked past the manager and his macaw and out his office window, down on the ball diamond below. What was it that writer had called it? "A lyric little bandbox of a ball park." The lummox smiled slightly, thinking, *Not for much longer.*

Spence sighed. Already, with spring training still months away, the lummox had let Boston's four-time Cy Young Award–winning free-agent pitcher slip through his fingers. He'd sold the Sox's twenty-game–winning sinkerball pitcher to Baltimore and traded their American League MVP left-fielder and beloved shortstop to Los Angeles for two utility players and an undisclosed but undoubtedly colossal amount of cash. The only reason the big lummox had not been able to dump Spence's five-time All-Star catcher, Sally Salvadore, was that his contract still had a year to run. But he'd more than made up for that unfortunate constraint by doubling the price of every seat at Fenway Park, whose ticket prices already, under the old man's tenure, had been jacked up to half again the amount at any other ball park in the majors.

In fact, Spence believed that the reason he had been summoned to this audience with Maynard Flynn Junior was to be fired, for good this time. He'd told the macaw as much just before they went up to the skybox office. What's more, with the dispersing of the great team that he and the old man had put together over the years, and along with it Spence's hopes of ever getting to a Series again, much less winning one, he no longer wanted to do the only thing he'd ever wanted to do all his adult life and had done so well for more than twenty years. He no longer wanted to manage the Boston Red Sox. Or so Spence told himself. After the fly ball that should have brought the championship to Boston had gotten into the sun and smacked his outfielder in the forehead — there had been talk in the front office of trying to hook up the player with the government witness-protection program to keep the more extremist members of the Red Sox Nation from lynching him — Spence's heart had pretty much gone out of the game.

Spence regarded the lummox. He was a good-size boy, give him that — six one, six one and a half maybe — with limp blond hair and wet-looking, protuberant eyes of a washed-out shade and something of a potbelly, even though Maynard Junior had worked out at a karate club downtown for years, attempting to exorcise the memory of a boyhood trauma.

Spence had been on hand to witness that event. It was young Maynard's first Little League tryout, to which the old man had literally dragged him over his mama's shrieking protests. He'd talked Spence into helping coach the kid's team, to give the lummox an advantage. At eight he was not really a lummox, just a scared little boy who at the tryout actually soiled himself out of stark fear of the ball. Worse, the old man had made him stay on and complete the practice. It was the one thing Maynard Senior had done that Spence deemed utterly unforgivable. In the manager's opinion, it accounted for much of the boy's subsequent behavior, including his recent decision to eviscerate the superb team his father had left him.

"Time to go fishing, Curse," Spence had said to the macaw just before entering the lummox's office. He was looking forward to it.

As the new owner smirked out at him from behind his departed father's huge desk, Spence remembered how the old man had sat there and pounded his fist on the green felt blotter and gone up one side of him and down the other and damned the Red Sox and the fans and the umpires and other owners, and he thought what a sad spectacle his out-of-place son, the professional graduate student of literature, made behind that same desk. Spence looked down at the canvas-covered playing field. A dusting of new snow lay on the tarp, and little white drifts had whisked up against the many odd nooks and crannies around the field. Spence remembered how Maynard Senior had loved to introduce his many threats with the phrase "By the time the snow flies in Beantown."

"By the time the snow flies in Beantown, Spence, you'll be history. I guarantee it."

Spence missed the old man.

The lummox put the tips of his fingers together like a church steeple. Spence suspected that much as he wanted to say "You're fired," he didn't have the guts. He was actually squirming in his chair. Spence was afraid that the boy might go in his pants again. Suddenly the winningest active manager in baseball realized that the final indignity of his big-league career might well be *having to broach the subject of his own dismissal because the lummox didn't have the sand to do it.*

"Look here," Spence said. "You want to give me the boot, go ahead. It won't hurt my feelings none. It won't be the first time I've been sent down the line."

The lummox reached for his hand-strengthening flexer, which he began to work quite sadistically. He said, "I am not, as you so elegantly put it, going to send you down the line. I want you to be around this coming season to see what happens."

Spence wondered what *more* could happen now that half of his team had been sold off or all but given away.

"Or, more precisely, what *doesn't* happen," the lummox said. "First, you will have a new general manager. I fired Henry earlier today."

Spence was speechless. Henry O'Leary was perhaps the finest general manager and front-office man in baseballdom. Also a longtime drinking bud of Spence's and the old man's.

"But I have an able replacement waiting in the wings," Maynard said, squeezing the very daylights out of the flexer.

"Who's that?"

"Moi," the boy said, standing up and coming around the desk and punching Spence in the arm with the knuckles of his index and middle finger. "Maynard Flynn II. New owner and general manager of the Boston Red Sox."

30

"How in the name of the Great Jehovah and the First Continental Congress can you expect to control your curve ball when you can't control yourself? Look at you. Drinking and tomcatting all night up to Canady. Not just once in a while, either. It's every weekend. You've got to get ahold of yourself, boy."

"Just the way you did," E.A. said, stumbling up against the Colonel's pedestal. He had the spins so bad he thought he might be sick right there on the common. He was just getting in from another all-nighter, and he couldn't deny a word the Colonel had said. Worse yet, Teddy was two weeks overdue. Usually he showed up by the second week of June, and E.A. was beginning to fear that he wasn't coming. That something had gone terribly wrong with his agreement with the warden, and he was stuck inside some hellhole of a Texas prison, maybe for the rest of his life.

At seventeen, E.A. was five ten and a half — a little taller than either he or Teddy had expected — and threw well over ninety miles an hour, with good movement on the ball and the same pinpoint accuracy that had impressed Teddy all those years before when they'd first played toss. He had a good slider and a fine off-speed breaking pitch, at least until last night, when he'd lost under the lights 8–1 to Trois Rivières. In the Common there was talk that of all the players who had ever come out of the village, E.A. was the one to watch.

"You're the one to watch, all right," the statue said. "Watch make a fool of himself. Staying out the night long at them over-the-border taverns. Hooring with French barmaids. Getting trounced by a bunch of Canuck stumblebums because you're letting yourself go to the dogs. Now you attend to what I'm going to tell you.

"For the past maybe one hundred years," the Colonel continued, "there has been a persistent myth in this so-called village that it has turned out many players who, but for some unforeseen stroke of misfortune, could have gone all the way to the top. But the fact is, there have been only two ball players from this forsaken village that had any kind of shot at playing any kind of professional ball at any level. And they are your father, who unfortunately spent his best years in jail, and you, who seem to be headed straight down that same path. If you aren't careful you're going to be part of the same sad little myth, E.A. Allen. Mark my words. With talent comes a high price. Self-discipline. Setbacks. Sacrifice. Risk of failing. If you aren't willing to pay that price, you don't have a snowball's chance."

"Well, I reckon you know just about everything."

"I don't know much," the Colonel said. "I don't even know what I don't know. But I know you have to take hold of your life, boy."

Despite his dressing-down from the Colonel, E.A. got drunk again the next Saturday after beating Sherbrooke, and he stayed over with Earl and Moonface at the Jolie Blon with a woman who didn't speak two words of English. Gypsy was waiting for him in the kitchen when Earl slowed down just enough for E.A. to stumble out of his car and stand shakily in the dooryard in the sunrise.

The 6:05 whistled at the railway crossing, reminding E.A. of Teddy. He felt bad. He felt like crying. Something was wrong, and it was more than just being hung over. He remembered learning how to read from the names on the sides of the boxcars, but he couldn't remember exactly how he'd gotten to the Jolie Blon or when they'd left. He vaguely recalled Earl and Moonface helping him into the car.

He stood in the dooryard, watching the freight pass like a ghost train in the mist. Gypsy sat at the kitchen table, watching E.A. out the window, Grandpa Gleason Allen's deer rifle in her hands, pointed at the door. Gran sat in her old-fashioned wicker wheelchair by the table. For the first time in years, she'd gotten up before ten A.M.

They watched E.A. drink out of the pump spout. They watched the train pass out of sight. They watched as Teddy Williams walked up from the tracks out of the mist, bat bag over his shoulder, and stopped a few feet away from E.A. Teddy looked different. Instead of the ratty suit coat, he was wearing a neat blue windbreaker, and there was no Crackling Rose bottle sticking out of his pocket. He wasn't smoking, and as hung over as E.A. was, he could see that Teddy was stone sober. Teddy slung the bat bag off his shoulder and down at E.A.'s feet and said in his raspy voice, loud enough for Gypsy and Gran to hear him through the screen door, "You look like death warmed over, Ethan."

E.A. said nothing.

"Jesus, Ethan. You're just getting in, aren't you? Why, your ma must be worried half out of her mind."

"What do you care about my ma?" E.A. said, staggering against the metal pump. "You misused her way worse."

"I never laid a hand on Gypsy, Ethan. Or any other woman."

"No. I reckon it wasn't your hand you laid on her."

Inside the farmhouse kitchen Gypsy figured Teddy'd be about ready to fly at E.A. She'd have to aim Grandpa Gleason's rifle at Teddy. But all he said was "Ethan. Listen. I know I weren't no good for Gypsy and I know I weren't no good father for you."

"You weren't *here* for me is what you weren't," E.A. said.

"That, too," Teddy said. "But it don't excuse this display."

E.A. said, "I'll tell you the same thing I told you a few years ago. I want you off these premises."

Teddy reached out and grabbed Ethan by the back of his neck and held his head under the pump. He pumped the handle until E.A. was soaked and spouting.

"Ethan," Teddy said. "I'll make you a deal. We'll go down to the ball field. You pitch to me. You strike me out, I'll leave. I get a hit off you, I'll stay on and work with you and you stay out of the roadhouses."

"You're on, mister man," Ethan said, shaking his head and shoulders like a drenched dog. "You got yourself a deal, Mr. Gone and Long Forgotten. Get your bat and stand in there."

E.A.'s first pitch was three feet over Teddy's head. It whanged off North Carolina, First in Flight, folding it up in the middle so that it looked as if it had been in a head-on collision. The second pitch just missed Teddy's head. The third pitch was a foot outside and ricocheted off Missouri, the Show Me State. With a 3–0 count, E.A. managed to get the fourth pitch over the plate, and Teddy took a short stride and a short, compact swing and hit the ball farther than Ethan had ever seen a man hit a baseball in his life. Over the dike of clay Devil Dan had thrown up, over the river, over the railroad tracks, into the willows behind the commission-sales auction barn in the village.

The ball must have traveled five hundred feet. Maybe more. Until that moment E.A. had not known it was possible for a batter to hit a ball so far. He thought of the ball Teddy had driven onto Old Lady Benton's porch above the drugstore. He could only imagine that hit. This one he'd seen, and he still had trouble believing it.

Teddy's mammoth home run over the river sobered E.A. up more than the pump — that and the dozen line drives and sizzling ground balls up the middle past the mound and between third and short that Teddy hit during the next ten minutes. He sent two more towering shots over the river. Each swing was economical, just a short step and then that lightning crack when the ball hit the wood of Teddy's Green Mountain Rebel. He swung only at strikes and didn't miss a one, and every ball he swung at was a hit. Finally E.A. threw a perfect slider that just clipped the outside corner before diving out of the strike zone. It was his nastiest pitch, but Teddy drove it on a line two feet over first base. A sure triple for a fast runner in any park.

Ethan heaved his glove at the old Packard seat slumped in the tall grass. He felt exactly the way he had the day Teddy told him he'd never be a major-league hitter. In ten minutes his dream of pitching for the Boston Red Sox had come unraveled. If he couldn't get a ball past an over-the-hill catcher for a prison team in Texas, how could he ever expect to pitch in the majors?

"I can't do it, can I? It was all a lie, me going all the way. What I am is just another Kingdom County loser."

"You're not a loser," Teddy said. "You listen to me, Ethan. You was hung over today and I had my batting shoes on. Ordinarily, you'd get me out half the time, maybe more." Teddy glanced up at the dooryard, where Gypsy stood watching, still holding the deer rifle. Speaking louder, Teddy said, "Now. No more breaking training. No drinking. No smoking. No staying out to all hours."

"You drink."

"I haven't touched a drop in five months," Teddy said. He reached into his bat bag and pulled out his catcher's glove. "We'll toss now. Then we'll run."

"I don't feel so hot," E.A. admitted.

"I don't imagine you do."

Somehow E.A. made himself head back out to the mound.

E.A. WENT TO WORK at the bat factory, tailing saws, sweeping up sawdust, stacking lumber. The Common was surprised. Gypsy had publicly vowed that her son would never set foot in the factory, which she feared would trap him, doom him to small-town life forever. Teddy said he'd see to it that didn't happen, but by God, E.A. was old enough to have a job where he had to show up every morning at seven and couldn't stay out all night drinking the night before. It was part of Teddy's plan.

Making a good wooden baseball bat, E.A. learned, was an art, from selecting the right ash tree in the woods to shaving the handle of the bat to the right thickness to give it maximum whip and strength. E.A. liked the heady, sweet scent of the varnish applied to the finished bats, which filled the whole village like the scent of bread near a bakery. He liked the thump and clack of the stamper impressing the words GREEN MOUNTAIN REBEL on the barrel of each bat. Best of all he liked watching Teddy shape a bat on the lathe, his big hands as capable and delicate as a surgeon's as, magically, the round barrel began to appear out of the wood. He worked to the rhythm of the throbbing belts and pulleys and shafts in the old mill. The planer screeched, the molders grumbled. Out in the factory yard the big log saw added its heavy rasping to the medley. The ripsaw whirred and Teddy's lathe buzzed, and the result of all this humming and whirring and roaring was the steady music of a wooden baseball bat being produced.

At noon Teddy ate on the bleachers or under the old elm on

the south end of the common. Occasionally E.A. ate with his father, but they didn't talk much. Even when he was working with
the other men at the factory, Teddy was a loner. Sometimes Baxter
Benton, the foreman, would bring him a finished bat that didn't
seem balanced correctly, and Teddy would shave the handle a little
thinner with a shard of glass from the bottom of a broken beer bottle, taper it just a little finer. "How do you know when it's right?"
E.A. said.

And Teddy said, as he'd said of the ash trees on Allen Mountain, "Oh, I know."

At seventeen, E.A. could not imagine anything better than
working days with his father in the bat factory and playing town-
team ball in the early evenings and on weekends. Except, of
course, playing for the Sox. In Baxter Benton's office was a glass
display case. Inside were a dozen or so bats with white smudges on
them, like some of the famous bats at Cooperstown, including one
that Teddy Ballgame had hit a home run with, one that Pudge Fisk
had used, one of Johnny Pesky's, and one that had belonged to the
Little Professor, Dom DiMaggio. E.A.'s favorite was a forty-inch
Green Mountain Rebel wielded by none other than Babe Ruth
himself, before he was traded to New York. E.A. always paused for
a few seconds to gaze at the Babe's bat when he went into the mill
in the morning and left in the late afternoon.

No one, least of all E.A., made much money at the baseball bat
factory. But it was important work, which helped maintain the tradition of wooden bats for the great American pastime, and E.A. regarded it as part of the apprenticeship that would lead to the day
he walked out to the mound at Fenway Park and threw his first
pitch in a Red Sox uniform.

E.A. had always loved everything about the Kingdom Fair, especially the early morning of opening Saturday. He loved the smells
of the trampled hay field where the fair was held, the fried food,
the animal barns. He loved the calliope music and the wheedling,

singsong spiels of the midway barkers, like the tall, pretty girl at the baseball-throw booth chanting into a hand-held microphone, "Hey, hey, can't do no harm to try your arm against Cajun Stan the Baseball Man."

She was about E.A.'s age, and with the hand not holding the mike she was juggling three brand-new baseballs. Her skin was the tawny color of E.A.'s old baseball glove and her hair, a deep, rich brown, hung straight to her waist. She wore a spangled denim jacket over a dark blue blouse, with white cowboy boots and tight jeans accentuating her slim legs. Beside her, next to a netted pitching cage with a radar gun, stood a slender, gray-skinned man with graying hair, wearing an elegant white suit with a blue handkerchief tucked into the breast pocket, a daffodil-yellow shirt, a light blue necktie, and spotless white shoes. Sitting on his head at a jaunty angle was a wide-brimmed white hat.

The juggling girl handed the mike to Cajun Stan, caught two of the balls in her left hand, tossed the third up ten feet, and caught it behind her back, flashing E.A. a grin and making an elaborate bow.

At the far end of the cage hung a canvas backdrop with a man's head painted on it. It was Stan's head — gray hair, rakish white hat, and all. The head's mouth was open. Above the entrance of the cage was a radar screen. "Try your luck against Stan the Baseball Man," the girl said to E.A. "Throw the ball faster than Stan, take all the money from the Baseball Man. Throw the ball in the Cajun's mouth, all Stan's moola going south. Five dollars to play, ten if you win. This is Stan, the fastest pitcher in all the land. I'm his daughter, Louisianne."

Teddy, coming along behind E.A., got out his wallet. "Go ahead, Ethan," he said, but before E.A. could step up to the cage, Earl No Pearl, already two sheets to the wind, shouldered his way front and center, handed Louisianne a crumpled five-dollar bill, and grabbed one of the baseballs.

"We got a pitcher here, folks," Cajun Stan said. "Going to take Stan to school."

Earl wound up and threw with all his might. The ball hit the white hat of the head painted on the canvas. The screen above the head flashed 79 mph. Earl shook his head in disbelief.

Stan took off his hat and handed it to Louisianne. He squinted in at the facsimile of his face, then lifted his hands high over his head once, twice, three times, like an old-fashioned pitcher from the early days of baseball. He kicked one skinny leg high and threw. The ball vanished into the mouth, and the radar screen said 92 mph.

Earl stared. "That pitch weren't no ninety-two miles per hour." He reached out to snatch back his five-spot from Louisianne. Instead, to his further befuddlement, he found himself holding Stan's hat. The bill had vanished.

"Thank you kindly," Stan said, taking back his hat.

"It didn't look *eighty* miles per hour," Earl complained.

"Course not," Stan said, readjusting his hat on his head. "A smooth pitcher with a smooth wind-up, no hitches, the pitch never gone look fast as it is."

E.A. suspected that the radar was rigged. Yet Stan's wind-up and delivery had been as smooth as fancy-grade maple syrup, and the pitch had been dead-on accurate. Maybe it hadn't been 92 mph, but it was fast.

Louisianne was chanting again. "Five dollars to ask Cajun Stan any baseball question. Stump the Baseball Man, you get back ten in your hand. No trouble to double your money. Any query at all, ladies and gentlemen. You'll find Stan the Man to be a bottomless repository of baseball trivia. He's here to astound and delight you."

Teddy handed her a five-dollar bill. "Try him, Ethan. Ask him a question."

Ethan figured Cajun Stan would probably know every hitter's batting average and every pitcher's ERA back to Ruth and before. He decided to throw the Baseball Man a curve. "How high is the Green Monster in Fenway Park?"

Stan laughed. "Why don't you ast something hard? Thirty-seven feet."

"Try again," Teddy said, giving Louisianne another five-spot.

"Longest recorded home run in Fenway?" E.A. said.

"What all this Fenway business?" Stan said. "Nobody care 'bout Fenway, Home of They Losers. Answer you sorry-ass question, old Teddy Ballgame's five-hundred-and-two-foot shot to right field. Crushed a fan's straw hat. This like grabbing a Hershey from a baby."

"Ask him something challenging, Ethan," Louisianne said.

E.A. looked at her quickly. How did this girl know his name?

But Teddy had another bill all ready to go, so E.A. said, "How many different angles does the playing field around Fenway have?"

Stan adjusted his radar gun, not looking at E.A., who was certain that this time he'd stumped him. Then the Baseball Man said, "Same number you is old. Seventeen."

"I can beat you throwing against that gun," E.A. said. "Double or nothing."

"Why, sure," Stan said. "You the local *he*-ro, right? The go-all-the-way-to-the-top boy. You probably right. You beat me. Stand back, folks. Give the local he-ro room. He about to take Stan to school, him."

From nowhere, Louisianne produced a baseball and tossed it to E.A. "Presenting," she said, "the one, the only, Ethan E.A. Allen."

The ball felt too light in E.A.'s hand, but he went into his compact wind-up and threw it into the head's mouth. The radar screen registered 93 mph.

"Well, now," Stan said. "Got us a regular Cy Young here. Got us a country boy can throw, all right."

Stan flipped his hat to Louisianne and went into his routine, pumping once, twice, three times, kicking, pitching. The ball hummed like a swarm of bees, and the radar screen flashed 100 mph.

"That can't be right," E.A. said.

"Oh, my," Stan said. "We got one here. Yes, sir. A bona fide Mr. Know-all." He looked at Teddy. "I ast you, Edward. How Stan gone teach this boy anything, he already know everything?"

Stan shook his head. "Yes, sir, E.W.," he said. "You gots a regular Alfred Einstein here."

"Albert," E.A. said.

Stan looked at him.

"Albert Einstein," E.A. said. "Not Alfred."

"Case closed," said Stan, and Louisianne picked up her microphone and baseballs and resumed her spiel, looking down the midway for another mark, as if Ethan had just fallen off the edge of the earth and she couldn't care less.

EARLY THE FOLLOWING morning, just as E.A. loped into Gran's dooryard after a five-mile run, a battered pink limousine with a loud muffler pulled in behind him. Printed across the driver's door were the words CAJUN STAN THE BASEBALL MAN. One of its headlights was bashed in. There was a deep crease in the front right door. The back bumper had fallen off, and the limo was rusting out underneath like a Kingdom County junker. At the wheel was Stan, wearing his snowy white suit and hat, a powder blue shirt with a pink tie, and a matching pink handkerchief. Louisianne, beside him, wore a short yellow sundress and matching heels. Sitting in back was Teddy Williams.

"Ethan," Teddy said, "this here is my old bud Stan. You met him yesterday. I and Stan played together in college. Back when I first broke in, I caught him."

Stan got out of the limo rather stiffly. "How do, bub," he said. "We meet again." Stan had the longest fingers E.A. had ever seen. His handshake consisted of three formal tugs, like a trout biting.

Gypsy came out of the house, shook hands with Stan, and gave Louisianne a big hug as though they'd known each other for years. Then Teddy and E.A. and Gypsy and Stan and Louisianne all went down to Fenway.

Stan sat down on the Packard seat. "No poison serpents round here, is they, E.W.?" he said. "I and venomous serpents is on the outs."

"It's too cold for snakes up here, Stan," Teddy said as he squatted down behind the plate to warm up E.A. "It's too cold for base-ball nine months of the year."

"Oh, it never too cold or too hot for baseball," Stan said. "Ain't that right, Louisianne?"

Louisianne winked one big, shiny, dark eye at her father. She stood beside the Packard seat and looked around the diamond with interest.

"I like your outfit, hon," Gypsy said. "It's very becoming." She grinned at E.A. "I'm not the only one who thinks so, either."

E.A. threw hard to Teddy for fifteen minutes while Stan looked at Devil Dan's Midnight Auto, looked across the river, looked at Bill's license plates on the barn. Like a bored kid staring around a schoolroom. Finally he walked out to the mound and stood behind E.A. like a softball umpire officiating a game alone.

"Boy," Cajun Stan said, "what you got to go with that heat?"

E.A. showed him his curve, showed him the slider Teddy had taught him.

"What you got for a straight change?" Stan said. "Can you get it over?"

"I can get any pitch over," E.A. said. Teddy set up low on the outside corner, flashed four fingers.

Louisianne said, "I give you E.A. Allen and his straight change."

E.A. hit the middle of Teddy's glove with a slow breaking pitch.

"No," Stan said. "That a let-up curve. Bona fide straight change, he gone fool most hitters. Let-up, they hammer it right over that thirty-seven-foot-tall fence we talking about yesterday."

"Nobody's ever hammered it yet."

"Who is they *to* hammer it round here? We talking two differ-ent brands of baseball, son."

Stan went back to the Packard seat, checking under it carefully before he sat down. "Throw from the stretch," he barked out. "Like you got mens on base, which you gone have pretty much all they time."

E.A. threw out of the stretch for five minutes. Then Teddy stood up out of his crouch.

"Well?" he asked Stan.

Stan sighed. He drew in his breath through his teeth and shook his head. "Boy got some old-fashioned heat, him. He got a good enough down-breaking hook, nice tight spin on the ball. Fair slider. Ain't got no change is the whole trouble."

"He learns quick enough, if I do say so," Teddy said.

Stan snorted, a mirthless noise. "E.W., what you mean? I ever in my life see a young fella that already knowed everything, here he is in the flesh. I ain't surprised. Apple don't fall far from the tree. Got red hair besides. That a bad sign. That the worst. You wants the truth, I never knowed a redheaded pitcher keep his composure out there."

Louisianne laughed. Everything her father said delighted her, and Gypsy seemed charmed by both Stan and his daughter. But E.A. couldn't tell whether Cajun Stan was kidding or serious. All he knew was that if he could learn something about pitching from the Baseball Man, he intended to.

They were sitting on the stoop, Teddy and E.A. and Stan and Louisianne, drinking ice-cold root beer. Gypsy and Gran were inside making Spam sandwiches on Wonder Bread. E.A. was showing Louisianne his baseball cards.

"So," Teddy said to his old bud. "Will you work with him?"

"Oh, I work with him all right," Stan said. "But they going to be a steep price. Know-all smart aleck like this young fella? I ain't studying no free teaching, no."

"When you get him signed, take your cut," Teddy suggested. "Fifteen percent."

"I going to. I taking my full fifteen percent. Maybe twenty. Meantime, Louisianne and I need to live, us. Pass me that there cigar box, boy. Let's see what you got."

E.A. handed him the box containing his baseball cards. Stan

riffled through them, muttering criticisms of the players. "Ted Williams," he said, holding up Ted's rookie card. "I strike him out in three pitches. Four at most."

Stan examined E.A.'s Cy Young. "Winningest pitcher of all," he read. "Huh. I take this. For payment."

Thinking Stan meant Cy Young, E.A. reached for the cigar box. Stan yanked it away. "I take *this*," he said, shaking the box. "Sell to a fella I knows down Shreveport, c'llects cards. In the meantime, my girl here hold on to it for me."

Louisianne took the cigar box. "Let him keep one," she said. She held the Cy Young out toward E.A. But when he reached for it, it vanished.

HIS FULL NAME was Stan T. Paige, no relation to Satchel, and he was from Tippytoe, Louisiana. He'd been orphaned at six and raised by an aunt, the madam of a local house of ill repute for whom he was, variously, an errand boy, general nuisance, and surrogate son. The aunt, retired now, was quite wealthy and entirely respectable. Louisianne, whose mother had run off with a voodoo band when her daughter was three, lived with her great-aunt during the winter and traveled with her father in the summer.

When Teddy met Cajun Stan, the Baseball Man was enjoying a three-to-five all-expenses-paid scholarship, courtesy of the state of Texas, for swindling the First National Bank of San Antonio out of $100,000. The money had been designated for a new American Legion baseball stadium. But Stan, in Las Vegas, had plunked it all down on a bet that San Antonio's double-A baseball team, for which he was pitching at the time, would win their league title. The fact that they did win was of little consolation to him when he was banned from the game for life and sent to prison for extortion.

Over the next several days, Stan showed E.A. a craftier pickoff move to first. He taught him how to push harder off the rubber with his right foot and demonstrated several different arm angles to come at the batter with. How to conceal the ball in his glove until the last possible moment, how to "cut" his fastball by positioning his top two fingers slightly off center on the outside of the ball so that the pitch ran away from righties and into lefties, how to surprise left-handed batters by throwing a back-door breaking pitch that started half a foot off the plate and then dived in to nip the outside corner at the last moment.

"How fast?" E.A. asked Stan, who was holding the radar gun, a week after his training started.

"Ninety-four," Stan said. "Second time around the league — second time around the *lineup* maybe — they gone jump all over that heat." Stan set down the gun and held out his hand for the ball. "Son," he said, "fetch you hitting bat."

"What?"

"You a hitter, ain't you? Fetch you bat."

E.A. got his bat. Cajun Stan took off his white hat and set it on the Packard seat. Louisianne helped him out of his jacket.

The Baseball Man walked out to the mound. "Stand in," he said.

"Aren't you going to warm up?"

"I been warm up forty year. Step into that batter's box, you."

As E.A. stepped up to the plate, Teddy squatted down behind him.

"Where's your gear?" E.A. asked him.

"Don't swing," Teddy said. "Just watch."

As delicate as a ballet dancer, Stan lifted his hands high over his head three times and pitched the ball. "Ninety-six," Teddy said.

"No," E.A. said.

"It's coming again," Teddy said. "Same place, right over the heart of the plate. Swing."

E.A. swung when the ball was in Teddy's glove.

"Swing again," Teddy said. "Now that you've seen it."

Again, Stan's hands rose over his head three times. His right arm came snapping down like a cobra striking. E.A. stepped out onto his front foot and started to swing, tried to hold back and couldn't. For the first time in his life he fell down in the batter's box.

Clap, clap, clap.

From the stoop, over slow, sarcastic applause, Gran said, "He's

205

ready at last. That's a stunt the Sox'll pay millions for. Look out, Boston. Here comes Ethan Allen."

Worse yet, Louisianne was making her palms-up stage gesture toward him, sitting on his ass in the batter's box, and Gypsy was laughing.

E.A. looked out toward the mound. "What in hell was that pitch?" he said.

"That," Teddy said, "was a straight change. That's your ticket to the top, son. If you can learn it."

34

MAYNARD E. FLYNN JUNIOR sat in his office overlooking the diamond. He was, at last, very close to completing his doctoral degree through the Pacific Northwest Internet Correspondence Program, in which he had matriculated sixteen years before. Better yet, he was even closer to disposing of the Boston Red Sox franchise. As the *Globe* had discovered, and published in this morning's edition to the consternation and outrage of all New England, for several months he had been negotiating secretly to sell the club to a consortium of Hollywood luminaries and political activists who planned to move the team to Beverly Hills.

A local group headed up by several former Sox players had also made a bid. In fact, a somewhat higher one. But the big lummox had no intention of selling the club to them.

Working his hand flexer frenetically, Maynard grinned. He loved thinking that he would be remembered as the man who, by eviscerating the Sox and then packing the whole kit and caboodle off to the far side of the continent, had with one bold stroke exorcised the curse that had hung over the team since the sale of Babe Ruth. Now the Nation would never again have to confront their great fear, that the Sox might actually win a Series and leave them with nothing to hope for. At the end of the season the team and their fans would go out in a blaze of defeat, leaving the people of New England happy losers for all time to come.

True, the Sox were somehow currently head-to-head with the Yankees in a battle for the lead in the Eastern Division race, largely because of the Legendary Spence's brilliant managing. Through a stroke of evil genius, Maynard had brought up Ted Williams's son, John Henry, who had played several undistinguished innings in a minor-league game in Florida, and insisted that Spence start him in left field. After a long session with Spence in the batting cage before the game, John Henry went 4–5 and belted two balls over the Green Monster. Thus far, that was the way the summer was going. The manager used every Spencerian trick for which he was famous and some no one had ever seen before. To enrage crowds at away games and whip up his own players, he'd patrol the perimeter of the diamond carrying a stick with a nail in the end. The boos descended on him along with the debris thrown out of the stands. "We do not need Mr. Spencer to pick up after the fans of Comiskey Park," the *Sun-Times* wrote. Never one to go by the book, Spence signaled notoriously slow runners to steal home, called for the double steal with two outs, started coaching third base himself, and routinely gave runners the green light to try to stretch singles into doubles and doubles into triples, often catching his opponents flat-footed.

Late one afternoon before a night game at the Fen with New York, a tall man, graying at the temples, walked into the clubhouse office carrying a thick book called *Einstein's Theory of Relativity and the Mechanics of Pitching*, of which he was the author.

He opened this tome to chapter five. "Did you know, Spence, that if we could attain enough speed, we could go back to 'seventy-eight?"

"What the deuce for?" Spence said.

"To play that winner-take-all game with New York over again. Throw Dent something else, an eephus pitch maybe. Or," the tall man continued, "back to 1920 and persuade Frazee to hold on to Ruth."

"I'd have to rename my parrot here," Spence said. "There wouldn't be any Curse of the Bambino."

"Macaw," the bird said indignantly. "Not parrot."

"With a little time travel," the author said, "think of the team we could put together. Myself, Yaz, Teddy Ballgame. In the meantime, Stan sent me down to help you out."

"I like the team we're putting together, Alien. I'm glad to see you. You feel like killing some Yankees tonight?"

That night the Alien Man, having come out of retirement after more than a decade, beat New York 8–4, throwing a five-hitter.

The lummox wasn't about to panic. He'd seen the Sox on the brink of success before, and he knew it would come to a screeching halt with the turn of the season and the first cool days and nights of fall. The boys of October the Red Sox were not. Nor had they been since 1918. Nor would they ever be, world without end, amen. Maynard E. Flynn Junior, B.A., M.A., and soon-to-be Ph.D., would see to that.

But shipping the team off to Hollywood was not all the lummox had in mind. By the time the snow flew, as his father used to say, he would have another surprise for the good people of Boston. Because immediately after the last game of the season at Fenway, the new owner intended to convert their "lyric little bandbox" to a museum dedicated to the abject failures of the Sox to win a Series.

In the foyer of this unique sports edifice would be, of course, a life-size effigy of Bucky Dent slapping his three-run homer off feckless Mike Torrez. The rest of the museum would consist of a replica of Fenway Park. Around this diamond the paying public — and if the lummox knew Boston, there would be no shortage of people willing to pay through the nose to see the Red Sox Century of Failure and Despair Museum — could stroll at their leisure. The tall figure of Bill Buckner would be off the grass at first base, stooped low, but not low enough, as the ground ball that should have ended the '86 Series with a championship for Boston scooted between his sore, aging legs. That this had actually happened in Shea Stadium was not a problem to the lummox; a little magic realism would not hurt the tableau he had in mind. From that same fateful Series he'd have young Calvin Schiraldi on the mound, glove on top of his head, an eternal, agonized wince on his face, having just given up a third consecutive base hit with victory one unattainable out away. And who was this but Teddy Ballgame, frozen in transparent blue-green ice inside a cryogenic tank in the on-deck circle, making an ungracious gesture at the press box. Don Zimmer, one foot on the dugout steps, rubbed the gleaming metal plate in his head that doubtless contributed to his decision to leave Torrez in to get shelled even after Dent's homer. The psychologically challenged Jimmy Piersall capered buck-naked in the outfield, his fingers wagging from his ears. Yaz stood at the plate, eternally popping out weakly to end everything in '78. And there would be more, much more, including a darkened night scene of the four-time Cy Young Award winner, All-Star shortstop, American League MVP, and Triple Crown–winning left-fielder, in tatters and chains, being ferried in a skiff along a dark stream by two evil-looking men in Confederate military caps, entitled SOLD DOWN THE RIVER.

The *pièce de résistance* was already completed. It stood a few feet away from the lummox's desk, covered with a white sheet. Maynard could scarcely wait to reveal it to Spence, whose clacking spikes he could hear, even now, approaching the door.

Spence gave his cheery shave-and-a-haircut, two-bits knock and stepped inside, the Curse on his shoulder. Maynard pretended to be hard at work on his ever-evolving thesis.

"Well, Junior," the manager said. "Still studying, I see."

"A student studies," the lummox said. "It's what we do. And kindly don't call me Junior. I believe that we've discussed that on prior occasions."

The lummox worked his hand flexer and gave Spence and the Curse of the Bambino his fishy stare. Spence wondered what the boy had concealed under the white sheet. Some new weightlifting apparatus, no doubt. He wished the lummox would quit knuckle-punching him and his players in the arm. Awkward though he was, he had a nasty way of catching you right on the muscle, making it smart like a bumblebee sting for twenty minutes afterward.

Junior's father had been a worthy adversary and sometime

friend to Spence. Often, after an exciting win, Spence and the macaw had joined the old owner in his office where, with their good friend Jack Daniel, they would visit and reminisce. The old man would shed real tears and say baseball wasn't what it used to be and get so drunk Spence would have to drive him home to Revere. One night, as Maynard Senior staggered through the door, he out and peed all over the boy's mama's twelve-thousand-dollar Turkish living room carpet, while the mama shrieked steadily and Spence and the child lummox looked on.

"Looky here, Junior," Spence began.

The lummox let out a great sigh. "I am growing *so* weary of requesting that you not call me by that detestable cognomen."

"Look, Maynard," Spence said, though that didn't sound right, either, "last night we lost another pitcher for the season. Torn rotator cuff and that's all she wrote. I'm down to three starters, counting the Alien. What I need here, I need me two, three more arms, we're going to make a run at the division, much less do anything in post-season."

"What earthly reason is there to suppose that even with thirty more arms, a ragtag assortment of has-beens, never-was's and never-will-be's like your so-called team could possibly 'do anything in post-season'?"

"Well," Spence said, "the boys are on a roll, see? Say we take the pennant again. Say we take the Serious. Why, then you wouldn't need to sell the team. Plus you'd get the credit for bringing the championship to Boston. The thing is, we need to move right now, before the no-trade deadline. After that we can't bring no more new players on board."

The lummox put his fingers together, making his little church steeple. "I am well aware of when we cannot sign additional players. Therefore I will give you thirty thousand dollars to use as you see fit. You may buy one thirty-thousand-dollar arm or three ten-thousand-dollar arms. The cash is yours to do with as you wish. A most handsome offer, I should say."

Spence stared at him, unable to formulate an appropriate reply. The lummox stood up and walked over to the sheet draped over the weight machine or whatever it was. Whipping it off with a flourish, he said, "Don't you think I've just made Mr. Spencer a handsome offer, pater?"

Before Spence's astonished eyes stood the stuffed figure — he supposed it must be stuffed — of Maynard E. Flynn Senior himself. He was wearing a three-piece suit and his Red Sox cap, and his recriminating index finger was thrust out at Spence as it had been a thousand times when the old man was alive. Spence's first clear thought was that the taxidermist had done a terrible job. The old man's nose overhung his lower face by three or four inches, and the eyes were as yellow and feral as those of a caged leopard.

"Wax," the lummox said. "For my museum."

Spence felt a tiny wave of relief. Wax was better than stuffed.

"Oh, there'll be one of you, too," the lummox said. "Dancing the hornpipe, or something along those lines."

Spence stared at the lummox. Then Maynard had another inspiration. He reached for the phone on his desk. "Get me my attorney," he told his receptionist.

With the famous Flynn sneer playing over his lips, he said, "I'm going to make you a sporting proposition, Mr. Spencer. If you can win the World Series this year, I'll sell the team to the local group. Otherwise, the whole operation, you and your overpriced contract included, will be heading west."

"If I win the Series you'll keep the team in Boston?"

"That's what I said. We'll finalize it with my solicitor *and* we'll make it public. Give those lowly journalists something to write about."

The lummox put down his flexer and placed the tips of his fingers together. "Here's the church," he said. "Here's the steeple. Here's Fenway." He opened up his locked fingers to show nothing but his palms. "Where are all the Faithful?"

So when Spence took three quick steps toward him, thrust out his hand, and said, "You got a deal, Maynard," the lummox was almost too surprised to knuckle-punch him on the arm, though not quite.

35

RECENTLY LOUISIANNE had been running with E.A. before his daily workouts with Stan. One morning, just back from a five-mile circuit to Kingdom Landing, they sat on the Colonel's pedestal on the village green, watching the sun come up over Allen Mountain, lighting up the Green Monster atop the baseball bat factory where Moonface was posting last night's Sox score. Boston had been in Montreal, looking for a sweep of a three-game series with the Expos in the last interleague contest of the season.

Louisianne wore bright red running shoes and red shorts with a matching halter top, her long, dark brown hair tied back with a red ribbon. As they waited for the score to go up, E.A. told her about the WYSOTT Allens' longtime feud with Devil Dan and Dan's threats to dozer down Gran's barn and house. But he couldn't stop staring at her slender, coffee-with-cream–colored legs. Although Louisianne seemed interested in the feud, finally she kicked E.A.'s sneaker and said, in a perfect imitation of her father's Cajun accent, "What you looking at, boy?"

E.A. turned as red as Louisianne's running outfit. She laughed and told him in her own voice to be careful or she'd make him disappear. As Moon put up the score, Boston 7 Montreal 3, she said, "Actually, Ethan, it's a lot harder to make someone appear than disappear."

"Who's going to appear?" he said.

She glanced up at the courthouse clocktower. "Stick around for a few minutes. You might be surprised." Then she jumped down off the pedestal and jogged back over to the hotel, where she and Stan were staying.

"Hook, line, and sinker," the Colonel said, as E.A. continued to ogle her bobbing dark ponytail and pretty legs. "I just hope she doesn't break your heart in the end is all. I don't mean to interfere. But you might better know now than later that women will generally do that to you. They will break your heart, or your spirit, or both."

"I'll thank you to keep your advice to yourself," E.A. said.

"Time was when you were happy enough to receive it," the Colonel snapped back. "I see those days are long — well, look at that, will you."

A dark, expensive-looking car was pulling up to the hotel. It stopped directly in front of the porch just as Cajun Stan, dressed in white as usual, came out and waved. The driver, a heavyset man in his sixties, built as solid as the brick shopping block, got out and nodded to Stan, then looked around the village, his gaze stopping on the Green Monster atop the factory with last night's score posted on it. He wore a Red Sox windbreaker and a Sox cap, and on his shoulder sat a large, multicolored bird.

As word began to spread that the Legendary Spence had appeared in the village, a steady stream of Sox fans appeared to get a look at him, get an autograph, take a snapshot, or just say hello. People like Gypsy and Gran and Bill and Frenchy LaMott, who ran the commission sales, and even Old Lady Benton, who probably wouldn't have walked across the street to meet the president of the United States, were eager that August morning to see the famous Spence in person as he and Stan walked down the common toward the baseball diamond. E.A. was already warming up with Teddy, who'd appeared with their gloves and a ball just after Spence arrived. The elderly bat boys, sitting out on the hotel porch in the morning sunshine, did not walk over to the diamond. That would have been beneath their dignity. But Fletch and Early and Late leaned forward in their folding chairs and watched attentively as Stan and Spence headed down the green past the statue.

"It's a nice pastime, Stanley," Spence was telling his old bud. "It's a very nice pastime when they can sell your franchise right out from under you the season after you've put an American League pennant banner over your home grounds and gotten to the last game of the Serious, not to mention we're leading the AL East by a game as we speak. Is that the kid?"

"That him," Stan said.

"He ain't too big, is he?" Spence said.

"You gone be surprised," Stan said.

"I doubt it," Spence said.

E.A., warming up on the mound, felt good. A little nervous, but ready.

"Okay?" Teddy said.

"Okay," E.A. said and threw a fastball, up and in on a right-handed batter.

"You go, E.A.!" Gypsy shouted.

"Ninety-four, ninety-five miles an hour," Stan said to Spence. "Hard to get a bat on."

"Any pitch five inches inside is hard to get a bat on," Spence said. "Tell him he's supposed to hit the glove."

"He sending the hitter a message," Stan said.

"The umpire will send him a message," Spence said. "Ball one."

"You're down on the count, kid," he said to E.A. "I don't like my pitchers getting down on the count. I don't like leadoff walks. A pitcher wants to stay on my right side, he better stay up on the count and not be walking no leadoff batters."

For the next ten minutes Spence watched E.A. throw. In only one instance — when a slider hit the dirt beside the plate — did Teddy have to move his mitt more than an inch or two.

The crowd of villagers, at least fifty strong now, was quiet. Everyone's eyes were on Spence, to see how he was reacting. The Colonel, away up the common in deepest center field, seemed to be leaning forward, holding his broken-off sword at an expectant angle, waiting to hear the verdict. Even Gran seemed to be holding her breath.

Spence stood near the pitcher's mound, wondering what exquisite new possibilities for disappointment this Vermont development offered. The night before, when he'd gotten back to his hotel in Montreal, a town where they didn't even speak English as their first language and they played hockey as their main sport, something had made him pick up the phone and call Stan. And Stan had somehow talked him into renting a car and driving down to see the kid this morning, leaving his team to fly back to Boston on their own. Now he found himself wishing he'd gone with them, not because he wasn't impressed with E.A. but because he simply didn't know how much more heartbreak he could take in a single season.

"Well," Stan said, "he can throw, him, yeah?"

"Oh, he can throw, all right," Spence said. "I'm desperate for pitchers and he can throw. Now" — reaching reluctantly for the contract in his back pocket — "we're going to find out whether he can pitch."

36

"I EVER TELL YOU folks about my all-time favorite baseball con?" Stan was saying. "When I con old George Steinbrenner out of his lemonzene?"

It was early in the evening. E.A. would be leaving for Boston the next morning, and Stan and Louisianne were departing that night in Stan's old pink limousine for a fair in upstate New York. The Paiges and Gypsy and Teddy and Gran and Bill and E.A. were gathered around Gran's kitchen table for a celebratory dinner of out-of-season venison and trout, woodchuck, Bill's dandelion wine, and a store-bought white cake on which Gypsy had inscribed, with chocolate frosting:

Congrats to Ethan Allen,
a Member of the Boston Red Sox

"If it hadn't been for Steinbrenner," Gran said, "Bucky Dent never would have put on pinstripes, and I'd be going dancing tonight instead of confined to a wheelchair."

Gypsy cut her eyes at E.A. and he grinned.

"Steinbrenner a bad one, all right," Stan agreed. "Mr. Moneybags. What wrong with baseball today, you ast me. For years it be my dream to con that man. Finally it come to me how.

"It spring training, back seven, eight years ago. Every morning, old George come to the ball park in a long, black lemonzene. That automobile most as long as a city block. You want the truth, I had my eye on it for a long while. So I go down by the entrance of the park with a big old valise in my hand, got the word DIRT wrote on it in red letters. And when George go by I hold up that valise, make sure he get a good look at it. About the third morning, that lemonzene stop. Driver says, 'What you got in the suitcase, brother?' I say, 'Dirt.' 'Dirt?' 'That right. Dirt on all the big players on Mr. Steinbrenner team, the World Champion New York Yankees.'

"'Mr. Steinbrenner ain't interested,' the driver say and pull through the gate. But ten, fifteen minutes later he come back and ast to see inside that valise. I open it up a crack, pull out a file on the New York manager, all full of made-up lies. 'Got one on every player,' I say, and stick the file back in the grip. 'How much you want for this stuff?' the driver say. I say, 'Man, I don't sell, but this what I tell, don't fret, 'cause I want to bet.' 'What that jive suppose to mean?' 'Mean this,' I say. 'Mean I bet Mr. Steinbrenner all the dirt in this little traveling bag 'gainst his nice black lemonzene I can strike out the three top hitters in they Yankee lineup.'

"Well, sir," Stan continued, "that big old bodyguard driver start to laugh. Then he tell me Mr. Steinbrenner don't never bet or gamble. So I say fine and get ready to go 'bout my business, me. But the driver call out, hey, *he* might bet me, gentleman agreement, if Mr. S authorize him. He tell me come back with the suitcase next morning, seven sharp. Before any fans or press get there."

Stan took a big bite of the store-bought cake. Louisianne was tossing a baseball from hand to hand. Abruptly the ball vanished and she looked at her father, waiting for him to tell the rest. Teddy had been staring out the window at Devil Dan, who was surveying his property line where it cut close to Gran's barn. Now he, too, shifted his gaze to Stan. Everyone, even Bill, was listening.

"So what happened?" E.A. said.

"Well, next morning I show up, go out on the mound with no warm-up. Slam bam, thank you, Stan — three Yankees up, three Yankees down. Nine pitches, nine strikes. Old George, he so disgusted he throw the lemonzene keys at my head and away I go."

"Wow!" Gypsy said. "That's the con of all cons."

"He furious at his players for striking out," Stan chortled. "Fine them a thousand apiece. Me, I have the lemon painted pink, and there it sits." Stan gestured with his fork at the battered, cotton-candy-colored limo in Gran's dooryard. It was hitched to a silver camper trailer with CAJUN STAN THE BASEBALL MAN painted on the side in rainbow colors, both camper and limo displaying Louisiana plates.

"That the best con of my life," Stan said. "Worth going to prison for all them other cons."

"No," Teddy said, watching Dan fold up his transit in the dusk.

"No?"

"No," Teddy said. "Nothing's worth that."

Teddy looked at Gypsy. Then he did something E.A. had never heard him do before. He spoke directly to her, by name. "Is it, Gypsy?"

Gypsy shrugged. "I wouldn't know," she said, and hurriedly got up and began to clear the table. If E.A. hadn't known her better, he'd have sworn she was fighting off tears.

In the awkward silence that followed, Gran wheeled herself back into her bedroom off the kitchen and Bill went out to his trailer behind the barn. Then Stan said, "Louisianne and I going to get over to that New York State fair, con some would-be baseball players out of they money, we gots to get a move on it. You ready, girl?"

Louisianne nodded. Two minutes later they were gone, having departed almost as suddenly and unaccountably as they had appeared.

Gran's place felt lonely after the Paiges pulled out of the dooryard, the single red taillight on Stan's camper winking out of sight as they passed Devil Dan's and turned toward the railroad crossing. Standing with his father on the stoop in the mountain twilight, E.A. missed them sharply, especially Louisianne.

Teddy lit a cigarette. Then he turned to E.A. "All right, Ethan."

"All right what?"

"It's time."

"To leave for Boston? I thought we were going in the morning."

"We are."

Teddy took a drag on his Lucky. "Tell your ma I need to make a call from her phone, will you?" he said. "It's time to settle up with old Davis."

Teddy and E.A. entered Dan's machinery shed, E.A. holding Gypsy's Battery Beam. Five minutes earlier, Devil Dan and R.P. had left the junkyard towing Dan's huge Bucyrus Erie crane on a flatbed. They had just received an urgent call from the Memphremagog state police barracks dispatcher (as the caller identified himself), telling Dan there had been a wreck on I-91 just south of the Canadian border. Two cars had plunged over a one-hundred-foot bank into the Kingdom River, the dispatcher said, and Dan and his Hook had to get there "immediately if not sooner."

The Blade loomed up in E.A.'s deer-jacking light. It was even bigger than he'd thought. Teddy climbed up into the cab and did something under the dash. Suddenly the engine began to rumble.

Ethan bounded up the steps and stood next to Teddy, in the leather driver's seat behind the controls. As Teddy eased the Blade out of the shed, E.A. was amazed by how high off the ground they were. The engine throbbed the way airplane engines in the movies do. The cab smelled like the inside of a brand-new car, like the deputy's new truck when he picked up E.A. and Gypsy to interrogate them. It smelled like the leather of a baseball glove and the Windex Gran made Gypsy use on the kitchen windows so she could spy on E.A. working out at Fenway.

E.A. and Teddy started along the Canada Post Road, the headlights of the earthmover illuminating a wide swatch of forest as they headed up Allen Mountain. They passed Gran's maple sugar orchard, passed the lane leading to E.A. and Gypsy's special place and the fork to Warden's Bog. Wild Woodsflower Gulf fell away to their right. Then they were on top of the mountain, parked beside Long Tom.

It was a warm night, the moon full and bright. Far below, Lake Memphremagog shimmered in the moonglow, which reflected off the cliffs above the water. Except for the light of a single motorboat two or three miles to the north, Memphremagog seemed as empty as it had been that day in 1770 when the Colonel first laid eyes on it and claimed every last drop of water, including the four-fifths of the lake that lay in Canada, for the Republic of Vermont.

"Hop out," Teddy said. "I'll be with you directly."

Ethan got down, and the Blade began moving along the concrete base of Long Tom.

"Teddy!" E.A. yelled. But his father was already emerging from the cab, jumping lightly onto the ground as the sixty-ton dozer unhurriedly nosed over the edge of the cliff. A third of the way down, it bounced blade-first off the face of the escarpment. Halfway to the lake it crashed into a projecting ledge. The cab sheared off and continued to fall separately, like a detached space capsule. The dozer hit the face of the cliff once more, dislodging a thunderous avalanche of boulders. Then it struck the surface of the lake, sending a geyser fifty feet high and disappearing into three hundred feet of dark and icy water.

★ THE LEGENDARY SPENCE ★

IT WAS UNUSUALLY hot that summer in Boston and in the other cities of the American League as well. Many days, and many nights too, were hotter then E.A. had ever thought possible. By the time he'd thrown five minutes of BP, he was wringing wet. Though his arm stayed loose and strong, just breathing was an effort in the sweltering weather. At home in Kingdom County there might be three or four really hot days a year, usually right in the middle of haying time. But northern Vermont heat was nothing like this heat, which radiated up from the crowded sidewalks and off the sides of the soaring buildings that blocked any breeze there might be and hung oppressively inside Fenway Park well into the evening.

The weather was just one of the unpleasant surprises for Ethan when he joined the Sox. He hated having to pitch BP day in and day out, never getting the nod from Spence for so much as a single inning in a real game. He hated having to answer the same questions from sportswriters in every city. Questions about growing up in the backwoods of Vermont and pitching to imaginary hitters and a swinging tire, about never playing high school baseball and subsisting on poached venison and moose meat and woodchucks. Though he liked his roommate, Sally Salvadore, he didn't like being odd man out in the clubhouses and hotels because of his age. Hardest of all was the terrible homesickness he felt for Gypsy and Teddy and the Colonel and even Gran and Bill. It swept over him several times a day like a debilitating nausea and kept him from sleeping at night and wasn't even entirely absent when he was throwing BP. True, he talked regularly on the phone to Gypsy and, occasionally and briefly, to Teddy. But he was now in a different world, about which they knew nothing and he as yet knew little. He looked forward to the last game of the regular season, with New York at Fenway, because Spence had given him two complimentary tickets, and Gypsy and Teddy were planning to drive down in the Late Great Patsy Cline.

In early September the Sox swept Seattle and moved a game ahead of New York in the American League East. Then they traveled to the Bronx, into the lion's den, and won three out of four. Riddled by injuries, without their Cy Young Award winner, without their American League MVP left-fielder, without their beloved shortstop, with the demise of their franchise hanging over their heads with every pitch, every at-bat, every chance in the field, the team somehow kept winning.

It had truly been a season not so much of impossible dreams as of downright miracles. The minor-leaguers Spence had brought up from Providence and Portland and Bristol, twenty- and twenty-one-year-olds who'd never faced major-league pitching, had played like seasoned veterans. They'd hit everything the opposing pitchers had thrown at them, then on defense had pulled home runs back out of the stands and turned game-losing singles up the middle into game-winning double plays. The dwindling pitching staff had shaved the corners and moved the ball in and out and up and down and, with Sally's uncanny ability to know what the batter was expecting and to call for something different, bluffed their way to one win after another. The Alien Man alone had won eight games in a row.

In most arenas of human endeavor, the Legendary Spence was probably the biggest optimist in the city of Boston. His romanticism even extended to the aesthetics of baseball. "Long's it has natural grass, I call a baseball diamond the most beautiful sight on the face of the earth," he announced at least once during every game. And of his wretchedly failed marriages, he continued to maintain that he could not understand "what went haywire," since after baseball, fishing, the macaw, and ice-cold beer in a tall red, white, and blue can, he had thought more of each of the three Mrs. Spencers than of anything else in the world. Yet despite these proofs of his boundless capacity for hopefulness, when it came to the chances of winning or losing a baseball contest, G. P. Spencer was a clear-eyed realist.

He was everywhere, chivvying his players and the umpires and the opposition. He had runners tag up and score after short fly balls. He used the hit-and-run and bunt with two outs, had his hitters swinging on first pitches and on 3–0 counts. In a thousand Spencerian ways, he defied all conventional baseball wisdom.

And he was lucky. In a game at Fenway with the bases loaded and Boston ahead by three runs in the top of the ninth, a high drive by Cleveland's cleanup batter that had grand-slam home run written all over it struck a seagull over second base and dropped into the glove of the Sox shortstop. After a prolonged and furious argument, in which Spence danced *two* hornpipes at home plate, it was deemed a ground-rule double, scoring two of the three runs Cleveland needed to tie the game. On came the Alien and struck out the next batter on a slider that swerved half a foot, stranding runners on second and third and giving Boston the win. The following night, with the bases loaded and the game tied, Sally smashed a high Baltimore chop off the dirt in front of the plate. He crossed first three steps ahead of the catcher's throw while the winning run scored. Boston hit pop flies over the Green Monster, easy outs in any other ball park. Their opponents drilled singles off the wall that would have been home runs anywhere but Fenway.

But even the Legendary Spence could have only so many miracles in him, and everyone in the Nation wondered how he could possibly summon any more when, as in '78, the division title came down to one game between the two fiercest rivals in baseball, the New York Yankees and the Boston Red Sox, with the Sox absolutely out of rested pitchers.

On Spence's desk beside his macaw was a small portable tape player, a present from a well-wisher in Newton, from which blared the voices of Willie Nelson and Waylon Jennings, singing "Luckenbach, Texas." Spence was tipped back in his office chair with a clean blue-and-white-checked engineer's bandanna over his face to keep out the light so he could think properly about the up-coming game. When the song ended, he reached out, groped for the switch, and turned off the tape player. "Thank God above," the macaw said.

Spence said, "I like them old honky-tonk numbers, even if the bird here don't. The ones you don't hear over the airwaves so much. You ever been there?"

Sally Salvadore, standing across the desk from his manager, looked at him blankly. After a minute, he said, "Where?"

"Luckenbach, Texas."

"No."

"Me neither," Spence said from beneath the bandanna. "Not really been there. I been through once or twice. But the winning-est active manager in baseballdom, you'd think he'd be able to say he'd gotten away just once to visit Luckenbach. You wouldn't think doing that or going fishing down in Florida" — he jerked his thumb at the picture of the old man in his Sox cap, standing beside the long-billed marlin — "would be out of reach for a fella that's managed the Boston Red Sox to one thousand nine hundred and eighty-four career wins."

"All that going to change now you got another good young pitcher ready to go," Sally said. "That new kid, from Vermont, she ready. She walk right through New York's lineup. You get you Se-ries ring, get to go fisha, go to Lucken with Willa and Waylie. This the year, chief."

"This is the year, all right," Spence said, feeling around in the picnic cooler beside his chair. He pulled out a tall boy, which he held out toward the macaw. The bird inclined its head and in a sin-gle vicious swipe ripped off the tab with its beak.

"Because win or lose, my friend, this old baseball whore is on his way after it's over," Spence continued. "To repeat. Win or lose. A little ice-cold beer, a little fisha, a little honky-tonk music."

"You throw the kid, we don't lose," Sally said. "I guarantee it."

"Ain't no such a thing as a guarantee in this game," Spence said. "You know that, Sally."

"Go with the kid," Sally wheedled. "We win today, win the playoffs and Series, you go catch you nice blue fish. Have some confida in the kid."

"Oh," Spence said, adjusting the bandanna so he could drink his beer, "I have plenty of confida in the kid. That ain't the difficulty. I just got *more* confida in them boys from New York."

"New York, number one," the macaw said.

Spence removed the bandanna, poured the remaining half of the pounder down his throat, and said, "What do you think, Curse? Who gets the ball tonight? My number-four knuckleball pitcher with the tired arm and pulled hamstring or Mr. Confida in Person from the Great State of Vermont?"

"Bud, the king of beer," the bird replied.

"You got that right, pal," Spence said.

"Give her the ball, chief," Sally said. "I been watching, she ready. She don't disappoint."

Spence sat up straight. He set the empty pounder down on the corner of his army surplus desk. Very carefully, he folded up his engineer's bandanna, patted down his bald head, wiped the sweat off his big, red, earnest face, and put the bandanna in his back pocket. "She don't disappoint," he said. "Well, now, Mr. Sally. I have managed the Boston Red Sox for the past twenty years and more, and I believe I could tell you a thing or two about disappointment. For instance, I could tell you what it is like to win one thousand nine hundred and eighty-four games and five division titles and three American League pennants and nary a World Serious. I could tell you what it is like to be fired on down the road twice by a man who died right here on these very grounds a year ago when that pop fly got up in the sun and played hob with our Gold Glove outfielder. And how that man's sorry son took over, and the first thing he did, he all but give away three of the premier players in the game today and then opened negotiations with a gang of picture-show radicals to move the franchise west if we don't win the Serious. And I could even tell you what a disappointment it might be if, by some one-in-a-billion chance, we do win the championship and I get rehired and have to come back and do this all over again."

"We win, you quit. Retire. Go to Florida," Sally suggested.

"Nope," Spence said. "I'm a lot of things, but I'm no quitter. I got a better plan."

"Spence has a plan," the Curse said.

"You're damn right he does," Spence said. Then, loud enough to be heard out in the players' dressing room, "ALLEN. GET YOUR SKINNY ASS IN HERE!"

As E.A. stepped through the doorway a minute later, Spence reached into his bottom desk drawer and got out the brand-new baseball that he'd intended all along, in the boldest move of the boldest season of an astonishingly bold career, to give the boy.

He stood up and flipped Ethan the ball. "Kid," he roared, "go get them pinstriped sons of bitches!"

Dusk was falling sooner now. By 6:30 that evening the stadium lights were on, and when E.A. came out of the tunnel from the clubhouse onto the playing field, his first impression was of color. The Home of the Boston Red Sox was the most colorful place he'd ever seen. The ball park as it filled up reminded him of the Kingdom in the fall, with each bright, short-sleeved shirt and top and cap a different splash of foliage on an autumnal mountainside. The square, gleaming white bases, the snowy chalk lines newly laid down on the red dirt of the infield, the shimmering emerald of the natural grass under the lights, the deeper green of the fabled wall in left field, the cardinal red of the players' socks — it was all dazzling.

And Ethan, warming up along the right-field sideline, just beyond first base, was excited by the presence of Gypsy Lee and Teddy, just up the third-base line and five rows back. What was a bit unsettling was that the Sox's owner, Maynard Junior, was sitting in a box several rows in back of first, in a section known in Fenway as the "posse" — a cadre of several hundred hard-core Red Sox rooters notorious for being as tough on Sox players who made miscues as on their opponents.

E.A. couldn't help feeling nervous. But he did not doubt that he could throw his 21st-Century Limited fastball past the Yankee hitters, at least for several innings, and he only wished that Stan and Louisianne could be here to see him.

He loved the steady rumbling and buzzing from the stands,

which he knew would rise to a thundering crescendo once the game began, punctuated by the sharp cries of the vendors — *pop-corrn, cold bee-ah hee-ah* — and the shouted advice and criticism from the posse. Nearby, in the Sox dugout, the Alien was explaining the physics of a breaking baseball to the macaw, who listened attentively. Spence was patrolling the perimeter of the outfield with his trash stick and a black plastic bag.

E.A. flipped over his glove hand to indicate to his warm-up catcher that a curve was coming. *Hold it gentle, the way you'd hold your galfriend's titty,* he heard Teddy say in his mind. The spinning breaking pitch dropped straight down six inches. With the Limited to set it up, that should do the trick.

"E.A., E.A., E.A." Earl and the boys were chanting his name from the bleachers in deep center field. The whole Outlaw team was on hand, all but Moonface, who had refused to leave his post atop the factory. Though he knew he wouldn't be able to hear them once the game began, Ethan was glad to have the boys here. As game time approached, he'd have been glad to have Gran and Old Lady Benton in the stands.

His fastball was popping, his curve was sharp, his arm was loose. The Alien ambled out of the dugout, watched him for a minute, nodded approvingly.

The applause when Ethan was announced as starting pitcher was polite. But as he trotted out to the mound, it rose to a prolonged ovation, and he understood that the fans were trying to help him. Psych him up. Suddenly he was scared. What if he couldn't find the strike zone? Or New York's leadoff man blasted a home run off him? A host of devastating possibilities raced through his head. Quickly he looked up at the grandstand and found Teddy, who touched his Sox cap. E.A. touched his cap back, and then threw his first warm-up pitch, as the Yankees' great leadoff hitter, a Cuban who got down the line to first like Willie Mays, walked out to the on-deck circle swinging two bats.

So far this season, New York's leadoff man had been hit by a pitch sixteen times. Tonight he crowded the plate even more than usual. E.A. was tempted to put one right under his chin. But while he'd have loved to establish with his first pitch that he couldn't be intimidated into giving up one square inch of the strike zone to an aggressive batter, he didn't want to risk putting the top base stealer in the American League on first just to make a point. What had Teddy told him when he'd pitched to the Yankee lineup in their imaginary games at home? "Their number-one man will crowd the plate, Ethan. But don't hit him early in the game. He'll be taking the first pitch anyway. He always makes the pitcher throw him a strike before he swings. Throw him a fastball right down the middle. The bat'll never leave his shoulder."

As the cheering intensified, E.A. put his right foot on the rubber and looked in at Sally for his sign. Sally signaled for the fastball.

E.A. went into his compact wind-up, rocked back, and exploded forward, just the way Teddy and Stan had taught him, to the screaming of nearly forty thousand people. Sally's glove never moved as the ball slammed into it like a stick of dynamite exploding. Up shot the umpire's right hand. The radar reading on the scoreboard flashed 96 mph.

"A fine way to start a big-league pitching career," the Voice of the Sox said, straining not to sound too excited, while up in Kingdom Common, Late and Early exchanged glances and Fletch looked straight ahead, and in the right-field bleachers at Fenway Earl and the boys, already two sheets to the wind, leaped up and hollered as if the Sox had won the world championship.

Then something magical happened. Ethan E.A. Allen, standing alone on the pitcher's mound, the top of the world when things are going well, the loneliest place imaginable when they aren't, forgot all about the crowd. He forgot about the umpire. He forgot about the up-again, down-again Red Sox tradition and saw only the crimson bull's-eye in the middle of Sally's black glove, framed by the catcher's fluorescent orange chest and leg protectors. He could have been pitching at home in the meadow. Or inside Gran's barn, throwing to his tire or Ted Williams's strike zone. Sally asked for a low curve on the outside corner, and the Yankees' leadoff hitter bounced out weakly to first.

The roar from the crowd rose higher, but E.A., breaking a few steps to his left in case he needed to cover the bag, was amazed by how fast the runner had gotten down the line and how close he made the play. As Stan had warned him, this was a different ball game from any he'd played before.

It was a new experience for the hitters, too, to face a pitcher who consistently threw over ninety-five miles an hour and could spot the ball on a dime. New York's two hitter, the best contact man in the major leagues, went down swinging on three straight fastballs, bringing the entire park to its feet.

E.A. got up 0–2 on the number-three batter. Sally signaled for him to waste a fastball up at eye level, hoping the guy might swing anyway, as his predecessor had. But E.A. shook Sally off until he came back with the slider out; the hitter swung four inches over it, and the Fenway ovation lasted for thirty seconds after E.A. hit the dugout.

⚾

"How's your arm feel, kid?"

"It feels like pitching nine innings."

"Now he wants to manage the team," Spence told the macaw. To E.A. he started to say, "I'll decide how long —"

Suddenly Spence lunged up out of the dugout, shouting "Go! Go, go, go!" The Sox leadoff hitter had cracked the first pitch of the inning on a line over the center-fielder's head.

With the runner safely on third and no outs, Spence turned back to E.A. "Next inning, I don't want you shaking Sally off no more. You leave him to call the pitches."

"I never shake off my catcher more than three or four times an inning," E.A. said.

"WELL, THAT IS THREE OR FOUR TIMES AN INNING TOO MANY!" Spence roared, his fiery face an inch away from E.A.'s. "NO MORE SHAKING SALLY OFF. PERIOD."

The Sox's two and three hitters both struck out, bringing Sally to the plate with the runner still on third and two outs. On the fourth pitch, up on the count 2–1, Sally blasted a line drive twenty feet up the Green Monster. The Yankees' left-fielder played the carom expertly, holding Sally to a single, so what would have been a two-run homer in any other baseball park resulted in only one run. Boston's five hitter grounded out, ending the inning. But there was E.A.'s lead, and it looked like the Sox had their hitting shoes on today.

E.A. couldn't remember what he'd done with his glove. As he searched for it, he felt, in between the bone and the muscle on his upper right arm, a stinging blow. "Good job out there," said the lummox, who'd slipped into the dugout while Spence had his back turned. "Very nice job out there, sonny boy. Keep it up." And before E.A. knew it, Maynard Junior had knuckle-punched him again, hard, right in the same place.

E.A.'s arm was still sore from where the thirty-eight-year-old boy owner had punched it. But the Yankees' leadoff hitter in the top of the second was far behind his first two pitches, and although Sally wanted him to waste a pitch, Ethan was sure he could strike him out with a slider on the corner. He threw the slider, and the hitter waved at it and missed. Caught by surprise, Sally didn't get his glove down, and by the time he caught up with the passed third strike, the runner was on first.

E.A. was unsettled. Not because of the runner, but because he realized that if he'd been determined to throw the slider instead of Sally's high fastball, he should have shaken off the catcher's signal and let him know what *was* coming. Not only had he disobeyed Spence, now glaring at him from the top step of the dugout, he'd done it in the worst possible way. Instead of one down and the bases empty, he had a runner on first and no outs. The crowd was buzzing. They were still on his side. But they wanted a strikeout or a double play, and this being Fenway, they fully expected one or the other.

The Yankees' number-five man batted from the left side of the plate. He quite frequently struck out, but he was popular in New York for his tremendous arm from center field and for his tape-measure home runs, one of which had recently struck the façade on top of the upper deck in right field at Yankee Stadium, near the spot where, many years before, Mickey Mantle's record home run had hit. As he stepped into the batter's box, Sally called time and came out to the mound.

"Look, kid," he said. "You want to shake me off, go ahead. Just make sure I know what's coming." Without waiting for a reply, the All-Star catcher said, "Now, this next guy got very quick hands. We don't want to let her see two fastballs in a row. So we going to mix it up. Maybe get her to bounce into a double play."

Sally went back to the plate. E.A. glanced around at his in-fielders, back at double-play depth. Then he went into his set position and leaned in for his sign. Sally wanted heat on the fists. E.A. checked the runner, not usually a threat to steal, and threw the ball right where Sally held his glove, up and in, 98 mph. The lefty fouled it straight back into the screen.

Sally called for the curve on the knees on the outside corner. But Teddy's motto had always been go right at the hitter with your best pitch. Challenge the man. If that meant going to the batter's strength, so be it. E.A. shook off Sally until he came around with the fastball again, Sally's finger hesitating before it went down, and he threw the same pitch as before except that this one tailed back toward the center of the plate and New York's five hitter did what no batter had ever done before in the history of baseball in Boston. He hit a fair ball out of Fenway Park in right field.

Ethan had seen mighty home runs before and had even had a few hit off him. But never anything like this. The ball was twenty feet high when it traveled over the red-painted seat more than five hundred feet from home plate where Ted Williams's record homer had crushed the straw hat of a fan. It cleared the façade with feet to spare.

Spence never moved. He just stared at E.A. from the top step of the dugout, continuing to stand there and stare as, shades of

Calvin Schiraldi in that fateful game against the Mets, E.A. gave up two more hits to the next two batters, a hard ground ball between third and short and a line drive up the middle. The crowd was now booing and hollering for Spence to get him out of there. E.A. had lost it. In front of his parents, his hometown baseball team, thirty-six thousand live fans, and millions of TV viewers, he'd gone from untouchable to unable to get an out. He walked the next batter on four pitches, his arm throbbing steadily from where the lummox had knuckle-punched it, but that didn't excuse shaking Sally off. And now, down on the count 2–1, with the bases loaded and no outs, here came Spence, tapping his right arm for the aging Alien in the bullpen, the great Yankee-killer, who had a sore arm himself. Meanwhile the crowd screamed bloody murder, enraged with E.A., enraged with Spence for starting him, enraged with the hideous, unspeakable, inevitable bad luck of the Boston Red Sox.

"Back to Vermont, woodchuck!" he heard the lummox holler. That was when the chant started. First the lummox, then a few of the nearby posse, then the entire section behind first base, spreading out and up through the stadium like a barn fire whooshing through dry hay, thousands upon thousands of voices lifted in derision.

"How much wood could a woodchuck chuck,
If a woodchuck could chuck wood?"

Over and over, the entire stadium up and chanting. Spence, his face as grim as E.A. had ever seen a man's face in his life, held out his hand for the ball. E.A. handed it to him and, head hanging, walked off the field to thousands of fans chanting that hateful woodchuck verse and showering him with debris. In all of his baseball fantasies at home in Kingdom County, he'd never dreamed of anything like this.

"'I WANNA GO HOME. I wanna go home. Oh, how I wanna go home.'"

The drunk in the black cowboy hat on the barstool to E.A.'s right had played Bobby Bare's classic "Detroit City" on the tavern jukebox six times. The same song Gypsy had sung on the water tank the day she'd told E.A. about Teddy racing the train. Now the drunk began to sing along.

> "I wanna go home. I wanna go home.
> Oh, how I wanna go home."

E.A. knew exactly how the guy in the song felt. He, too, wanted to go home, home to the Green Mountains of Vermont. What's more, he wanted to stay there for the rest of his sorry life. Never mind that the Alien Man, sore arm and all, had come in and shut down New York for eight innings, until Sally's three-run homer in the ninth won the game and the Eastern Division championship for the Sox. Never mind that the entire city of Boston was now going crazy. For Ethan E.A. Allen, this was the worst night of his life. He'd gone from pitching a perfect inning to pitching like what he now knew he was, a hick woodchuck from the sticks who'd almost certainly never throw another ball off a major-league mound in his life.

"'I wanna go home,'" the drunk started up again. "I wanna nother roun'. You ready for another roun', old buddy?"

Staring at the faded autographed pictures of old Red Sox stars over the bar — Earl Wilson, who in June of '63 was the first African American to pitch an American League no-hitter, Johnny Pesky, the great manager Dick Williams, and several dozen others — thinking that *his* picture would never be there, E.A. nodded.

"Ethan."

He whirled around on the barstool. Somehow Teddy and Gypsy had located him in this alleyway dive off Boylston Street, wedged in between a pawnshop and a bail-bond office, a place so out of it that the only other customer, even on this night of all nights, was the singing drunk.

"Listen, Ethan," Teddy said, slipping onto the stool to his left. "You might not think so, but you done fine out there tonight. You had a great inning your first time out. Then you had an off inning. That's all. That's baseball. Don't shake Sally off from now on." Teddy grinned. "That's why he's catching for the Boston Red Sox and I'm running a lathe in a bat factory in Vermont."

"Who's this guy?" the drunk in the hat said, leaning out around E.A. and staring at Teddy. "Some homeless? He looks like some homeless."

"Ethan," Gypsy said, giving him a hug. "Listen to your dad. He knows what he's talking about."

E.A. had never heard Gypsy refer to Teddy as his dad before.

"Sweetie," Gypsy said, taking a sip of his beer, "you know what I think you should do next time they start up with that woodchuck bullshit, pardon my language?"

E.A. was pretty sure there wouldn't *be* a next time. The next time he pitched a baseball game would probably be for the Outlaws, back in Kingdom Common.

But Gypsy said, "I'm going to tell you how to get an edge on the crowd, honey boy."

"Hey," the drunk said to E.A., "you drinking with me or talking with them?"

"I thought getting an edge on people was Teddy's department," E.A. said.

"What you do, hon," Gypsy continued, "next time that woodchuck business starts, you spit in their soup. That's what Gran used to tell me when kids at school ragged on me. You spit in their soup by enjoying it."

"Enjoy having thousands of maniacs calling me a wood-chuck?"

"How much wood could a woodchuck chuck," Detroit City sang at the top of his lungs.

Teddy was staring straight into the mirror behind the bar at the drunk.

"Absolutely, baby doll," Gypsy said. "Here's what you do. You remember who you are. You're Gypsy Lee Allen's boy, which makes you one-quarter Gran Allen's grandboy. That gives you twenty-five percent pure WYSOTT Allen meanness to draw on when you need it. Do you think Gran would care what the grand-stand shouted at her?"

"She'd probably like it," E.A. said.

"If woodshuck could shuck wood," warbled the stumblebum. Teddy's eyes, the color of ice on an asphalt road, had not left the florid countenance of the singing drunk in the mirror.

"Gran would *definitely* like it," Gypsy said. "She'd enjoy hearing those idiots holler at her and make fools out of themselves."

"Who you calling fools and idiots?" the drunk said.

"Were you at that game tonight?" Gypsy said.

"'Course I was," the guy in the cowboy hat said.

"Were you calling my boy here a woodchuck?"

"'Course. Everybody was."

"Well, then I'm calling you an asshole." Gypsy turned back to E.A. "Red Sox fans are all as mad as hatters, Ethan. I've always suspected it, but I never truly realized it until today. Turning on their own players. Shouting derogatory epithets. Even we WYSOTT Allens don't do that to our own. If the Sox ever should win the Series, hon, their fans will burn this city down. I really believe they will, the crazy sons of bitches."

"Who you callin' sons bitches?" the drunk said. "You callin' the goo' people of Boston sons bitches?"

Teddy leaned out around E.A. and gave the drunk a hard, direct look.

"What you staring at?" the drunk said to Teddy. "What you staring at, mister? You don't like my hat? Why don' you try knock it off?"

The drunk grabbed a fistful of E.A.'s shirt and said, "Drink up, Slick." As Teddy started to stand up, Gypsy yanked the drunk off his stool. He swung at her wildly and missed, and she knocked him cold with an uppercut to the jaw.

The barkeep reached for the phone. But Teddy laid a twenty-dollar bill beside E.A.'s beer glass and said they were gone.

On the way out, E.A. said to Teddy, "Well, you going to pump me sober?"

"Nope," Teddy said. "Way I figure, son, after a night like the one you've had, a man deserves a few beers if it'll make him feel any better."

Then Teddy and Gypsy and E.A. headed out into the packed streets of the celebrating city, whose team not even the most devoted members of the Red Sox Nation could have predicted would beat the Yankees and reach the playoffs.

40

MUCH LESS the World Series. Yet magically, miraculously, incredibly, that is exactly where the Red Sox found themselves in mid-October. Up in Vermont, over coffee at the Common Hotel early on the morning that Moon made it official by putting up on the Green Monster the words SOX TAKE SEVENTH GAME FROM TWINS, WIN PENENT, Judge Charlie Kinneson told his brother the editor and Prof Benton and the elderly bat boys that yes, Boston was on the most remarkable roll he could remember. But the preponderance of the evidence led him to only one conclusion: no team in baseball was going to win four of seven games from Boston's opponent in the Series that fall, the New York Mets. The Mets, who had taken three of four games from the Sox back in early July during interleague play, were loaded with talent and depth. For starters, they had the best pitcher in baseball, Mario "Pancho" Villa. In addition, they had two other twenty-game winners on their pitching staff, the fearsome Japanese submarine pitcher, Suzika Koyoto, and the fastest pitcher in the National League, Doc Sweetwater Jones, who consistently threw 98 mph and patterned himself on Sal "the Barber" Maglie, throwing on the fists, grazing the hitter's chin, knocking his knees out from under him, and then, when he moved off the plate, spotting the ball on the outside corner where he couldn't have reached it with a mop handle. And they had a tall, pinch-faced long-ball hitter and Gold Glove first baseman named Miller Jacks.

Jacks had played briefly for the Sox six years before. Spence had personally run him off the field during a night game with the Orioles in Camden Yards for not hustling out a comebacker to the pitcher. Jacks had just stood at the plate, disgusted, while the pitcher threw him out, and Spence had flown out of the dugout and grabbed him by the neck and the seat of his uniform pants and charged into the tunnel with him, hurling him into the dressing room and trading him to New York the next morning. The old man had backed Spence one hundred percent, even paying the manager's hefty league fine for attacking one of his own players. Afterward, as they watched the tape of Spence giving Miller Jacks the bum's rush in front of fifty thousand delighted Baltimore fans, the old man repeatedly pumped Spence's hand and said it was his finest moment in baseball. As far as Spence was concerned, not running out a ground ball was a cardinal sin, tantamount to, say, badmouthing Willie Nelson. Though it was about what he'd expect from a fella who had a last name for a first name and a first name, or something close to it, for a last name. Spence was greatly looking forward to taking Jacks and the Mets to school in the Series and then cashing in his baseball career forever and going fishing.

Late on the Friday night before the opening game of the Series, E.A., who since his debacle against the Yankees had been relegated to throwing BP again, lay in bed in his hotel room listening to Sally snore and thinking about baseball. How he'd run on the village green in the evenings to build up his legs when he was just a tyke. Gotten the game-winning hit off the four-eyed schoolteacher in the championship game against Pond in the Sky. And thrown all those no-hitters against the Outlaws' rivals. Sometimes in the late innings, when a game was in the bag, he'd pitched like Dazzy Vance of the old Brooklyn Dodgers, tipping way back and shutting his eyes and hiding the ball behind his leg so it seemed to come at the hitter out of deep center field. Or like Walter Johnson, who came from the side faster than anyone but Feller had ever come over the top. He could kick his leg higher than Juan Marichal, spin around like the great El Tiante, and throw an eephus pitch like Rip Sewell's or the Alien's, up, up, and up, then right down over the plate, a perfect strike, while the batter watched with his mouth open. And that's when the inspiration came to him.

"I ain't about to be badgered, not today of all days," Spence told E.A. the next morning, just before the Sox were set to take the field for BP. "If you're here to badger me about pitching, kid, we've been over all that before. Like I said, you've got a future with the game. But not this year. You need a season at Bristol, then one at Providence, working on getting that fourth pitch. Now skedaddle. I got to get the boys ready for that underhanded pitcher going against us."

"I can help with that."

"You're a hitting coach now?" Spence said.

"No," E.A. said. "But I can pitch BP just like Koyoto."

Spence's face turned the shade of a cooked lobster. Just before he blew, E.A. said, "Watch and see for yourself."

Then he left, fast, before something really unfortunate happened.

E.A. told the groundskeepers he'd throw BP off the mound that morning, and he asked them to roll the batting cage up to home plate. As Sally stood in to take his raps, E.A. stepped toward third base, swung his arm in an arc with his fingers nearly brushing the dirt and his arm sweeping underhanded across his body so that the pitch appeared to shoot *up* toward the plate from out of the grass somewhere between the mound and third. Sally was so surprised that he let the ball go by, belt-high over the heart of the plate. Then he grinned and slammed the next one and the next one and the next one deep into the outfield gaps.

From the stands, a few early arrivers, members of the Fenway posse, called out something about woodchucks. E.A. thought of Gran, smiled, and pitched like Koyoto, duplicating the swinging arm and wicked sidewinding upshoot, and when the game started the Sox hitters jumped all over Koyoto and sent him to the showers in the top of the third inning.

SOX TAKE SERIES OPENER AT FENWAY 10–4 BEHIND ALIAN MAN, read the sign on the bat mill in Kingdom Common early the following morning.

"No small thanks to our boy," Earl No Pearl was saying over his first cup of coffee at the hotel. "According to the Voice of the Sox, yesterday old E.A. give the boys BP just like that Jap fella. I imagine he'll do it again today. Only it'll be Sweetwater, not Koyoto."

"E.A. can do Sweetwater?" Judge Charlie K said.

"Hell, yes, he can do Sweetwater," Earl said. "Here down to Woodsville one afternoon a year ago, E.A. thrown like Doc Sweetwater for two, three innings. Them New Hampshire boys couldn't touch him."

Sweetwater Jones stood six feet eight inches tall and weighed two hundred and fifty-five pounds. Besides leading Arkansas to a Division One National Championship in the College Baseball World Series, he'd caught more TD passes than any other player in the Razorbacks' history. He threw 98, 99, and occasionally 100 mph, coming straight over the top, with a peculiar hitch at the apex that disconcerted opposing hitters nearly as much as the fact that in the off-season he practiced dental surgery in Little Rock. Something about a dental surgeon who could make the ball sing like a high-powered dental drill as it hurtled toward the plate scared the daylights out of hitters. In his four seasons with the White Sox before going over to the Mets two years before, Doc Sweetwater had lost to Boston only once.

E.A. naturally came straight over the top himself, and he'd practiced Doc Sweetwater's idiosyncratic hitch, which was actually a very calculated hesitation — analogous, perhaps, to checking to be sure that the drill bit was positioned exactly where he wanted it before ratcheting it up to full bore. BP pitchers had tried, unsuccessfully, to mimic Sweetwater's hitch before, but E.A.

had him down perfectly, and on the last six or eight pitches of each hitter's raps, he threw his 21st-Century Limited to help them fine-tune their timing.

Sweetwater's change was only moderately effective — he had never mastered the technique of maintaining the same arm speed that he used for his fastball — and the second game of the World Series began with the Sox leadoff hitter taking the former Razor-back's first pitch high over the Green Monster. For Boston the game got better and better. In the meantime E.A. fumed silently in the dugout. He'd helped the Sox get their 3–0, 6–2, and 8–3 leads and their 8–5 win. Yet he still hadn't thrown a single pitch in a post-season game.

For the third game, in Shea Stadium, the Mets had saved their best pitcher, who had pitched the first, fourth, and part of the seventh game in their National League championship series against Atlanta. All-Star Mario "Pancho" Villa was the most unorthodox pitcher in major-league baseball. During the regular season he had compiled a record of 32–4.

Villa hailed from Mexico City and had grown up watching tapes of Luis Tiant and Fernando Valenzuela. Like Tiant, he spun around and looked at the center-field wall, tipping his chin sky-ward, leaning back nearly parallel to the ground, throwing his glove straight up and his left elbow out toward the batter and re-leasing his humming fastballs and sinking off-speed deliveries (it was said he had eight distinct breaking pitches) from no one knew exactly where. His release point was one of the great mysteries of baseball.

Pancho Villa, E.A. discovered, was difficult to imitate. He seemed to be part baseball pitcher and part prima ballerina, but that wasn't the tough part. The tough part was that he was also part illusionist. At some point during the Mexican hurler's serpen-tine gyrations, the hitter lost track not just of the baseball but of Villa's throwing hand, so that the ball seemed to come at them sometimes from the scoreboard, sometimes out of Villa's left spike, but more often than not out of thin air about halfway to the

246

plate. While E.A. rendered a fair approximation of Villa's motion at BP during the Sox off-day practice at Shea Stadium, and again the next morning before the game, what he couldn't duplicate was Villa's release point.

VEAH STYMEES SOX Moon's headline read the morning after the Mets took game three 6–0 behind Villa's three-hitter and Miller Jacks's two home runs and four RBIs. But the Alien won again the next night in New York, 7–4, and Boston now had three opportunities to win the one remaining game they needed to become World Champions.

The following night at Shea the Sox started where they'd left off the night before, taking a 4–1 lead into the bottom of the fifth inning behind a young pitcher named Sullivan, who had played at Boston College and started the year at Bristol. That was as far as they got, though. Jacks homered again in the fifth with two men on, then doubled in a run in the eighth, giving the Mets a 5–4 win. Sullivan, for his part, pulled a groin muscle in the last of the eighth and was out for the rest of the Series.

Back at Fenway in game six, Spence used two journeymen minor-league pitchers who had helped the team in August and September but were no match for the Mets' powerful lineup. Jacks, who was hitting .640 in the Series, was, if anything, inspired by the cascading boos from the Fenway Faithful each time he came to the plate. He blasted three home runs and knocked in seven runs, and the Mets won 18–2 behind Koyoto, with Villa scheduled to pitch the seventh game against the Alien, whose arm had been on ice for three days.

Having come so close that he could nearly taste the champagne (not that he liked it), the Legendary Spence appeared to have lost his last shot to win a championship and keep the Sox in Boston.

IN KINGDOM COMMON the morning of the seventh game of the World Series dawned bright and sunny, with the wind backing around out of the southeast. The wind snapped and popped the red-and-white bunting on the hotel railing and the second-story porches of the brick shopping block and the streamers on the Colonel's sword and hat and the huge, rippling banner on the bat factory saying, GO SOX. Teddy and Gypsy, leaving for Fenway in the Late Great Patsy Cline as the sun rose, were pushed all over the southbound lane of I-91 by the hard-gusting fall wind.

Across the state line, in the mountains of New Hampshire, the colors had peaked a week and a half before, then held there, the fall foliage more brilliant than anyone could remember, and the little towns along the interstate were colorful with bunting and with huge placards hanging outside businesses that said BOSTON RED SOX, NEXT WORLD CHAMPS. Closer to Boston, biplanes and crop-dusters trailed huge letters across the cloudless blue sky proclaiming BOSTON RED SOX WORLD CHAMPIONS. And every other car and pickup sported bumper stickers depicting the Curse of the Bambino saying BOSTON, NUMBER ONE. Life-size stuffed macaws in Sox uniforms, right down to bright red socks, were the most popular souvenir item throughout New England.

Outside Fenway the line of spectators waiting to get into the stadium stretched all the way down Boylston past Kenmore Square. People without tickets had packed into Lansdowne Street in hopes of acquiring a home-run ball.

Around noon E.A. started throwing BP. The wind in Fenway had dropped somewhat, and already several thousand fans were on hand to watch him pitch like Pancho Villa. Miller Jacks watched E.A.'s contortions from the sideline and sneered. So did the big lummox, sitting behind the Sox dugout with the wax effigy of his father, Maynard Senior, beside him.

E.A. had never heard anything like the tremendous rumbling of the crowd thronging into the stadium for game seven. It sounded like the ocean during a huge storm. Or like a hurricane approaching.

"Welcome to Fenway Park, folks, on a warm and very windy fall afternoon. A good afternoon for baseball, Red Sox fans," said the Voice of the Sox. "And what a day it is as the Boston Red Sox take the field against one of the most feared teams in recent baseball history, the National League Champion New York Mets, in the seventh game of the World Series . . ."

The waves of applause seemed to extend out into Boston and beyond, where Red Sox fans by the hundreds and thousands were watching or listening to this last hurrah. From the deep conifer forests of northern Maine to the seashore villages of Cape Cod to the resort towns of the White Mountains, New England looked half abandoned. Everyone who wasn't at the game was in front of a television screen or next to a radio.

The Gloucester fishing fleet was watching the game on small portable TVs. Bars were packed. Town halls and fire stations were showing the game on large-screen sets, and through the worn old speakers of the Philco, Gran could see the big tubes pulsing green and gold and red and silver. The colors reminded her of Christmas, a detestable time of year, in her estimation, when everyone except her pretended to be cheerful and generous.

". . . here in Fenway, as the Alien Man prepares to take the mound against Mario Villa, the mood can only be described as electric . . ."

Bucky Dent leaped up onto the warm, curved wooden top of Gran's old console and got ready for a long catnap, while back in

Boston the PA announcer boomed out, "And managing the Red Sox, the one, the only, the Legendary — Spence."

Out of the dugout, cap already off for the national anthem, came the winningest active manager in baseball, and cheers shook the hallowed old ball park to its foundation.

In and out, up and down the ladder, from more different angles than the Faithful had seen since the days of Luis Tiant, the Alien mixed his 75-mph fastball, his incomparable slider, his curve, and his change, pitching less with his throbbing arm than with his heart and simply outfoxing the Mets over the first three innings. By the time he set down the ninth hitter, the Fenway crowd was on its feet for every pitch, screaming as if that would be the pitch to bring them their championship.

Pancho Villa was as sharp as ever. E.A. imagined he could hear Villa's fastball humming all the way from the bullpen, where Spence had sent him to watch the game. Traveling from the pitcher's hand to the plate in just over a second, the baseball was a pale blur. Despite the BP session with Ethan that morning, the Sox hitters were unable to touch him. Going through their order for the first time, Villa struck out eight and got the ninth on a weak grounder to short. Even Sally was unable to muster anything more than a long foul ball against him.

The Mets left two men on base in the top of the fourth but failed to score. In the bottom of the inning, the Sox leadoff hitter walked. On a 2–1 count to the number-two hitter, a good contact man, Spence, coaching third, played one of his hunches by starting the runner. The two hitter got a fastball on the outside of the plate and drove it into the gap in right center, not far from where E.A. was standing in the bullpen. The crowd was up and thundering. New York's right-fielder chased down the rolling ball, his back still to the plate, as the lead runner rounded second. Spence never hesitated. Windmilling his arms, shouting, "Go go go," he waved the man around third, running a few steps beside him in foul territory.

The throw came in to the Mets' second baseman in shallow center, who relayed it to the catcher, and the runner slid under the tag to score. Villa came back and struck out the next three Sox hitters, but the way the Alien was pitching today, E.A. thought one run might well be enough.

In the top of the fifth, with two outs, Miller Jacks doubled into left center but was stranded when the Alien struck out the next hitter on a sky-high eephus pitch that brought down the house.

Spence went out to the third-base coaching box to yet another thunderous ovation. No more than half of the fans at Fenway could have known what a brilliant call he'd made on the hit-and-run that had gotten them their lead. But they all knew their team was ahead by a run, with the game half over.

They knew, too, when Villa struck out the side again, that a single run might have to suffice.

In the dining room of the Common Hotel, even the mounted cougar, moose, deer, and trout seemed to be watching the TV screen. At the end of each half inning the men leaned forward in their chairs and peered out the window to watch Moon, hunkered down on the bat factory roof like a gargoyle, Sox cap pulled low over his ears, stand up and climb his homemade ladder to post another big white wooden o in the proper column. Only then did the score become official in the Capital of the Red Sox Nation.

With two outs and two runners in scoring position in the bottom of the sixth, the score still Boston 1, New York 0, the plate umpire rang up Sally on a slider out and down. The ump had appeared to pause for a split second before raising his arm. Maybe it was this hesitation. Or maybe Spence was looking for an opportunity to ratchet up his team and the Fenway Faithful for the last three innings. But as the umpire's right hand rose heavenward and Sally headed back toward the dugout and the crowd howled its displeasure, Spence started down the base line from the coach's box, walking as slowly toward the plate as a gunfighter, holding on to his cap to keep the wind from blowing it off his head. The crowd's anguish changed to wild applause. Every man, woman, and child in Fenway Park, plus millions of TV viewers throughout New England, believed they knew what was coming next.

Sally ran back up the line to intercept his manager.

"Exactly where was that pitch?" Spence demanded.

Sally shrugged. "Close. Maybe a strike. My pitcher throws it, I want it for her. I don't pull the trigger. My bad, chief."

"Maybe a strike," Spence said. "And maybe not a strike." He stared hard at the umpire, who stared back. But this time, to everyone's astonishment, Spence did not press the issue.

In the top of the seventh, the Alien walked the Mets' leadoff hitter on four pitches. He struck out the next man, the crowd now chanting, "Eight, eight, eight" — eight outs to go. But the next man in the Mets' lineup hit a double off the right-field wall, sending the runner on first to third, and as much as he hated to go by the book, Spence did, signaling for the Alien to issue an intentional walk to set up a force at every base. The following batter hit the first pitch directly over second base on one sharp hop. The Sox's rookie shortstop dived for the ball, which miraculously disappeared in his outstretched glove, the glove coming down hard on top of the base, the shortstop bouncing to his feet like a trampoline artist and gunning out the batter by four steps, turning what had looked like a certain two-run single into an inning-ending double play.

Boston failed to score in the bottom of the seventh, and though the lummox would have loved to sneak into the Sox dugout and knuckle-punch the Alien Man in the arm, as he had E.A. during the division playoff with the Yankees, he couldn't figure out how to get away with it. He was still pretty sure that the Mets would get to the Alien anyway and that the Sox, true to form, would find yet another ingenious way to lose the game and the Series. History, after all, was on his side.

"SIX, SIX, SIX," chanted the crowd as the graying pitcher walked out to the mound and got ready to put the lid on the New York Mets for the next to last time that afternoon. The wind was blowing harder now, gusting first from one direction, then another. It added an eerie melody to the crowd noise, as if the old ball park were crying out to the team to do at last what they had failed to do for so many years, failed to do for a lifetime, actually, for fourscore years and more. At home in Vermont, E.A. thought, the deer and moose on Allen Mountain would be disoriented by the wind, which confused scents, made it difficult to hear predators and prey alike. He felt something of the same disorientation. What had the Colonel once told him? That it was no fun to fish or play baseball in the wind. It made what should be fun a chore.

In the top of the eighth, the Alien got the first two Mets on long flies. Both started out to straightaway right, but the wind pushed them toward deep center, where they were catchable, though they jittered about like Wiffle balls, and an inexperienced fielder might not have corralled either one. Now there were only four — "FOUR" roared the crowd — outs to go.

Next up was Miller Jacks, who, on a 1–2 count, smashed a line drive straight back at the mound. The crack of the ball shattering the elbow of the Alien's pitching arm was audible in the broadcasting booth and so was Spence's roar as he charged out of the Sox dugout toward Jacks, now jogging down the line toward first and jabbing a taunting finger at the Alien, sitting on the mound and rocking and holding his elbow, his face stricken with anguish and disappointment.

Sally tackled Spence just before he reached Jacks, but it took the umpiring crew and the police five minutes to separate the surging scrum of battling players. The Alien was carried off the field on a stretcher, Spence accompanying him into the dugout.

He picked up the phone to the bullpen and stared at it for a moment. Then he said into the mouthpiece, "Say, kid. You feel like getting in a little work this afternoon?"

JOGGING IN from the bullpen, E.A. heard some scattered boos and a few "woodchuck"s, but there was applause, too, led by Gypsy Lee, now standing on her seat and shrieking, "That's my boy, you'd *better* clap for him!" There was so much debris on the field that E.A. thought the posse must be showering him with it. But it was just the work of the wind, now blowing a blizzard of hot dog wrappers and paper napkins and beer cups thrown out of the stands during the melee.

Spence met E.A. at the mound, placed the ball in his hand, and said, "One out at a time, kid. Throw to Sally, not the hitters. Whatever happens, I'm behind you. You're my pitcher."

E.A. looked up at Teddy and Gypsy. Teddy touched his cap and E.A. touched his. Then he threw his warm-up pitches.

Sally trotted out to the mound. "This lefty five hitter, she don't like the curve out. We set her up with heat on the fist, then get her with a back-door curve, nick the outside corner. Don't forget you got a man on first. Go from you set position. You going to get these out, win the game."

E.A.'s first pitch to the lefty, a 98-mph fastball, caught the inside corner, on the letters, causing the umpire's right hand to jerk out and up, and it was as if he had thrown a switch activating the loudest cheering E.A. had ever heard. The next pitch was a slider, also on the hands, which the hitter fouled weakly into the Sox dugout. Then Sally called for heat at eye level, trying to get the hitter to bite at a pitch out of the strike zone. He wouldn't, and the count was 1 and 2.

Through the cheering, E.A. could hear Miller Jacks calling "woodchuck" at him from first base. E.A. remembered that he was Gran Allen's grandson. The thought made him feel strong and mean as he snapped off the back-door curve that would, he believed, catch the lefty flat-footed, leaving the Sox one inning away from the championship.

It was a perfect pitch. It started four or five inches outside and several inches high, dropping down and in to nip the outermost corner of the plate at the last moment. The hitter waved at it feebly and popped it out behind the Sox shortstop, into mid-left field. E.A. turned, the crowd now screaming, "THREE THREE THREE," and started off the mound, watching over his shoulder as the left-fielder took three or four steps in. E.A. watched the fly ball reach its apex, watched a Red Sox hat that he suddenly realized was his own sail several feet over the infield grass toward shortstop, the shortstop reaching out automatically and catching it by the bill, watched as the fluke of wind that had blown off his cap flawed the outfield grass like the choppy surface of a windblown lake and carried the pop fly over the Green Monster into Lansdowne Street.

New York 2, Boston 1.

AT FIRST, no one in Fenway seemed to comprehend what had happened. The park was utterly quiet. E.A. realized that the wind had died as abruptly as it had come up. There was no breeze at all, just bright fall sunshine on a packed and silent stadium.

E.A. knew it wasn't his fault as Jacks crossed the plate with the home-run hitter close behind him. He knew that the curve ball he'd thrown had been a perfect pitch. The batter had connected with it, however poorly, through sheer luck, and the quirk of wind, later estimated at between 60 and 70 mph, had turned a pop-up to shallow left field into a two-run homer.

"That's baseball, kid." Spence was standing beside E.A. on the mound.

As bad as E.A. felt, and as completely as he understood that a right-handed pitcher simply cannot throw a better curve to a left-handed batter than the one he had thrown, he was determined not to make an excuse. "Sorry," he said. "I caught too much of the plate with that hook."

Spence shrugged. "You ever see that old picture show? *Big Wind from Winnetka*?"

E.A. shook his head.

"Well, that was it. The Big Wind from Winnetka. Now it's behind us. It ain't even breezy no more. See?"

E.A. nodded. This was the Legendary Spence at his best. No raving, no storming. Just straight baseball talk.

"We'll get them runs back for you," Spence said. "This weren't your fault. Don't worry about it."

The Legendary Spence swatted E.A. on the butt and trotted off the field. E.A. walked the next batter on a 3–2 count with a pitch that could have gone either way, but before the woodchuck chant could get up a head of steam he got the next hitter on three straight 21st-Century Limiteds. The third fastball was well out of the strike zone, but the Mets' seven hitter swung at it from his heels and missed by a mile, and now the crowd was up and cheering for a Sox rally in the bottom of the eighth. For one more miracle in this miraculous season.

With one out, the Sox's shortstop and three hitter, who'd saved the day in the seventh with his double play, hit a line drive high up on the wall. It was fair by thirty feet and would have been a home run in any other baseball park in the world, but the Mets' left-fielder snagged the rebounding ball with his bare hand, whirled, and threw a strike on one bounce to the second baseman, holding the runner to a single.

The next hitter struck out on a pitch that E.A. could have sworn Villa literally pulled out of his hat, leaving the Sox one out and one last at-bat away from yet another devastating failure.

Eduardo Salvadore walked to the plate to a tintinnabulation of foot-stomping and hand-clapping, intensifying into a roar louder than the roar after Fisk's Shot Heard Round the World, as the Sox superstar took a short stride, head tucked down, swung compactly, and drove Villa's first pitch over the right-fielder's head. The outfielder raced back, reached up over his shoulder — and the ball skipped off his outstretched glove, over the fence.

Boston 3, New York 2.

Euphoria.

E.A.'s FIRST MISTAKE in the top of the ninth inning was to try too hard to keep the ball low, in order to avoid a repeat of the pop-fly home run. As a result he pitched around New York's number-eight batter and walked him. He'd violated a cardinal rule of baseball by issuing a free pass to the leadoff hitter.

The nine hitter, a decent contact man who only rarely hit the long ball, fouled off several very good pitches. With a 3–2 count, E.A. walked him as well, on a slider on the hands, another pitch that could have gone either way.

"Time to pay a little social call on the umpire," Spence said to the macaw. He reached up, grabbed the side of the dugout, and heaved himself onto the field. The crowd's howl of anger over the called ball four changed into a roar of anticipation. Here came the Legendary Spence, his uniform shirt and pants torn and grass-stained from the brawl the inning before, the macaw perched on his shoulder, making a beeline for home plate.

The organist played a riff of "Spence's Hornpipe." More debris rained onto the field. All over New England, people were off their barstools and couches, cheering for the Legendary Spence. The umpire stood waiting.

"Sally," Spence shouted. "Where was that last pitch?"

"One little inch off the corner."

"Has Blue been squeezing my pitcher?"

"She no squeeze."

Spence took several quick steps out around his catcher toward the plate. His chest nearly touched the umpire's chest, his face jutted into the umpire's face, and his arms hung straight down at his sides like an Irish dancer's, like Gypsy's when she did the River Dance on the cab roof of Devil Dan's Blade. Thinking of Gypsy, E.A. glanced at the box seat just up the third-base line. There she was, waving her red cowgal hat and shrieking for the umpire's head along with the rest of the Faithful. The lummox, too, was standing up, motioning for Spence to go sit down, get off the field.

"You're squeezing the kid, Blue," Spence shouted. "This ain't the time or place for it."

"That last pitch missed, Spence. Go back to the dugout where you belong."

"I got two eyes in my head," Spence shouted. "I can see. You're squeezing the kid."

"I don't want to toss you, Spence. Not in the last game of the Series. If you persist in this, I will."

To signal that the conversation was over, the umpire turned a quarter revolution toward the plate. So did Spence, gearing up the Faithful to a new pitch. They knew what was coming. The organist launched into the first bar of the hornpipe. The umpire turned again. Careful not to bump him or say what couldn't be unsaid, the Red Sox manager followed suit. Fenway was going wild with joy. In all baseballdom, only the Legendary Spence would risk being tossed in the last inning of the last game of the World Series.

Sally jumped in between the two men. All three were now revolving around home plate like clockwork figures. In the on-deck circle, the waiting hitter glanced out toward the mound and exchanged fleeting grins with E.A.

Suddenly Spence was through. The hornpipe was over and he was heading for the mound. "How you doing, kid?" he said.

"Good."

"Can you pitch your way out of this?"

"You just watch me," E.A. said.

"All right, Mr. Ethan," Spence said. "I will." And he returned to the dugout.

E.A. reviewed the situation. The Sox were up 3–2, with two New York runners on base and no outs in the top of the ninth inning, the top of the Mets' order coming to bat. He checked Teddy and touched his cap. Teddy touched his.

As New York's number-one hitter stepped into the batter's box, E.A. found himself envisioning the pattern of baseballs Teddy had painted on canvas for him to throw at in Gran's barn. Ted Williams's representation of the strike zone. He could smell the hay and old manure and sawdust of the barn, and he remembered the Colonel's telling him that games were won on the practice field. Practice was something he'd had plenty of. In his mind he'd been in this situation a hundred times. He could hear the rain on the roof of the barn, hear the pigeons muttering in the cupola, the thud of the ball on the painted canvas draped over the hay bales, and he struck out the leadoff batter on four pitches and the number-two man on five, the fifth pitch a fastball on the inside corner, which hit 99 mph on the radar gun.

Everyone at Fenway was on their feet. "ONE ONE ONE," screamed the crowd and then, as the Mets' three hitter stepped in, "THREE THREE THREE," calling not just for an out but for another strikeout. Down 0–1, on the second pitch of the sequence, the three batter beat the ball on the ground to the Sox's shortstop, who charged the ball, fielded it cleanly, then couldn't find the handle on it to make the toss to second for the force out. The sort of freakish mishap that happens once or twice a season had happened to the shortstop at the worst possible time, leaving the bases loaded with two out and Miller Jacks, the best clutch hitter in baseball, coming to the plate.

Sally called time and went out to the mound while the crowd's agonized groans turned into cascading boos for Jacks. "Keep it on the fists," Sally said. "We don't want that first pitch too far over the plate, where she can get solid wood on it. I give you a good target on the letters on the fists on the inside black, kid. She don't dare let go by, but she don't do much with it. Don't try too hard to keep the ball low, we can't walk this guy and tie up the score. We got to go right at her and win the game here. Okay?"

E.A. nodded. He looked up at Teddy, who touched his cap again.

Sally signaled for the fastball in, and a fraction of a second before E.A. lifted his hands to his chest to start his wind-up, Jacks raised his right hand and stepped out of the batter's box. The umpire threw up his hands for time. Just as Teddy had taught him to, E.A. threw the ball anyway in order not to make any abrupt movements that could injure his arm. The pitch was right where Sally'd wanted it, on the fists, 98 mph. Sally held it framed, but the umpire said, "Time was called," and though the crowd was enraged, there was nothing anyone could do. The debate on whether Miller Jacks had called for time before E.A. started his motion would rage on in baseball circles for years. But the call had been made and the call stood. Jacks had accomplished what he'd set out to. He had seen E.A.'s best pitch. Now he was ready to hit whatever the boy might throw him.

E.A. stepped back on the rubber. The runners took their leads. Again Sally signaled for the fastball in and up. The pitch was a couple of inches high, a couple of inches inside. The crowd groaned and booed the call. But there was no quarrel from Sally or from E.A. As E.A. had suspected, Sally's plan was to move Jacks off the plate with that first pitch, keep him from digging in, then work him away with a slider on the knees. The slider cut the corner as Jacks watched it go by. The umpire's right arm lifted, and the Faithful set up an oceanic roar. The next pitch was a high, hard fastball, which Jacks fouled straight back into the screen, and the Red Sox were one strike away from winning the World Series.

Ethan thought Sally would want him to use high heat again to put Jacks away. Instead, the catcher flicked down two fingers. E.A. set, kicked, and threw a curve low off the plate that hit the dirt, so Sally had to block it with his body to keep the runner on third from scoring. Two and two.

The next pitch was a fastball, 100 mph, the swiftest recorded pitch E.A. had ever thrown, and up around the letters. Jacks followed the ball into Sally's glove with his snakelike head but didn't offer. Sally held the pitch. E.A. waited for the umpire's arm to go up.

It did not. And true to his word, Spence stayed in the dugout.

This matter was now between Ethan and the umpire and Sally and Miller Jacks.

With the count full and the bases loaded, E.A. was thinking only about his pitch selection. He felt he had to challenge Jacks with his best pitch, fastball pitcher against fastball hitter. But when he put his foot on the rubber and got set, Sally, to his astonishment, signaled for the bases-loaded pickoff play, a sign he could only have gotten from Spence. It was the oldest trick in the book, and making it work required perfect timing. E.A. stepped back on the rubber and started the count in his head. One thousand one, one thousand two, one thousand three, and he stepped toward third, bluffed a throw, whirled, and fired the ball to his first baseman, catching the Mets' base runner flat-footed three feet off the bag. The first baseman's glove went down and slapped the runner, lunging back too late. The oldest trick in the book had worked. The World Series was over.

45

Except that it wasn't.

The first-base umpire hesitated. Still hesitated. And finally extended his hands waist-high, palms down.

"Time out," Sally shouted, as Spence burst from the dugout. Until the tag went down and the umpire gave the safe sign, the Red Sox manager had not known how much he'd wanted the championship. Now he felt as if a lifetime of baseball had been snatched away from him.

"Appeal," he shouted. "The runner was out by two feet. Appeal!"

"He hooked in around the tag, Spence," the first-base umpire shouted over the bedlam. "The tag was up on the shoulder. The runner already had his hand on the bag."

The replay went up. Spence studied it, jaw thrust out; everybody at Fenway studied it. You couldn't tell, really. E.A. couldn't tell. But the tag *had* been high, and it did appear that the runner might have grabbed the bag first. It looked as though the first-base umpire was right.

"Appeal!" Spence shouted again, turning to the home-plate umpire.

The umpire shook his head. "I was too far away, Spence. I couldn't make a judgment. The call stands."

Later Spence would confide to the Curse that at this point he realized that, unlike his friend old Maynard, he was probably not destined to die of sheer disappointment over the outcome of a baseball game, even the seventh game of a World Series. So he did the only thing he could do. He grinned at E.A. and went back to the dugout, with the count 3–2, two outs, and the bases loaded, while Sally signaled E.A. to challenge Miller Jacks with his best heat and let what was going to happen happen.

The instant E.A. released the pitch, he knew it was a good one. Better than good. Miller Jacks knew it, too, and he hit E.A.'s best fastball as hard as it is possible for a man to hit a baseball. His bat moved so fast that afterward E.A. could not remember seeing it move. The ball was twenty-five feet high and climbing as it left the infield.

As the Sox left-fielder raced to his right and back, Jacks broke out of the batter's box toward first. Then he did a near-perfect imitation of Fisk in '75. Jumping, waving, conjuring his home run fair, gesturing with both hands, willing the rising baseball to stay fair. From his angle, E.A. couldn't tell whether the ball was fair or not as it sailed high over the pole on top of the Green Monster. But there was no delay on the part of the third-base umpire, who immediately and emphatically signaled that it was a foul ball.

Jacks was beside himself. He continued to gesticulate and jump as the replay went up, and the Fenway organist played a couple of bars of "Spence's Hornpipe," which made Jacks angrier still.

Meanwhile E.A. played catch with his third baseman to keep his arm loose. He'd glanced once at the replay, which continued to flash up on the scoreboard, and it seemed to him that Jacks's home run was foul, just as it had seemed, on the pickoff play at first, that the runner had gotten in just before the tag.

Sally was on the mound, reminding him that Jacks's blast was just a long strike.

"He *pulled* it," E.A. said, his teeth gritted. "He didn't just get his bat on it. He pulled my best pitch."

"Don't worry," Sally said. "That's all she can do with one on the fists. That don't hurt. Now look. This guy looking for one on the corner away now, so we give what she don't expect. Same pitch as before. See? Spence already send me the signal while Jacks cry and hop around. She going to strike out for sure. You get you win.

We get our rings. Spence get to go fisha. Club stay in Boston. Okay?"

"Okay," E.A. said.

"No, not okay," Sally. "Not yet. Look, kid. This Jacks, she got some six sense. Somehow, I don't know how, she always know where I set up. So when you wind, I setting up on the outside corner. Then when you release, I move glove back in toward fists and you hit it. Okay?"

E.A. nodded. They all had such confidence in him, he thought. Not that he'd ever lacked confidence in himself. After all, he was a WYSOTT Allen. But they all had such great faith that he could throw the ball wherever they asked him to. Sally. Teddy. Spence. Even Stan had believed in his control.

"Well," the Colonel said in his head, "what are you waiting for?"

"Teddy," E.A. said, scanning the stands. "I need to find Teddy."

He searched the stands. Teddy and Gypsy weren't there. E.A. stepped off the rubber.

"What is it?" said the Colonel. "Why are you delaying the game?"

"I'm waiting for Teddy."

He knew ahead of time what the Colonel was going to say.

"You're on your own, boy. Get up there and throw the ball."

E.A. stepped back on the rubber. Sally ran through the signals, stopped with one finger down, pointed in. Fastball on the fists, as they'd agreed.

Once more E.A. scanned the seats, but now everyone was standing, it was too packed to see any one individual. The crowd blurred into a faceless sea of color.

Then E.A. knew exactly what he was going to do, and he knew he would not be giving the best fastball hitter in the National League another opportunity to hit his fastball. As the Fenway fans clapped and stomped, louder and faster, faster and louder, screaming "ONE, ONE," for one more strike, and Gypsy Lee clasped her hands together and prayed to Our Father Who Art in Heaven, and Teddy watched with an unlighted Lucky in his mouth, and Spence watched with one foot on the top step of the dugout, on his shoulder the bird named for the jinx that either would or would not be lifted in the next seconds, and the Commoners two hundred miles to the north watched the snowy old hotel television, and Gran, just across the river, listened to the Voice over the Philco, waiting to leap out of her wheelchair and kick up her heels when Jacks connected, and Moonface watched his portable radio beside the ladder on the factory roof, and even the lummox in his box seat suddenly understood, for the first time in his life, what being a Red Sox fan was all about and wanted the Sox to win more than he'd ever wanted anything, even his Ph.D., Ethan adjusted the ball in his glove. He lifted his hands, kicked, brought his arm whipping down with all the speed of his 21st-Century Limited, and everything else was easy.

Miller Jacks looked ridiculous. The best fastball hitter in the National League lunged out on his front foot and waved at E.A.'s change-up like a Little Leaguer in his first at-bat, swinging when the baseball was scarcely halfway to the plate. Sally was taken off guard and dropped the ball, then picked it up and tagged Jacks hard on the back, really hard, but it didn't matter. With first base occupied, Jacks was out the moment he swung and missed.

The Boston Red Sox had won their first world championship since 1918.

It was reported in the special edition the *Globe* put out that evening that the windows of the Pru and the Hancock shook and the car horns and sirens and church bells of Boston joined in a medley of pure, heavenly noise, radiating from the Old North Church to the farthest reaches of New England. In Aroostook County, Maine, loggers started their chain saws and waved them over their heads. One hundred miles offshore in the Atlantic, the Gloucester fishing fleet blared their foghorns, bringing up the swordfish to see what the ruckus was. Reliable longtime fishermen reported that humpback whales rose to the surface and sang, in unison, a song that sounded like "Spence's Hornpipe," which the Fenway organist was blasting out for all the world to hear. The Faithful were dancing in the aisles, and a million more citizens of the Red Sox Nation were dancing in the streets of Boston and Bangor and Burlington, and of Concord, New Hampshire, and Concord, Massachusetts, where Thoreau had traveled much and seen much, but never anything like this. The tugs and freighters and liners in Boston Harbor blasted their whistles. Locomotives hooted. At correctional centers, escape sirens shrieked.

Sally ran out to the mound and pressed the game ball into E.A.'s hand, and here came the lummox, clambering down over the roof of the Sox's dugout. Pumping his big-knuckled fist, he made his way toward the celebration between the mound and home plate.

As he was lifted on high by his teammates, E.A. saw Spence head toward Miller Jacks, who was standing at home plate open-mouthed and stunned, his bat still in his hands. Maynard Junior was just a step or two away. "Spence, we did it," the lummox blubbered and knuckle-punched his manager in the arm, twice.

Spence dropped the open Budweiser pounder in his hand at the lummox's feet. "Oh," he said, bending over. "Sorry."

But instead of picking up the beer can, Spence straightened up and socked the lummox in the stomach as hard as one man can punch another, driving the boy up off his feet and into the arms of Miller Jacks and knocking them both to the ground in front of fifty million television viewers.

"You're fired, Spence," the boy owner wheezed, struggling to his feet. "You'll never set foot on a major-league ball diamond again."

"Let's hope not," said the former manager of the World Champion Boston Red Sox as, without breaking stride, holding tight to the legs of the macaw on his shoulder, he fought his way through the celebrating fans and players toward the tunnel and freedom.

★ IMPOSSIBLE DREAMS ★

"DRIVER," SPENCE SAID from the back seat of the taxicab, hunkered down in his fishing hat and sunglasses. "What's all this hullabaloo?"

"You don't know? God love you, man, where you been? The Boston Red Sox have just won the World frigging Series."

"Well," Spence said, holding out his first pounder of the long trip south for the Curse to open and feeling the tension begin to drain away from him with the air whooshing out of the beer can. "Will wonders never cease."

The cabdriver, who'd picked Spence up on Boylston Street and agreed, for a thousand dollars and expenses, to take him to Florida, twisted the dial of his radio. The ebullient Voice of the Sox came into the cab. ". . . punched the owner . . . in front of an estimated fifty million television viewers . . . unconfirmed reports that he's being held at precinct headquarters on assault charges . . . the people of Boston threatening to march on the station to free the Legendary Spence . . . Bastille Day . . . mayhem . . ."

"Punched the owner?" Spence said. "I never heard of such doings. What is this fella, some kind of raving psychopath?"

"Oh, yeah," the driver said happily. "Oh, yeah, he is."

As E.A., now in his street clothes, drove over the bridge, he could hear the victory procession behind him, winding downtown like a great, happy dragon. He threaded the car he'd borrowed from

Spence through the complicated back streets of Cambridge into Somerville, where he picked up I-93. An hour later, in the slant late-afternoon sunlight of this perfect October day, he was in New Hampshire. Cars were still honking madly, drivers and passengers giving each other thumbs-up, the tollbooth operators at Manchester giving the drivers high-fives.

Two hours later he got off the interstate at Littleton and stopped at the state liquor store he and Gypsy and Gran used to visit on their wrong-way whiskey runs. He spoke briefly with a guy in a hunting jacket headed into the store, then gave him a bill. On the street, cars and pickups with GO SOX banners and CURSE OF THE BAMBINO bumper stickers were lining up for a parade. Three or four minutes later the man in the hunting jacket came out of the store and handed E.A. a brown paper bag.

Crossing the Vermont state line, he felt good to be heading home.

The sun dropped behind the Green Mountains. Off in the distance sat a farmhouse with a sideways window under the eaves, like his window at home. He would cut some wood for winter, he thought. Set up a better place to throw in the barn. Maybe hunt partridge. Get in touch with Louisianne if he could.

He stopped for gas in St. J, his cap pulled down over his eyes.

The guy at the counter shoved his money back at him. "Gas is free to anybody wearing a Red Sox cap, dude."

"Why's that?" E.A. said.

"You don't know? Local kid, an Allen from up in the Kingdom, just won the World Series for the Sox. He got the Mets' big hitter with a change-up, but you know something? I've seen the replay of that pitch maybe thirty times. You ask me, I'd say it looked as fast as his other pitches."

"It's supposed to, I reckon," E.A. said. "That's the trick."

"Oh, we got an expert here," a guy beside him said.

E.A. grinned at him. "Get a bat," he said.

"What?"

"Have a good day," E.A. said.

"Say," the guy said. "Ain't you —"

E.A. was on his way to the car.

He didn't get back on the interstate. He drove the rest of the way up old Route 5, wanting to immerse himself in this homecoming, in the experience of home, feeling the pull north as surely as the geese now going south would feel that pull in the spring. The mountain villages were pretty in the falling darkness. He'd played town ball in some of these hamlets just a year ago. Here and there pumpkins sat on lighted porches, and colorfully dressed harvest figures slumped in wheelbarrows. Outside the towns he kept his speed down to about forty-five in order to savor coming home, so he was surprised to see flashing blue lights coming up behind him just south of Kingdom Landing. The cop approached the window in the dark, a tall man, a few years older than E.A. Ethan had his license out and ready. The policeman looked at it, looked back inside at E.A., then began to laugh.

"E.A. Allen," he said. "You don't remember me."

"No, sir," E.A. said. "I sure don't."

"Well, I don't blame you," the cop said, giving him back his ID. "I'm Orton Horton."

"Good God." E.A. got out of the car and shook hands with Officer Horton. Now they were both laughing.

"I heard the game on the radio," Orton said. "It was great."

"I didn't feel so great standing out there wondering what to throw Jacks after he'd just hit that four-hundred-foot foul home run."

"E.A.," Orton said, getting out a ballpoint pen and tearing a citation out of his book. "I've got a boy, his name's Travis — no more Ortons or Nortons. He's three and he likes to toss with me. I wonder . . ."

E.A. took the pen and the citation. Then he had a better idea. He handed the citation back to Officer Orton Horton, got something out of his jacket pocket, and wrote on it "To Travis Horton, a heck of a ballplayer. E.A. Allen." He handed the Series-winning ball to Orton and told him what it was, and at first the policeman couldn't say a word. Then he wanted to give E.A. an escort into the Common, lights flashing, but E.A. said no thanks, he had some private business to take care of, so they shook hands again, and E.A. got back in the car.

Orton started toward his cruiser. Then he came back and said, "E.A., Norton and I were a pair of little pissants, weren't we?"

"Nah," E.A. said.

"We weren't pissants?" Orton said.

"Oh, you were pissants, all right," E.A. said. "You just weren't little. Good luck to Travis."

He pulled into the Common about eight o'clock. It was full dark now. The stars were out, and a great round orange harvest moon was coming up behind the courthouse. The air smelled like smoke from the celebratory bonfire just burning itself out on the baseball infield. Now and then a car driving through town blasted its horn. The hotel barroom was jammed with people watching a rerun of the game. Tattered banners still hung from the brick shopping block. The lights were on in the *Monitor* office, and through the big window E.A. could see Editor Kinneson typing at his desk.

He parked in front of the courthouse, across from the east side of the green. He wondered if he'd regret giving the ball to Officer Horton. He thought not. He'd already decided to give his Series ring to Louisianne if she'd take it. He put the paper bag from the Littleton package store into his jacket pocket and headed across the common.

"Here," he said. "It's from Barbados."

"I gave all that up a long time ago," the Colonel said. "It was what killed me, you want the truth."

"One bottle won't hurt. To celebrate."

"Celebrate what?"

"You know good and well what."

"Oh. That. They rang the church bell over yonder for twenty minutes. You'd think the British were coming again. Set it down here by the pedestal. I'll see it doesn't go to waste."

"I bet you will."

"They say you got Jacks with a change," the Colonel said.

"That's right."

"Everything changes. Even here in the Kingdom."

"Like what?"

The Colonel thought. "Devil Dan has his place up for sale," he said. "Since they ran off with that Blade of his. Of course, you wouldn't know a thing about that."

E.A. grinned in the dark.

"Things change," the Colonel said again. "They did for me. They will for you. Don't expect it always to be this way."

"I don't."

"I hope not. Because you'll have good seasons and off seasons. Good games and off ones. The team won't all stay together, and you may or may not stay in Boston. You might like the new manager, you might not. Change, boy. It's what you can count on. Thankee for the rum."

"I'm the one who ought to thank you," E.A. said. "For sending me Teddy."

"Whoa," the Colonel said. "I never sent you Teddy."

"Of course you did," E.A. said. "You said you'd send me a fella. To teach me baseball."

"And so I did," the Colonel said. "But it wasn't Teddy. Good Jehovah, boy. Is that what you've been thinking all these years? I never said a word to Teddy. The fella I sent was Stan."

"*Stan?*"

"Stan," the Colonel said. "Teddy came on his own, son. Because he was your pa."

THE PHONE RANG as E.A. stepped into the farmhouse.

"Hi, hon. Congratulations. E.W. and Patsy and I are on the road." Gypsy Lee broke into song, imitating Willie Nelson. "'On the road again. I can't wait to get on the road again . . .'"

"Where are you, ma?"

"On the road, hon, like the song says. We're on the interstate, coming up on New York and headed for Nashville. We stopped at a Wal-Mart and bought a quart of blue paint and a brush, and E.W. painted *The Gypsy Lee Allen Old-Timey Country Music Show* on Patsy. Music City, here we come."

"Well. Good luck, ma. In Nashville."

"Thank you, sweetie. So long. I'll call you from Guitar Town."

"So long, ma," E.A. said, and hung up the phone.

"I've come home," he said to Gran.

"I can see that," Gran said. "I haven't lost my eyesight, you know. Just the use of my legs."

"I thought you weren't ever going to finish up down below," Bill complained. "That baseball game run way on along into the late afternoon, and I never did catch up on my evening chores. Where's Gypsy?"

"Headed for Nashville with Teddy," E.A. said.

"Gypsy and Teddy," Gran said. "They make my ass ache."

"We listened to it all," Bill said. "There's one thing I don't understand. Why grown men would stand out in the hot sun playing a boy's game don't make a particle of sense to me."

"We get paid well to do it, Bill."

"I was hoping you'd bean Jacks," Gran said. "Bounce one right off his noggin. Did you remember my paper?"

E.A. handed her the *Weekly World News* he'd picked up when he stopped for gas.

The headline said, SPACE CREATURE THROWS OUT FIRST BALL AT WORLD SERIES. Below was a doctored picture of Spence on the mound at Fenway, shaking hands with a bubble-headed creature about two and a half feet tall. On one of the creature's splayed, twelve-fingered hands was an old-fashioned baseball glove.

Bill shook his head and headed out to his trailer.

E.A. went up to his room and looked out the sideways window. In the moonlight he saw a tall man leaning against the barn door smoking a cigarette. He saw a kid taking BP from a pretty young woman. He saw the moon's pale reflection off Gone and Long Forgotten in the family graveyard.

He went back downstairs. Gran had fallen asleep. He pulled her quilt up around her, and in a sharp voice, her eyes shut tight, she said, "You ruined our losing streak, E.A."

"Don't be too disappointed, Gran," E.A. said. "There's always next year."

Spence and the taxi driver had had an altercation the other side of New York City over Spence's drinking beer in the vehicle. So Spence had paid him two hundred dollars and was now hitchhiking through the pitch-black night. A big man in a windbreaker and a Red Sox cap, carrying a gym bag, with a large tropical bird on his shoulder. He'd left his fishing hat and sunglasses in the cab. He was thinking that if he didn't get a ride he'd hoof it to the next truck stop and talk some semi driver into carrying him and the bird into Philly, jump a Greyhound from there to St. Pete. With any luck he'd be on the Gulf in three days.

He walked with his back to the streaming traffic, left arm stuck out, thumb up. That was how he and Stan used to hitchhike to their games in Texas and Louisiana when they were just breaking in. Later the whole team had a '43 Nash coupe with wide running boards. You could only fit six inside, so the others would ride on the boards, linking hands over the roof so as not to fall off if one man went to sleep. "That was what responsibility was all about," he was telling the macaw. "You held a fella's life right in your hand, you know."

"I ought to know, you've told me a hundred times," the Curse said.

"Are you cold?" Spence said. "Is that it? Do you want to come inside my jacket?"

"I want to know where we're going," the bird said. "What the plan is."

A vehicle stopped, a beat-up jalopy with writing on the doors. Spence couldn't quite make out what it said. Then he recognized the fella driving. It was the kid's old man. Beside him was a young redheaded woman strumming a guitar.

Spence got in back. "Where you folks headed?"

"Down south," the driver said. "Tennessee."

The song the woman was playing had an old-timey sound, and Spence found himself tapping his finger to it. "That's a nice number, if I do say so," he said.

"I'm going to sing it at the Opry," the woman said.

Spence thought for a minute. "I like that song a lot," he said. "It's way better'n most of what you hear on the radio. I hope they listen. At the Opry."

"Oh," the driver said. "They'll listen."

Spence nodded. "I'm going south, too," he said. "Fishing."

The driver lit a cigarette. They rode on for a while, the woman singing a sad song called "Nobody's Child," about a woman who'd lost her lover, killed in a trucking accident on a mountain. She was left with a baby, but then the baby died, too.

"Night turns to day and the day finds the evening
And once I looked up when I heard someone breathing.
And I saw them fly away over the pines."

"Oh, yeah," Spence said when she was finished. "You just bet they'll listen."

Later they stopped for coffee. "Look," Spence said, closing the door gently so as not to waken the macaw. "Will you just look there." Behind the truck stop was a lighted softball diamond with a late-night game going on. Old-timers, it looked like. Men up in their forties and fifties, just dubbing around having fun.

Spence stood stock-still, watching the softball players.

"You want to watch an inning?" Teddy said.

"I might at that," Spence said. "I like to watch me a little ball from time to time. Course, it ain't *base*ball."

"No."

"Thank the Judas, no," Spence said, walking fast now, toward the softball park.

As he pushed through a gate, a batter hit a lazy fly ball between the left- and center-fielders. It fell in for a hit. A runner who'd been on first rounded second, and the left-fielder picked up the ball, which Spence figured should have been caught anyway, and lobbed it back in to the second baseman, allowing the runner to advance to third.

"Hey," Spence shouted. "You out there in left field. You *never* throw behind the runner. Not unless he's already headed back to the base. You just gave him another bag, free for the taking."

The outfielder, gray at the temples, looked like a local real estate agent.

"Yeah? I suppose you could do it better," he said.

"I could take that cowplop you call a ball so far over the wall you'd never find it."

"Get a bat and stand in, old man," the pitcher said.

Spence shucked out of his windbreaker.

"Serve it up," he said, leveling his bat. The pitcher did, and Spence belted it fifty feet over the center-field fence onto some railroad tracks. Then he and Teddy and Gypsy had their coffee and got back in the car.

Teddy drove, Spence and the Curse dozed, Gypsy worked on a

new song to sing as an encore at the Opry. When Teddy stopped again, in Harrisburg, Gypsy was asleep, too. He picked up the morning newspaper. On the front page was a wire photo of Ethan, looking in at Miller Jacks, under the headline SOX TAKE IT ALL. And halfway down the page, a photo of Spence punching the lummox.

They drove on into the dawn. In Front Royal, Virginia, the sun lifted over the Blue Ridge, illuminating fall colors nearly as bright as Vermont's. Something in Patsy's engine began to tick. The odds were they wouldn't make it another fifteen miles down the line, much less to Nashville.

Then again, just maybe they would.